Choppiness on High Seas

Choppiness on High Seas

Arvind Wadhera

T

Troubador Publishing Ltd
Unit E2 Airfield Business Park,
Harrison Road, Market Harborough,
Leicestershire. LE16 7UL
Tel: 0116 2792299
Email: books@troubador.co.uk
Web: www.troubador.co.uk

ISBN 978 1836281 337

British Library Cataloguing in Publication Data.
A catalogue record for this book is available from the British Library.

Printed and bound by CPI Group (UK) Ltd, Croydon, CR0 4YY
Typeset in 10.5pt Minion Pro by Troubador Publishing Ltd, Leicester, UK

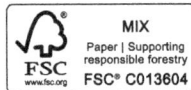

In memory of my mother

1930

Gail Stephens

Behold a filth hole of desolation! There was mud and blood on slippery, damp floors as an open gutter's stench mixed with the strong fumes of ethanol and ammonia. Expectant mothers screamed and wretched in labour; the stocky midwives, thinking nothing of it, delivered one baby after the next, snipping at the umbilical cords before the placentas slopped out and splashed on the floor.

Gail Stephens was far too strong a woman to suffer a mishap in childbirth. She had earned this child even if it meant delivering him in a shelter for unmarried women. As soon as he was placed on her breast, she smiled. "You are my boy, Matthew. We will be each other's strength from now on; do not worry about anything. Mummy will always be there."

Next, the shelter put them in a maternity ward in an adjacent warehouse. There were two rows of beds on either side of the long corridor. The babies were placed in cots alongside their mothers as the midwives instructed the first-time mothers about nursing and feeding. Repeat mothers needed no such assistance and happily instructed their new sisters. Poverty may be a scourge, but motherhood ignored misery and united them all. Gail was not alone in having opted to keep the baby of a deserter. The sisterhood of bastard bearers did not believe in the stigma society callously applied to them.

The rest at the maternity ward did her good. Gail was a picture of health when she left the hospital and returned to her lodgings in the old stone house granary. She scrubbed herself with soap and water and dried her hair before the coal fire before choosing a clean dress with small floral patterns, its pleats pressed by the coal-heated iron firmly until crisp. She fed Matthew, cleaned him and put him back in a makeshift cot, where he quickly drifted into slumber.

Gail's occupation was in keeping with her social status but was conducted in a parallel world. Gail cleaned the houses of wealthy London families. Her encounters with mahogany, marble, velvets and silks did not ignite envy; they only provided affirmation of her son's destiny. "My son will live this life one day. I need to work hard to give him a good start. He must study so he can get an office job." And work hard she did. The houses she cleaned were immaculate and often received the admiration of guests: "Please ask her if she has some free hours."

She wore one of her two cardigans and grabbed her shawl before heading to Mr Burroughs' house with Matthew wrapped in a blanket. Mrs Burroughs welcomed her, calling out to her husband. Mr Burroughs looked at mother and son. "What a beautiful baby. Should you be working so soon, Gail?"

"Thank you, Sir. I had an easy delivery and am well rested. I brought Matthew with me today, but from tomorrow, I will leave him at the infirmary's baby centre."

Mrs Burroughs smiled. "Gail, this is the first baby we have had in this house. Please bring him here as often as you can. If you cannot come to work one day, please do not worry. Your wages will be paid."

"Oh, Madam, Sir, that is very kind indeed. Thank you. But I am a strong woman in good health." Looking at Gail, one could hardly imagine the modesty she left back home every day; there was a sense of purpose about her, not the resignation of her peers.

The Burroughs had been a godsend after the tedious and unpleasant households she had worked for previously. Work was not difficult to find but was tricky to hold on to. A well-built, tall, handsome woman with an unblemished complexion and fine face did not go amiss on men. The emergence of a certain level of unease often made her leave the job herself. On other occasions, the lady of the house would ask her to leave. These were times when unmarried women with a child were presumed to be of questionable trait: prey for men, an unnecessary risk for their wives.

The wages were low, though. Wealthy people would spend vast amounts on indulgences but remained parsimonious regarding servants and cleaners.

There was little money, but Gail had her son christened at the local parish.

Matthew was moved to a charitable nursery at the age of eight months. The nursery had been set up by one of her clients. It was like a play school for children of working mothers until they were old enough to go to school. Many children had been put there to receive a meal at least once daily. They were laughing, smiling and crying, oblivious of their misery. A child needs love, company and the occasional scuffle. They partook in the one celebration the nursery could provide, a cake at birthdays, even though the cake distribution would be chaotic. The children did not know any other way. Good manners were not a natural trait amongst their lot. The child carers and teachers would adopt a stern stance and did not shy away from mentioning the dreaded punishment of no dinners. It had never been implemented, but the threat was formidable in its impact on the young cohort.

Along with the nursery's other charges, Matthew grew from a baby to a toddler, from a toddler to a boy. Matthew stayed there until the age of six. Finances remained grim, but Gail was determined that her son learn manners and undergo full schooling, something she herself had been deprived of.

In the morass of their misery, the improbable education of Matthew Stephens took root.

Gail registered him at the local primary school. Schooling was not compulsory, certainly not for six-year-olds, but Gail believed education was the only way out of destitution. Moreover, all children at school were provided free school dinners, so there would be one less meal to worry about, just like when he was at the nursery. Matthew spent the next three years becoming a good student.

But then, war broke out. There was initially fear but shortly after, Britain's pugnacity took root and the public believed that they would win, however difficult things got. The National Service Act conscripted citizens between 18 and 41 years of age. This initially created panic and hurt amongst families but soon a sense of truculent defiance to Hitler and duty to Britain came into play. Although single women were not exempt from conscription, women who had children living with them were exempted. Gail nevertheless wanted to play her due role and registered with the local makeshift hospital to offer cleaning services.

In anticipation of a concerted air attack, the government evacuated children to rural areas in Operation Pied Piper. Matthew was separated from his mother. Gail did not resist as she wanted her son to be in a safer place. Matthew continued his schooling in the countryside and Gail continued to work.

The authorities set up air raid shelters in London. Despite the evacuations and the numerous blackouts, a sense of normality prevailed. The people made it through the severe winter. There were no sirens as the air raid had yet to materialise. The summer was as pleasant and active as one could get during wartime. The British bulldog spirit remained unsubdued but it could not prevent the vast number of injured soldiers that came back. The community organised itself to provide support and assistance. There were soldiers from all over and new relationships were forged. Somehow, life continued. People would still go to their work and then gravitate in the evenings around pubs.

On September 7, 1940, came the Blitz. The City of London as well as the broader London Civil Defence Area were attacked. The ground shook and buildings crumbled. Fires broke out and the din of air raid warnings and fire engine sirens settled wistfully in everyone's ears. The government enforced a blackout. Darkness only amplified the firing from the anti-aircraft guns.

The Spitfires and Hurricanes engaged to defend their motherland and roared into whatever the Luftwaffe could throw at them. The German bombers dropped not only bombs but also incendiary devices. London was alight and during almost three months of unrelenting bombing, the Docklands were pulverised and Gail's accommodation was destroyed. She was quickly rehoused by the still functional social services. Despite immeasurable damage, the unrelenting fortitude of Londoners kept the wheels of business and efficiency turning. Many London landmarks survived although St. Paul's cathedral suffered considerable damage. The surviving symbols of Britain and London lifted the spirits and fed the sentiment of invincibility. Unlike London, other cities fared worse.

The Tube sheltered thousands until May 1941 by when the Royal Air Force had won the battle of Britain.

After eight months away from each other, Matthew and Gail were reunited.

Matthew's schooling in a quickly constructed local school was relaunched.

The war had brought forward latent generosity and support for the less fortunate from across the social spectrum. Gail's employers provided the clothes, shoes and satchel. Although they had previously been demanding in their expectations of her work and had been stingy when discussing wages, they felt sorry for a woman trying to raise a child alone in such times. She enjoyed the empathy of her clients as she was diligent in her work. As she had to go to work every morning, Matthew would have to make his way to school on his own. Some sacrifices had to be made in the upbringing of her son. The street was narrow, and being shoved and pushed aside was routine for him. He did not mind and took all this in his stride. He emitted a glow of quiet confidence, a characteristic rare in his world. He had not felt the absence of a father and was connected to his mother's maxim: "Get a good education, work hard and prosper."

Before he set off each morning, Matthew washed his face with a clean, wet rag and combed his hair back tight with a side parting. A deceptively proud proponent, his poise and straight-backed confidence stood out from the world around him. He was not treated like a street urchin but someone better than his surroundings.

The years at school and at home in Gail's company forged a rounded youngster. By the time he was twelve, Gail no longer looked at him as a child. He was a young man who would make his way in this world, fending for himself a lot better than she had for herself. He would be educated, broaden his horizons, and grab the opportunities encountered. And then one day, he would meet a nice girl, marry her and set up their home.

Undoubtedly, there would be difficulties, but he would get through them. He was her son!

Gail refused to identify Matthew's father: "No one who abandoned us can be called your father. I know it was thirteen years ago, but I remember his departure as if it were yesterday. I do not want to be secretive. I just do not want you to have any notion that you ever had a father."

The stevedore who seduced Gail had left on a ship for America a few days after he learnt she was with child. Gail had loved him and was hoping that they would get married. There was hurt and bitterness, but Gail decided to go ahead with what was hers. Stevedore or no stevedore, her son would be hers. Domestic turmoil would be absent. But adversity would stay.

His birthday called for an extravagant meal of roast beef and gravy and a glass of ale. A celebration at the Stephens household was exceptional, but this was a special landmark for a proud mother and her young man. The fact that she was running a fever could not detract from marking her son's day.

The following morning, Gail still felt weak and asked Matthew to get some provisions from Mr Strike, the grocer. "Tell him that I am not feeling well, and I will pay him later. And please put that hammer away. I forgot it next to the cooker; it should be on the shelf next to the street door so we can find it when needed."

Matthew did her bidding. Mr Strike gave over the provisions and gave him a small paper chit with the list of items shown with the total price. Matthew returned, put the things in their place and cooked soup for his mother.

"Thank you, Son. I am feeling a lot better than this morning. So, I can clear up while you do your schoolwork."

"No, Mother, it is all right. I did my work at school yesterday."

There was a knock on the door. Mother and son looked at each other questioningly. "Who is it?"

"It's the grocer."

Matthew opened the door to Mr Strike and another man who worked in his shop.

"Mr Strike?"

He moved towards Gail. "Your son said you were not well, so I thought I would look you up. You are in bed; how convenient."

"If it is about the money, I can pay you tomorrow. My wages are due."

Mr Strike's companion stayed by the door behind Matthew, who was facing his mother. But Alan Strike walked to the bed and stretched his hand to Gail's forehead. This was strange, but she was lying under a quilt. She felt his palm on her forehead.

"You do not seem to have a fever anymore, so you will be fine. You have such a beautiful complexion." His hand moved down the side of her face.

Gail snatched her face away, but Mr Strike's hand kept moving down her shoulder under the quilt till it reached her breast. Gail kicked her quilt away and jumped up. Matthew tried to move towards her but was restricted by the man behind him. He was stuck in a firm arm hold across his shoulder, tightened around his throat.

Alan Strike put all his weight on Gail and, grabbing both of her wrists, pinned her down on the bed while wedging his torso into position between her legs. Gail screamed. Matthew stamped his heel onto the man's foot, who momentarily loosened his grip. Matthew bit his hand hard and was let loose. He grabbed the hammer from the shelf and raced towards the bed. He swung the hammer onto Mr Strike's head. Blood spurted out immediately. He turned towards the door, but the other man was gone.

Gail screamed again. The man who had collapsed on top of her had moved. Matthew darted back and swung the hammer again and yet again. This time, a wallop of blood-drenched brain appeared through the broken skull. Seeing his crushed head and the pool of blood spread on the bedsheet, Gail pushed him back and realised that her assailant was dead. Matthew was crying. Gail took him in her arms and then moved to look at him. "Do not cry. You did well, Son. You saved my honour. There is no greater act."

Matthew could not speak and looked back at her in shock and fear, the hammer still in his hand.

Gail got to work. She and her son wrapped the body in the sheet, washed the hammer, and sat the body against the door. They then cleaned themselves to remove the bloodstains and put on fresh clothes. As night fell, Matthew went to the coal merchant and returned with an empty wheel cart with empty gunny sacks. Once they ensured no one was within earshot, under the cover of darkness, they heaped the body onto the cart, covering it with gunny sacks and wheeled it to a maintenance hole covering the drain pit. They removed the gunny bags, put them aside, opened the manhole cover, and, with considerable effort, pushed the body through the opening and let it go, hearing a splash. They put the sacks back in the cart and wheeled it back to their house.

Once back in their room, she said, "Son, this will never be mentioned to anyone. We will both die with this. That man was a monster and needed someone to finish him."

"Did I not murder him, Mother?"

"No, Matthew, you do not murder monsters; you slay them."

"But what about the other man?"

"He will not say anything. If the people around here learn that he was part of an attack on a mother and her son, they will lynch him. We may be poor here, but we value each other."

Gail was right. The shop did not open the next morning or any other morning. The other man disappeared as well. A few days later, the sewage collectors found a body. When they identified the body, the neighbourhood quickly assumed that the missing shop hand had had something to do with this. They used to argue all the time. Someone had even seen the two men in each other's arms.

"Good riddance to filth. We do not like their sort over here in any case."

Life was cheap in this part of town, and the police were extremely willing to accept a plausible motivation. The case was opened, shut, and filed into the archives within the week.

Mr Burroughs

The stress of the Strike encounter weighed on her health, and Gail suffered a relapse. Only this time round, she coughed and coughed and, after a few days, ran a fever. Matthew trusted his mother's judgement and did not feel the guilt and remorse he had expected. His mother had cleared any moral dilemma quite conclusively. But she was unwell. In typical fashion, though, she continued to work as a housecleaner at two houses. Matthew was at school, and they both had to eat.

Her cough and fever got worse. One of her employers would not pay any advance on wages. "You are in no state to work. Please get some rest. We will get someone to replace you until you get better." How was she going to get better without any money?

Doctor Harris said the same thing again. "Ms Stephens, I cannot just keep giving you medicine. You need rest. If you want, I can talk to the Burroughs family. I know them well. They are very reasonable people... OK, I will not. You need that job. But to do your job, you need to get better."

Mother had to continue working irrespective of her condition. School was fine, but what was the point if Mother was getting more unwell by the day? Mother was right, though: if he studied, he would get a decent job. Then she will not have to work at all.

Gail's eyes were prickly. They were stinging, and her body was burning, successive shivers shaking her spine even though she lay under a thick quilt. The room was cold, and the icy wind whistled through the curtainless window's gap. The door was closed, but the stone floor transmitted the chill from outside into the heart of the room. Gail Stephens' living space was a stone granary with ill-fitting doors. Home for a lone mother and her son could not have been more modest.

The following morning, as soon as Gail had left to join the long queue at the free dispensary, Matthew went to the house of his mother's other employer. Surprisingly, the head of the household himself, Mr Burroughs, opened the door. He led him into the study: "You are the cleaning lady's boy? What is wrong?"

"Sir, she has a burning fever and a very bad cough. She will not be able to come today."

"Hmm, who's taking care of her?"

"I am, Sir. She has gone to the dispensary, Sir. I put chilly water compresses on her forehead every night. I also give her a tablespoon of the cough mixture three times a day. The doctor said that she needs to have soup and rest. But if she stops working, she earns no money. There is not enough at home to eat. So, one of us must earn. If you let me, Sir, I can do the cleaning until my mother is well again. I remember what she did from the times she brought me here. Sir, you can pay me less than what you pay my mother. I could also do other tasks, Sir."

"Hmmm."

The man walked towards his bureau and started writing on a sheet of paper. He then blotted out the ink and put the first sheet aside to start writing on another one. He opened a little drawer and took a small green velvet pouch tied with a piece of red string. He gathered the two sheets of paper and gave these along with the bag to Matthew. "Can you read, err… what is your name, young man?"

"Matthew Stephens, Sir! Yes, Sir, I can read. My mother has put me through school. She does not want me to work because she wants me to keep attending school. I tell her that I can work during the day and go to school at night, but she will not have it. Now, of course, she is extremely sick…"

"Matthew, take this first piece of paper to McGrath and Son in the high street for food and groceries for yourself and your mother. The second paper is for Doctor Harvey. Ask him to have a look at your mother. This pouch has some money. Keep it safe and use it to take care of her. Stay at her side for the next few days. Go to night school as soon as she starts sleeping all right and return to day school when she is ready to return to work. And do what she tells you to do."

"Thank you, Mr Burroughs, Sir. Where can I start, Sir?"

"Young man, go home and look after your mother. Take these notes to their addressees, and do not let your mother out until she is well again. Tell her this is an order."

This was fantastic; Mother was going to get better. "Oh, thank you, Sir." He bowed and left the house in a hurry.

Doctor Harvey: "It is not what I feared. There is no blood being expelled when she coughs. Moreover, the cough is dry. I can give her something that calms the cough and reduces the fever. She can stop taking what Dr Harris has prescribed. Your mother needs to drink a lot of water and sleep well. This cough syrup should help with her sleep and the cough. Keep her warm and give her tea during the day."

Once the doctor had left, Matthew stoked the fire in the pitifully small room. Its tiny size should have made it easy to warm up, but the floor remained cold. Matthew opened the wooden chest in the corner and took out old blankets and shawls. He put one over the window to block the wind and then folded the other at the foot of the entrance door to cut out the wind. He made a soup of potatoes and lentils and took a bowl to his mother.

She smiled. "Thank you, Son. And people used to say that it would be difficult taking care of you. If only they could see my young man now."

The war ended and a sense of relief echoed throughout the populace. For mother and son, though, the objectives remained as before.

Looking after one's mother alone at thirteen was rare, even in war-battered London.

Gail started sleeping through the night within a week. The cough and fever both subsided. Matthew returned to school at night. A fortnight later, Gail's recovery was complete. She returned to work, and Matthew was back at day school.

It was difficult to stop thinking of how important money was. He was studying to earn; what if he tried to get a job with one of those offices near the docks? Not all the people who work there went to school. In any case, after school was done, he would be looking to work, so why not start now? If things do not work, he could carry on with his studies.

"Matthew, education is the main priority. I do not want you to have to do household chores for others. My parents thought that I would meet a man who would look after me. But then they died, and I fell in love with a scoundrel. An education would have come in handy. There are many jobs now for women. If you had been a girl, I would have done the same, Matthew."

"But Mother, I just want to try. I can always go to night school after work."

"But I won't see you at all then, Matthew."

Matthew was surprisingly at ease in his schoolwork

for a youngster with unusual responsibilities. He went to school early each morning, finished his lessons, stayed on to complete his homework and left his schoolbooks in a cupboard in class. He then headed home, stopping at the market to buy vegetables. He would purchase tea and honey if he had money left over. Once home, he would clean the room, take out the toilet pans to the drain, shake out the quilt and blankets and put them all back. He would also go and fill water from the hand pump outside on the street and carry water pails back into the room. Once the house work was done, he would light the coal fire, heat the water and have a quick bath. The room would be warm for his mother's return. The fire would heat up the stove and allow Matthew to make a soup using leftovers from the previous day, adding potatoes and salt.

The Stephens coped. They may not have had much, but they had each other.

Gail looked at her son and wondered why he was so confident. Was it because he was doing well at school or managing the household? Or was it just that he was so good-looking? Matthew had toned pink cheeks over which deep blue eyes gazed out from under a fringe of dark hair. Young or not, he was a strapping male with a handsome face. His thick neck supported a face with chiselled features, high cheekbones, a small nose and ample eyebrows. The most remarkable features, by far, were his deep azure eyes that had a will of their own. They gazed undaunted, concealing what was mulling behind them. When his eyes slid into a smile, the mouth followed faithfully, revealing perfectly aligned teeth. His radiance amidst the contextual grime was as conspicuous as an isolated water lily floating unblemished in a swamp.

Matthew Stephens

At seventeen, Matthew Stephens secured an apprenticeship in the London office of the East Asia Company as a shipping clerk. The application had been surreptitious as well as audacious. Gail had no idea that her son had just turned up at the offices and asked to speak to the boss and that the manager had agreed to see him.

She thought it was too soon to work, but Matthew promised to continue with his technical college studies of accountancy in the evening sessions after work to secure his diploma. Moreover, the fact that the manager had liked him must mean that he was ready to start work.

The company had many trainees but none as young. The first few weeks were an initiation. "Senior colleagues," a term that included everyone, asked him to make tea. Others laughed at him, calling him names: Kiddo, Junior, Matt the Brat. The girls found him "dashing."

He was assigned to a team in the shipping department that verified the documentation for cotton shipments from India and Egypt to England. He also learnt to prepare the shipping manifests for outbound shipments of textiles and machinery. The 'Kiddo' executed his work with gusto, a sense of purpose, diligence and rigour. As for the jokes aimed at him, there was little to get upset about. It was all meant affectionately. In any case, pride was not a characteristic with which he was familiar.

His greatest strength was his attitude of 'just getting on with it.' That is what he was being paid for. And once he finished work, he still had his evening classes. It was a full day but one that would lead to something more worthwhile. His employers had yet to capitalise on his accountancy skills. But that did not matter. He was able to carry out the work he was given. Matthew was not more intelligent than his peers but certainly keener. There was no task that he could not take on. He did his work well, and his employers were pleased with his single-mindedness and sense of purpose. Throughout, he remained grounded and eventually won over his colleagues; whenever he had a free moment, he would offer to make tea for everyone. There was still much to learn from all these people, and remaining humble and respectful was important.

Work was enjoyable and paid a salary that helped his mother and him. And that is what really mattered. Matthew's concerns revolved around his mother. She was his moral anchor and the bedrock of integrity over which his childhood had flown. There had, of course, been the occasional ripple, but the ground had not moved. Gail had shown him that adversity was not something to avoid but to acknowledge and face. She had always remained calm, listened and given advice on all the simple things in life.

At the office, Matthew became good at his job and even had an opportunity to use the basic cost accounting he was learning at technical school at night. He understood the basics of double-entry accounting and would draw up a monthly profit and loss account for his department. The company's assistant accountant would review Matthew's work, make some corrections after discussing them with Matthew and then file them with the monthly accounts of other departments. Matthew realised that every business action anywhere within the company would find its way into the accounts.

After two years at his desk, Matthew started computing the cost of holding a ship at port while it waited to be filled with cargo. The shorter the turnaround time, the lower the docking costs. Matthew also put the concept of 'opportunity cost' to working out the cost of sending ships out earlier than when they were filled, with unused capacity. His peers and superiors did not consider this nice, hardworking young man a threat. They let him get on with it and encouraged him to present his work directly to the manager. The latter admired what he did and started trusting him, openly commending his efforts. The boy who had just shown up asking for a job was coming good a lot sooner than expected.

Matthew was assigned to the East Asia Docks at the age of twenty to supervise the stevedores at work; his job was to verify that incoming shipments completely accounted for the incoming cargo manifesto and that the outgoing cargo was fully manifested. Matthew knew there had been discrepancies in the past, and his appointment there had been an expression of trust. Dockhands approached him to continue the practice of his predecessors, but Matthew was in this for the long term and did not want any blemish on his reputation. He thought, 'Reputation is all I can build at this stage. The Company trusts me, and I must meet their expectations.'

Loading and unloading cargo involved hard labour, but the wages did not adequately reflect the physical efforts of the workers. But, even at the poor pay rates, crowds at the gates asked for work each morning. This had been going on for generations. Some labourers belonged to the same families, sometimes even father and son on the same crew. Why had the sons decided to continue the tradition despite being poorly paid? Education had obviously not been a priority for their parents. Instead, the latter had opted for getting their offspring to chip in with daily wages. In their eyes, education did not pay immediately, whereas manual labour did. In families where a mouth to feed was one too many, working alongside one's father or uncle was commonplace. There was acceptance of one's situation. Matthew saw it differently; surely, if one's parent is putting his back into raising a family, it is important to move on and do something more satisfying and better paid. Given his mother's precarious financial situation and the low wages paid to the workers at the dock, it was clear that he would work extremely hard but have to find a different path to making money. He would have to use his brain more than his back.

During the year working at the docks, Matthew observed that the freighters were never filled on the way out. Moreover, on long-haul trans atlantic or Indian Ocean routes, major earners for all big shipping companies, the smaller batches of cargo were denied shipment if they did not correspond to the standard size of crates and wooden bulk boxes. In the old days, bespoke shipping had allowed individual items to be shipped. There had been no standard prices, and the tariff for each shipment was negotiated. The handling costs had been higher, but now, with more standardised shipment, minimum sizes, and standard rates, the unintended consequence was unutilised capacity. Matthew saw such spare capacity as a potential source of revenue. He explained to his superiors that such capacity could be sold cheaper to customers because the only additional costs associated with using spare capacity were the handling and loading charges. Lower prices would deviate from the standard tariff structure but would find customers who could afford to ship at the last minute or could despatch their cargo piecemeal. Any such bookings would bring in additional revenues and would go straight to increasing profits. He formally presented this idea to his supervisor, who then offered it to his boss. Ironically, Matthew had found a way to make money effectively out of a past practice.

The idea worked. The timing could not have been better. Exporters and importers no longer wanted to put all their eggs in one ship. It was best to ship smaller quantities. Goods were no longer sold at a wartime premium, but freight rates and margins at each stage still remained high. The supply chain had so many links, each claiming their pound of flesh. Post-wartime business was booming, and there were rich pickings for those picking their moment.

The selling of excess capacity took off and became a business activity: a special 'piecemeal despatch' department was created, headed up by twenty-one-year-old Matthew Stephens. His salary increased almost two-fold. He felt vindicated in his ethos of avoiding manual labour and focussing on cerebral opportunism. The quest for business opportunity came from uneasiness about manual work. It was not that he looked down upon manual work. How could he? It was the most honest type of work; his mother had earned her living doing that. It was also the surest form of work, which everyone could do. But Matthew Stephens did not want to be everyone.

He wanted to be someone.

Gail and Matthew moved to a new home, a one-bedroom flat with a wooden floor, a tin bath and windows that closed shut, keeping the wind out. Gail stopped working for the Smithson family but continued at Mr Burroughs' house. Although the gentleman was parsimonious with idle chat, he made an exception in the case of Matthew Stephens' mother and often asked after her son. "Gail, you should be proud of that boy. Please ask him to stop over for a cup of tea." Matthew would always visit promptly and provide an update on what he was doing at the East Asia Company.

"How much money does each shipment make?"

"This is confidential information, Sir. But theoretically speaking, if the running cost of each outbound ship to Singapore is one hundred thousand pounds and the revenue at full capacity is three hundred thousand, then at an average of 80% capacity utilisation, we are looking at revenues of two hundred and forty thousand pounds and a margin of one hundred and forty thousand. There is also the return journey for additional revenues. Of course, from this, we must take out our fixed costs and depreciation of the vessel itself. We aim to have about fifteen long-haul roundtrips per annum for each vessel. And we have twenty-three ships plying this route."

"Interesting business. Do ships get lost at sea?"

"No, Sir, they get damaged, but the shipping sector is very well served by the insurance companies. Moreover, the exporter insures all the cargo. The standard pricing for goods is on a CIF: cost, insurance, freight basis."

"What are the main risks?"

"Sir, the main risk is obvious: the break-up of the British empire. If the British colonies were to become independent, trade would not be guaranteed to continue with such regularity. Right now, our businesses enjoy a captive market."

"But trade is trade."

"Yes, Sir, trade is trade. But the Americans, Germans and the Japanese are gaining in importance. Tomorrow, it may be the Chinese and the Indians."

"Matthew, you are very young, yet you have picked up so much in your work environment. Of course, caring for your mother at such an early age has matured you beyond your years. And yes, you are right. We cannot afford to be complacent or arrogant. Empires rise and fall. Just like the waves on the high seas. We should always be prepared for turbulence."

"It is a very stable business, Sir, if trade continues even at its current levels. The war has anchored the importance of shipping in our lives. Transporting arms to far-flung territories would not have been possible otherwise. International trade is set to grow even further, especially as the war finishes. Our economies run on natural resources that are produced all over the world. The future lies with oil from Arabia, tin from Indonesia, rubber from Malaya, iron ore from Australia, and copper ore from Chile. Europe's industrial base presents immense opportunities only if we can get a regular supply of raw materials. If I had the means, I would raise finance and start a shipping company."

"You are incredibly young, but why not! Finance is always available for good business opportunities. How difficult is it to acquire a sturdy ship? And a dependable crew to run it?"

"Sir, ships can be acquired on lease through major banks active in the sector. Crews can be engaged with 'merchant navy contractors.' These companies engage crew from all over the world. Many of them do not speak English, but they learn very quickly."

"Would you like to be my partner in a shipping venture, Matthew?"

"Why, yes, Sir, but am I not too young?"

"Think about it for a few days, and then let's discuss this in more detail."

"But, Sir, what line of work are you in?"

"Tea and spices. I was born in Calcutta in India. We still

have tea estates in Darjeeling. Have you ever been there?" asked Mr Burroughs.

"No, Sir. I avoid travel because of my mother. In any case, I do not have the means for such a voyage."

"Soon, you will. Darjeeling is like a piece of Scotland. But then you have probably not been to Scotland."

"No, Sir, I have only gone as far as Brighton."

"Brighton is a good start. What did you think?"

"It was raining all the time, but the Pier is impressive."

"It certainly is, as is the Royal Pavilion."

"I did not get to visit it, Sir. I was in a long queue and had to return to the station to catch the train back."

"Do not worry. When you can travel, there will be many amazing treasures to discover."

"Yes, Sir."

Travel was an attribute that needed to be emulated. Matthew now had the means but still used his mother's presence as an excuse, maybe because he was single and had no real family or friends with who he could travel. His colleagues often spoke of the Lake District, Sherwood Forest and the Scottish Highlands. They had been to Marseilles in France and Genoa in Italy. One had even gone as far as Istanbul. He had listened and remembered the names of these places, but visiting in person was something quite different. He was reminded of the cargo offloaded when coming in from far-off locations. There was often an odour, a fragrance that came with it, a sensory, exotic identity that exuded its origins. When the cargo arrived at the docks, it was still surrounded by accompanying goods from the same region. Once offloaded and despatched to the receiving party, London's air would rapidly find its way into the fibres, grains and spices and change their chemical make-up just as London's own composition would metamorphose.

One day, he would travel to some of those lands and put his five senses to work. For now, he had to employ his sixth sense and sniff out business opportunities. Of course, age was not on his side, but with Mr Burroughs' patronage, that handicap was easily overcome. There was so much to learn at work.

Mr Burroughs was a well-known businessman with excellent social, business and government contacts. His name often featured in the local newspapers as he sponsored education and healthcare projects. The Mayor of London had called him a local treasure. If he saw something in Matthew, that meant something.

Gail Stephens was pleased. "Matthew, Mr Burroughs seems to have taken a liking to you. If you ever do anything with him, please ensure you work hard and show absolute sincerity and honesty. But be aware that he is part of high society, and such people have much more to them than meets the eye. Please do not do anything that goes against your values. Mr Burroughs will respect you for that. And you will have peace of mind. In the end, that is all that matters in life."

Mother was cautioning him at various levels here. It was not clear what she knew, but she was right. Success had to be built on the foundation of hard work and integrity. So far, things had worked out. With his mother by his side, they would continue on that track.

Matthew had stepped out and was walking towards the pub when he came across the local church. Although he had never been religious, he felt a curious urge to go in. The inside was empty and very silent. He walked through the aisle towards the altar and sat on one of the benches. He looked at the cross and the candles and felt drawn to them in a manner he could not comprehend. It was as if he was moving closer to them without moving from his bench. He smiled and closed his eyes. But even when he shut his eyes, he could still see the cross and candles quite clearly. He then felt a tingle in his feet that moved through his legs and up his body. When the tingle died out, it was replaced by a feeling of total relaxation. Matthew brought his hands together and said the Lord's prayer. The "Amen" brought him back to normality. That was quite something; he thanked God for everything and prayed for Him to stay by his side while he launched his life.

Matthew then walked back and let himself out, stepping back into the mayhem of the street.

Gwendolyn

"Congratulations, Matthew, on your appointment. It is very good news."

"Thank you, err."

"Gwendolyn. I work in accounts and know you from the reports you submit."

"Of course, Gwendolyn. I see you often. Well, thank you very much. I am pleased indeed."

"You should be. It is rare for someone to be promoted. You must be happy having been appointed manager."

Gwendolyn, an attractive but shy bookkeeper, worked in the accounts department at the East Asia Company's offices. They had often nodded acknowledgement towards each other at the bus stop. Gwendolyn had curly auburn hair, dimpled cheeks and deep brown eyes. She was slim and looked frail in her straight skirt and plain blouse.

The same evening, they chatted as they left through the front door around the same time as everyone else. After a few days, they started walking together from the office to the bus stop. Their conversation remained punctuated with extended pauses of silence. Although Matthew had gone through the travails of a hard childhood without flinching, anything bolder than a nervous walk alongside a timid female colleague was something life had not reared him for.

Occasionally, their hands would brush against each other; Matthew would apologise rather than grab the opportunity to dare something more adventurous. Gwendolyn would not respond; anything she said may give an unintended message: a "No, it's OK" may be construed as: "Oh, please go right ahead." An unspoken, quick withdrawal of her hand may be looked upon as "Don't you do that again." The glamour of the movies and the publicised romances of celebrities were all around, but these were two very ordinary individuals. What happened in films did not transfer directly into one's day-to-day existence. Unlike the movies, where things moved at an astonishing pace, their togetherness manoeuvred its path through awkwardness.

This, however, did not stop wild speculation in the office grapevine; it is bewildering how an innocent walk from the office to the bus stop can be transformed into a torrid assignation. Routine companionship for a few minutes became a lofty tale of lust and passion. The protagonists of the scenario were aware of the interest they had ignited amongst their colleagues, but nothing could placate the rumour mill. One evening, on the way to the bus stand, Matthew enquired, "You do realise that everyone back there thinks we're together?"

Gwendolyn did not look at Matthew. "Yes, I know, Matthew; people will always talk."

"Does it not bother you?"

"No, why should it? Does it bother you?"

"Well, we are not together, so it's a bit strange."

Matthew realised that what he had just said had not quite come out as intended. Gwendolyn did not say anything.

"I meant that we are not together as yet.."

Gwendolyn did not react particularly to the "as yet," but continuing to walk alongside Matthew without looking at him, she replied, "We walk to the bus stop and we talk. Beyond that, rumours are rumours."

Matthew decided that his caution was becoming quite an obstacle. "Well, what I meant is, what if those rumours were no longer that? What if there was substance to it?"

"Is that what you want?"

"Is that what you want, Gwendolyn?"

"Do you normally answer questions with questions?"

Gwendolyn smiled at the irony of her own response. They had reached the bus stop. Other people were around, and this abruptly ended their discussion, at least on that matter. Instead, Matthew spoke about a particular shipment that had to be sorted out. Gwendolyn's bus arrived. As she got on the bus, she heard Matthew calling her name.

Matthew called out, "Yes! Yes, Gwendolyn, that is exactly what I want."

Gwendolyn smiled and turned to make her way through the aisle to find herself a seat. As the bus started, she imagined that Mathew's eyes were trying to locate her, but she chose not to look back. The following day, they took the familiar path to the bus together; Gwendolyn did not mention the previous day's half-finished matter, nor did Matthew. Nor was the matter raised for the rest of the week. Matthew remained remarkably cautious in his approach towards Gwendolyn. He realised that he was very fond of her, but however romantic he would feel about her, his behaviour with her remained nervous and restrained. In his mind, though, he had decided that Gwendolyn would be his lady, and he would pursue her for as long as it would take. But how does one pursue someone? When with her, all his ambition and hard work, his ingenuity in finding new earning opportunities for the shipping line and his precocious self-assurance receded. Instead, he became a considerate albeit diffident walking companion who would often just be happy to faithfully walk by her side, even if it involved a stretch of silence. She must have liked him, but he was unsure if she wanted something more than just liking him.

Their togetherness played out in three different contexts: one in the office environment, the other in the daily walk to the bus and lastly, in the realms of thought.

Gwendolyn surprised him when they stopped at the bus stop. "What are you doing tomorrow, Matthew?"

Matthew's pulse raced, but he maintained an appearance of calm. "Nothing much. I will come into the office and work on the shipments register."

"But it is the weekend. What do you normally do on Saturdays?"

"Well, I normally work on the shipments register."

"Every Saturday?"

"And Sunday, actually."

Gwendolyn looked puzzled, but then the creases on her forehead straightened, and her face broke into a smile. "Tomorrow, we are going for a walk."

"With whom?"

Gwendolyn laughed. "With no one, you ninny, just you and I."

"Great, but... I'm not a ninny."

"Of course, you are, Matthew Stephens. You are a lovely, shy ninny. Let us meet here at this bus stop tomorrow at, say, two in the afternoon, OK?"

He felt a weakness that was unusual for him. Most challenges could be dealt with, but this! He had no experience with women. Self-assurance at work in dealing with colleagues had given the false impression that he was a worldly person; ironically enough, colleagues at work assumed that Gwendolyn had been an easy piece of work:

that Stephens chap has got that girl wrapped around his little finger. That walk to the bus stop bit is just a façade. Lucky man, though; she is all right, that one.

Gwendolyn thought that imagination is healthy until it becomes a rumour. Characters got pinched, and reputations got punched by slander. Beyond that, imagination can play havoc, and rumours can blemish character. Even amidst working-class libertarianism, such blemishes often damage. But Gwendolyn remained unperturbed.

Other girls at the office had shown interest in Matthew. It was nothing predatory, but Matthew was a good-looking chap with decent career prospects. He was always polite but had never reciprocated any approach or responded to innuendo. Behind his cheerful façade, he was preoccupied. He worried incessantly about his mother and his work and had not succumbed to the proclivities of a normal young man. But now, that was all changing. He had met Gwendolyn. He would stay on course and not settle for anyone else. He would replace rumour with reality.

Back at home that evening, it was difficult to steer his mind away from the anticipation of meeting Gwendolyn the following day. She must certainly like him. Otherwise, why propose an outing together? But then she thought that he was a ninny. Or she was just being mischievous and teasing him. Either way, he just had to be himself. If she were to like him for who he was, there would be no pretence or falsehoods.

Matthew was at the bus stop at a quarter to two. He wore a smart set of chestnut brown trousers, a white cotton shirt with small checks and a beige V-necked sweater under a brown, single-breasted woollen jacket. His shoes were a deep brown and were polished and neatly laced. His Brylcreemed hair had been combed with a parting down one side. His face was clean-shaven, and he had even dabbed on his Old Spice lotion. Matthew Stephens had prepared himself with the diligence becoming of him, even if it had taken him hours to put his clothes and everything else together.

Gwendolyn's bus stopped at two minutes to two. She wore a red jacket over a white dress with red piping. He had never quite seen her like this. Under a sun playing hide and seek behind a waft of clouds, Gwendolyn radiated a rare glow. "You look so handsome, Matthew." She took his arm and led him in the direction of the Thames. Within an hour of their walk, Matthew had gathered the courage to hold her hand. Gwendolyn put her fingers through his, and they walked on, clasping each other's waist. Gwendolyn paused by the banister at the riverside and pulled Matthew beside her. She turned to face him, looked straight at him, smiled, shut her eyes, and got her face even closer to his. Matthew kept his eyes open as he edged closer until his lips touched hers. For Matthew, this was a first kiss: the sense of lip on lip was sweet, sensual, and so delicate. Her perfume was subtle. Matthew's arms went around her waist, pulling her gently, and her arms clung to his shoulders. Matthew became aware of his arousal and arched back his hips to not appear vulgar.

Matthew did not want to ask, but, at that moment, he thought, 'Maybe I am the first chap she is kissing.'

They broke away from each other and walked side by side.

The next time they kissed was just before Matthew dropped her home. "The next time, we can go to a restaurant."

He thought to himself, 'I will ask for her hand only once I'm ready.'

When he returned to his room, he changed into his pyjamas in front of the mirror. He looked up at his reflection and caught a questioning look. 'That was great, but what is going on? You really like this girl, don't you?'

The face that looked back at him was handsome: chiselled

features with dark hair. The eyes were a deep blue. There was a hue of pink on his cheeks that bore testimony to his youth. The eyes sparkled with curiosity as if questioning what he was feeling. As he turned away to go to bed, his mind filled up with the image of Gwendolyn.

He lay there looking up into nothingness. But the void soon gave way to the subject of his infatuation. It was as if a cinema projector was beaming images of her onto the ceiling and that someone was spraying her perfume around his pillow. The mind is capable of intense sensorial pleasure, and it was particularly generous to Matthew.

"Do you like this restaurant, Gwendolyn? I do not know much about restaurants."

"Yes, it is quite nice. I never go to restaurants. What with the rent for the flat I share and for my contribution to my parents, I try to save. I go to the pub with my flatmate sometimes, but I do not like the smoke. But tonight is different. I have always wanted to try Italian food. And I have great company. I hope the food is good."

"I hope so, too. You are right about being cautious with money. We all have responsibilities. But when one has great company, one must make the most of it. We met, and here we are. My mother says we must accept circumstances and get on with it. Life must be lived."

"Of course, Matthew. Sorry, I did not mean to sound grim on our evening out. Let us make the most of it, eh?"

"I am a bit hungry, so I am considering ordering the veal dish. I have never had an osso bucco before."

"Have you been to Italy?"

"No, I have not travelled at all. One must cross all of France before one gets to Italy. It is only for rich people. Not for people like me, especially not at my age. Why? Would you like to go to Italy, Gwendolyn?"

"Call me Gwen, Matthew. It will feel a lot closer."

"Only if you call me Matt. I already feel close to you. I only have my mother for company and have never really known anyone else."

"Oh, that is a bit sad. But you have me now."

"Thank you, Gwendolyn, I mean Gwen."

"Matthew, Matt, have you ever been with a girl?"

"Oh, God, no. I have not. Have you?"

"With a girl? No, I have not."

"Sorry, Gwen, I hope it's not too awkward a question."

"It is. But I often wonder what it would be like."

"*Ecco*, the fish for the lady, vegetables, Miss? And for you, Sir, our *osso bucco*. *Grazie, Signori*. Enjoy your meal."

"Thank you. This looks nice."

"*Certo*. It tastes even nicer than it looks." Looking at Matthew, he said, "Your lady friend is *bellissima*, Sir." He bowed and left them to continue their questions.

"They are so charming, Italian men. My food looks nice. The place is lovely, as is the company. We can come here again if you like."

Things were getting interesting just before Romeo had butted in.

"Gwen, you were saying…"

"That Italian men are so charming?"

"No, no, about wondering what it would be like."

She giggled. "Oh, you remembered. My flatmate talks about men all the time. She is older and has been with many, but she feels depressed. And I am sorry if I called you a ninny. You are not a ninny at all. You are intelligent, and you are a gentleman."

They finished the meal, Matthew paid, and they then left. "I will walk you home. Do you live with your parents?"

"No, Matthew, I moved out to share a place with a

friend. My parents live and work in an inn near Liverpool Street. Some of the travellers were not very gracious in their behaviour towards me. My parents could not say anything because they were only employees there. So, I decided to move out when the possibility presented itself. They are quite busy but we try to meet often. I am their only child."

"As am I."

They walked along a broad pavement lit by sulphur streetlamps, a yellow darkness.

"Matthew, tonight, there is no one at home. My flatmate is visiting her parents. You can stay over if you like." She reached for his hand and clasped it as if she did not want to let go.

Matthew's heart skipped a beat and then resumed pumping with anticipation. Gwendolyn was leading, and he just had to follow. At no stage should he take the initiative and risk botching things up.

Gwendolyn's flat was neat 'girly' accommodation with lace curtains and tablecloths on the coffee table. There were even lace cushion covers on cushions neatly placed against the back of the dark grey fabric-covered sofa. It was a comfortable, small flat nicer than where he and his mother stayed. Mother and son kept their place clean but never decorated it. Before his salary rise, they had gotten used to extremely basic living, and after the raise, they had not aspired to a pretty house, just something warm, with running water and a bathroom.

"Please take a seat, Matthew. I will join you in a moment. Would you like something to drink? I have some sherry."

"Yes, please. This is all very nice. I am sorry, but I have no experience of such situations and am a bit nervous."

"I gathered. I always said that you were a ninny. For me, having an older flatmate helps. Although I have never been with a man, she gives me tips." She came and sat next to him and put one hand on his thigh. "Today is the occasion to use them. Do not worry. It is only me." Matthew grew bolder and put his arm around her back. She looked up at him. He kissed her. She kissed back. Soon, both their mouths opened and gave way to curious tongues. This was delicious. His hand moved to her waist, pulling her even closer. She got up, took his hand and led him towards her bedroom.

"Matthew, I am sorry. This is all too fast."

"What? You are right. I am sorry. I should have been more careful. I do not know how this goes. I should be leaving."

"No, Matthew, I am hastening things. I am behaving like a loose woman. I really want to, but…"

"So do I, Gwen, but we should wait. I can never think of you as a loose woman. It is my fault. For so long, I even hesitated to hold your hand. So, this is quite daunting."

"Do you like me?"

"Like you? I am crazy about you. I think of you all the time."

She kissed him and drew him closer.

"Are you sure, Gwen?"

"Yes, Matthew."

They undressed each other and gingerly moved onto the bed. Gwen lay on her back as Matthew gently lay on her, using his arms in a half push-up to not put all his weight on her.

The sensation of flesh on flesh was exquisite. How could skin be so alive? And he had never felt himself as hard. It was as if all the blood had rushed to one spot. She led him in and then arched her back to push herself against him. Matthew had obviously thought of this moment but never expected the ecstasy he felt. He had always imagined that making love was one-sided, with the man doing everything, but here, Gwendolyn was moving in a way that was intensifying the sensation. Man and woman were deriving pleasure by giving, bodies and minds engaged in exquisite confluence.

Just when it could not get better, there was an explosion. Their senses resonated in a chorus of intensity. The fact that they both sighed in unison meant little to the inexperienced lovers. They stayed in each other's arms, each feeling a fullness that tingled throughout them. For the new lovers, just gently caressing each other was enough to awaken their senses again.

Gwendolyn leaned over onto Matthew's sculpted torso and crossed her leg over his. Matthew had his hand on her back at the level of her waist. "You have such lovely skin," he said, caressing her back from waist to shoulders. He felt Gwendolyn respond as she shifted on to him, moving up to his waist and letting her legs rest on either side of him.

Matthew was aroused even before moving his hand up to her breast. She smiled and sighed as she descended on him. Matthew gasped a gasp of intensity. She was moving gently on top of him. She started moving quicker with a surging sense of urgency. There was an air of abandon as she began sighing; this aroused Matthew even more, and he felt himself approaching a crescendo. As pleasure took over their senses, the imminence of another orgasm ignited simultaneously within both.

"I love being your ninny," he whispered.

She kissed him. "Shh."

She savoured the moment she had been waiting for. She felt spasms repeatedly. Matthew was also riding the wave and followed suit. The rapid breathing slowed down gradually as they lay on each other, lulled onto a tender cloud of nothingness, before falling asleep in each other's arms. But then, one of them woke up and aroused the other with the movement of yearning. And so, the next hours were spent drifting in and out of sleep, every waking moment, another act of passion.

The sky outside had started to light up.

Matthew had spent the whole night making love to the woman who was now his. Everything he had ever wanted was lying next to him, but fatigue was setting in, and even desire was losing its edge. Pleasure was an intoxicant that had to be consumed in moderation.

It would have been easy to stay there and forget everything beyond the perimeter of such exaltation. But there was still his mother and his job that needed his attention. Matthew kissed Gwendolyn and left for his own place to bathe and get ready for his life as a man, not before arranging to see Gwendolyn later that afternoon by the river where they had first kissed.

"I know it is Sunday, but as I did not go to the office yesterday, I will go home, bathe and then go in for a couple of hours. We can meet later this afternoon if you like."

"The ships will not stop sailing if you do not go in today. How can you even think of the office at such a moment? You really are a ninny. I will see you by the riverside at two."

He pecked Gwendolyn on her dimpled cheek and left. On his way home, Matthew stopped to buy groceries. Gail had a day off, but she had gone to church and then would stop at the tea house for her cuppa. She would then go for a walk along the canal before heading back home later that afternoon. Normally, Matthew would be at the office and not eat with her. But this morning, he cooked a big breakfast and smiled as he devoured the toast and eggs. This must be the best Sunday morning of his life. He could not stop thinking about the night. He bathed leisurely, humming like a little boy, and then wiped himself dry. As he stepped out, he smiled to himself. He was in a cocoon of well-being, and everything he looked at seemed bright, clean and happy. A light-headedness had set him afloat. The air was fresh, and the sky was a clear blue.

He headed to the office.

The familiarity of the musty smell of leather and paper in the office was reassuring. He had to squint to adjust to the room's darkness, especially on a Sunday. He flicked on the light switches, and he was at home. There were stacks of files and paper on many desks, but his desk was immaculate as always. Everything had been filed in the hanging folders in the file cabinet behind his chair. He looked through the week's shipment records.

But his mind kept going back to the night. He felt aroused just thinking about it. "I am here to do some work. So, let us get on with it." He scrolled through his files for two hours, making notes of cargo discrepancies on a sheet. Once the list for the past week was done, he put the papers away, tidied his desk and got up to leave. On his way out, he switched off the lights and locked the main door. As he walked to the river, his mind wandered. 'How had she felt? Was she in love with him? She seemed quite sure of herself. Had she told him the truth? Had there really been no one else? Are there still others?'

'Should I tell her I love her? Or should I just play emotionally detached? Will we make love again tonight?'

Gwendolyn was waving towards him. As he approached her, his only thought was, 'She is here. That is all that matters.'

As he kissed her, he recognised her skin's taste and smell and the light perfume she was wearing. "Oh, Gwendolyn, I missed you."

"Then you should have just stayed with me instead of shooting off to the office."

"Yes, I know…"

"It does not matter, and we are here now, you and me. Are you going to take me to your place?"

"Eh? Why, o-of course."

"Not right away, you ninny. Let us walk a bit and get something to eat first."

"O-of course, th… that's exactly what I had in mind."

"No, it wasn't."

"Err, Gwendolyn, would you like to come to my place this evening? It is very modest, a lot less welcoming than yours."

"I wouldn't expect anything else from you, living alone without a woman and all that."

"No, in fact, there is a woman, but it is my mother. She is old and not very well. She has always worked, and we have never had much money to do anything more than live a basic life."

"And I thought you were living a bachelor life, and I was just another girl. Matthew, I do not come from riches either. My parents live in London. They both work at a travellers' inn near Liverpool Street. I don't want your mother thinking you are spending time with a woman of easy character."

"No, no, Gwendolyn, she would never think that. In fact, she will be happy to meet you. We can all arrange to meet at a park one of these weekends. And we can go to a nice pub for a drink and a wholesome dinner."

"Yes, of course. What did you tell her about last night?"

"I would have told her that I went out with a colleague, and it was too late to return home. When I got home, she had already left to go to church. She often wanders around on Sundays because I go to work. During the week, she cleans the house of a wealthy couple and helps with other household tasks there every day of the week."

"And your father?"

"I do not know him. He left my mother when he learnt she was with child. They were not married. There has never been any contact."

"Oh, I'm so sorry, Matthew."

"Do not be. For me, it has been quite normal to have one parent. But for my mother, it was very difficult. Society looks down on single mothers. People took her to be a loose woman and me to be her bastard. I did not care about myself; my mother was seen as easy prey. What annoyed and hurt me the most was the shamelessness of men when they encountered her."

"Men, ugh."

"Not all men. Especially not the ninnies."

"I hope not, Matthew. I have never been with anyone else. So, I do not have any experience."

"And you will not ever be hurt by me. I am so happy to be here with you."

"I have been fond of you for quite a while, Matthew. Although you are quite popular and sociable at the office, you were slow, even hesitant with me. Do you know what, that is what I like about you. I like your modesty and sincerity."

"I am both Gwendolyn. Why would I not be? And I am hesitant because I do not want to do anything wrong. I never knew that you liked me."

She kissed him on the cheek. "And here I was about to apologise for calling you a ninny. Let us walk a bit."

Even the grey sky seemed romantic, clouds cosying up to each other to keep the sun to themselves. The breeze was refreshing against the intimacy of a tight clasp around each other's waist as if on the deck of a ship staring on to a new horizon. Matthew thought, 'Why is being together in the moment all that matters? How can we feel so strongly about someone and experience joy rather than pain?'

Another restaurant meal completed the evening. "I will pay this time, Matthew. I insist."

Matthew walked her back to her place but did not go in. Instead, they stayed at the entrance while Matthew explained that he should return home.

"Of course, Matthew, I am not going anywhere. You should make sure that your mother is all right."

It was good that Gwendolyn understood his responsibilities towards his mother. A lingering embrace was sealed with an enthusiastic kiss before they managed to separate themselves and bid each other goodbye.

Matthew sat on his bed, leaning back against his pillow, but the previous night's lack of sleep was taking its toll.

Gail had put a kettle on to prepare her sleep powders.

Sensing movement, Matthew's eyes opened. He walked to the kitchen and found his mother. "Mother, I spent the afternoon with Gwendolyn. I am sorry if you were alone."

"Not at all. I had a lovely day, although the walk was a bit chilly. Gwendolyn? Is that not the girl who works with you?"

"Yes, Mother."

"You often talk about her. Do you like her?"

"More than that. I love her."

"Does she love you?"

"Yes, I think she loves me as well."

"It is wonderful to love and even better to be loved back. It is not for everyone, but for those who experience this happiness, it is a true gift. You are being nice to her, I hope?"

"Of course, Mother. I told you I love her."

"We often hurt the ones we love, Matthew. We need

to try and show our love so that we can start building a relationship of trust and confidence."

"Yes, of course. I am hoping to marry her one day."

"My son is talking about getting married. How nice. But marriage is a huge responsibility. Marriage is not just about love and passion. It is about compatibility, about adjustment, about honesty and support. Are you ready?"

"I will soon be."

"You are the best judge of that, my son. All I know is that you need to be with someone who can live with your poor past, your modest present and your searing ambition. I hope that you find both love and success. It is so nice to know that love can blossom amidst such simplicity."

The words had hardly been uttered when the siren broke out, warning of the rounds of the police. Fire brigades were scrambling past, and the quiet had given way to a cacophonic panic. Not another gang bust! Things were getting quite edgy in London, and the rise of gangs was playing havoc with local communities. These were times of prosperity, but communities that had arrived from eastern and southern Europe were goaded. The grievances against them were that they were stealing jobs. And they worked odd hours; this was unfair. They were taking our trade. They should go back to where they come from. Back to Poland, back to Italy, back to Portugal. Son and mother went out onto the street. A few streets away, flames were creating a menacing glow. It was a Catholic school for Polish and Italian children. They had even accepted Caribbean kids.

Explosions and flames were becoming the new normal. Intolerance and victimisation of the newly arrived became routine. All these families were trying to do was to make a living and get an education.

They returned to the house, and Matthew's mind suddenly switched back to the more pleasant subject of Gwendolyn and himself. All relationships were a responsibility. His mother and he had been each other's responsibility. Now, there was Gwendolyn. One day, they would start a family and buy a house; the duties were unending.

Matthew's life would now have three pillars: shipping, mother and Gwendolyn. It all seemed daunting, but then most men had to juggle irreconcilable demands made at each turn of life. Mother had managed in the most demanding situations, buoyed only by her love for her son. He was all she had. He hoped that Mother did not feel that her importance in his life would be affected in any manner. 'We have gone through so much together. And she is the only person who knows everything about me. Everything.'

Mother and son cleaned the kitchen, tidied around them, and each went to their respective beds.

Once in bed, his eyes remained open and stared at the darkness, the image of Gwendolyn playing out on the ceiling. "You're still a ninny." Matthew felt himself aroused. So, he just turned to the side, grabbed a pillow and closed his eyes, smiling. Sleep remained elusive as all he could think of was the love he had made the previous night: a rare feeling of sensual pleasure, happiness and completeness that he had never encountered before. How could tenderness be so powerful? How could the memory of flesh and the perfume of skin be so evocative that it aroused yet again?

Fatigue eventually smoothed the edges, the weight of eyelids bearing down on inner vision. Breathing became calmer and deeper, and the body and mind surrendered to slumber.

Lie deep, embrace the night.
Cease the worries for the morn.
Happenings that well might
View the stars that adorn.
The windows to your inner eye
Give way to the glitter, that light.
Let worry and care take flight.

He arranged for the ladies in his life to meet in a park. They were both exceedingly polite with each other until they started an exchange of 'ninny' jokes at Matthew's expense. It was evident that there was strong mutual approval.

Gwendolyn became a regular visitor to the Stephens household. Gail asked her to stay over, but Gwen felt that would not be appropriate.

Matthew was tasked to accompany her back after every visit. He did not always come back home after taking Gwen to her place. Gail was happy with the way things were. He had found a lovely girl; they should make it through life together. After all this time, things were taking a turn for the better. Calm and peace of mind had remained elusive in the Stephens household. Destiny had never played them a decent set of cards. But this time round, the sun was shining over a calm ocean.

Her son had got through a most improbable education: day school, night school, college and then he had got a decent job in a great company. And if all that was not cause for celebration, he had met a lovely girl: a strong companion who would stay by his side till the end.

She, Gail Stephens, could now look forward to a family wedding and grandchildren. At last, she would be like everyone else. Vindication was a potent validation of her life choices.

'So what if I had been left alone? I decided to keep what was mine, and it proved to be the best decision I ever made,' Gail thought.

Gail

Although the piecemeal department grew and his relationship with Gwendolyn deepened, Matthew Stephens' salary stagnated. The general excuse being bandied about was that these were times of severe competition and that the boom years were laced with the cut-throat behaviour of the powerful. What was conveniently left out of this rationale was that the government had maintained its custom for its wartime carriers and continued offering quasi-exclusivity for the massive reconstruction of the post-war years. So much had been destroyed, and entire cities were being rebuilt. There was also the post-war legacy on the seas where the warring factions had previously caused intended damage with sub-surface sea mines. So, ships were still being lost, causing considerable financial damage. Combat aircraft had engaged in aerial conflicts only for attack and defence purposes. There was no psychological advantage in having aircraft fly over vast stretches of the ocean with no one to encounter but merchant ships.

Good times or tough times, remuneration at the East Asia Company was based on seniority, not on revenue generation. Merit was commended, but there was no tangible pecuniary reward. For Matthew, what was the point of being appreciated if one was not remunerated? A pat on the back makes no sense if that same hand is empty. If you generated income for your employer, then surely there was entitlement to its riches? So what if there was competition in the shipping industry? The company still enjoyed strong government patronage and in turn ensured that its main client was being served round the clock.

Matthew was playing his due role diligently. But this was being taken for granted. That is how it worked. There were the owners, and there were the workers. The owners would pay the workers whatever the market rate was. They would get rid of staff when there was no such need. Paying anyone financial rewards would only spoil the person and give much importance to someone who was just doing his job. Isn't that what the salary was for? Keep them in their place, lest they start aspiring to a chair at the table. One should not be misled about one's place in the world.

This lack of potential for a higher income made Matthew uneasy. He toyed with the idea of another job or even starting up on his own in this post-war period. War or no war, there was a market for buying spare capacity and then reselling it in bespoke quantities to shipping agents. Matthew knew twenty-three shipping companies with offices in London and over a hundred freight agents. He would have to consolidate this network and gain complete market trust. Trust was the most important capital when one had no wealth.

While he was contemplating a change in his career, his mother took ill once again, only this time the affliction was worse; there was pain, loss of weight and rapid physical deterioration. Mr Burroughs helped to secure an appointment with a well-known private physician. After examining the symptoms and conducting certain medical tests, the doctor confirmed that the disease had already progressed and would continue to spread rapidly.

The doctor explained that her condition was the subject of research in many countries and suggested surgery as a potential first step. He cautioned that the surgery did not guarantee that the disease would stop.

Gail would not have it. She did not want to take the risk of an unreliable operation, which would only burden her son. The inevitability of her fate needed acceptance, not denial. She would rather have access to morphine to deal with the pain and live out the time she still had.

The affliction was aggressive and sapped the features on her face; her hair had thinned, and whatever strands were left bore the consistency of brittle hay. Even the light in her eyes had dimmed. Without surgery, the disease attacked the liver and shortened the last stages of her illness.

"It has been a difficult life, Matthew. But now it is time to leave. I will find it easier in the afterlife. You know, Son, fortune and misfortune skip generations. You will live a great life."

"I am sorry, Mother. I have let you down. I do not want you to leave." Matthew had hardly ever cried, but this was his mother bidding farewell to him.

"No, Matthew. There is nothing to cry about. You can finally live your life the way a young man should. Just remember to care for others as you have cared for me."

Her feeble voice uttered the message with conviction.

Gail Stephens had been the compass of Matthew's existence; she had defined the direction of his travel so far but would no longer be there to show him the way. It was lamentable that his mother's main companion throughout her life had been hardship. She had been very unfortunate. Her travails would not be consigned to futility. Matthew had developed his values from her; her strength in adversity was a remarkable feature and would be difficult to emulate.

He would do his mother's bidding: live his life. But how? A life without her by his side would not be a life. He would have to adopt her sense of human dignity fervently. And he would have to believe in her presence even when she is gone.

There would always be that star in the night sky that would shine brighter and help him navigate the high seas.

Gail STEPHENS (1887-1952)
Loving mother, hard worker, honest woman.
"Life is about accepting one's lot and getting on with it."

The only people who attended the church service were Matthew, Gwendolyn and Mr Burroughs. "Losing your mother is a tragedy indeed. But do not forget that she will always watch over you. All you need to do is call out to her." Matthew was looking into a void while his ears took in Mr Burroughs' words. He nodded until he just broke down, eyes and nose streaming. Gwendolyn looked at Mr Burroughs and hugged Matthew as he sank his head into her shoulders. He was still sobbing as Mr Burroughs looked at Gwendolyn in compassion and patted Matthew on his shoulder before nodding a farewell to Gwendolyn.

Gwendolyn and Matthew stayed there for a few minutes before they started walking away from the grave, her arm around his waist, her head against his shoulder.

Matthew went through the next few days in a daze. He returned to work, but the condolences at the office only extended his despair. Once home, he would go to Gail's room, sit at the edge of her bed and feel the emptiness. His mind darted back to when she was fine, and then it would envision the frail body of a suffering mother whose life was slipping away beyond reach.

Gwendolyn came to his house with him after work. She cleaned and put things back in their place before returning to her place. She started staying over at weekends and, soon enough, even during the week. Matthew was expressionless and had retreated into a cocoon of isolation. Gwendolyn chose not to say much as she did not want to intrude. Matthew would need to accept that life ends, but death is eternal.

She had to be there for him because that is what one does. She was spending days and nights at the house. Matthew was grateful for Gwen's presence, but his grief was compounded when he thought of Gail's lonely life. He and Gwen had each other. But Gail had had no one.

Gwendolyn and he would visit the cemetery every weekend, clean the tomb and change the flowers. They would look at Gail's burial place for extended moments. Gwendolyn would walk away after a few minutes while Matthew would linger in silence, his head bowed in memory and respect.

He would play out the times his mother would get ready and leave for work after having put everything in its place, the rare times she would accompany him to and from school, the times he would go to Mr Burroughs' house with her as a child and then by himself as an adult, the abuse she had faced at the hands of Mr Strike, the quick-thinking and decisive manner in which she had reacted, the day in the park with Gwendolyn, the day the doctor had said that the disease was incurable.

A life like no other, it would not go in vain.

Matthew Stephens and Co was established in Old Street with a staff of three clerks under a twenty-five-year-old boss and his young lady accountant. The financing had come from Matthew's savings and a substantial loan from his benefactor, Mr Burroughs. Trade was erupting, but the first shipments were still difficult to secure. Matthew had to contact agents to ask what and where they were waiting to despatch and then had to find out what space remained on outgoing ships; he had a shipping list where he mapped demand from exporters and the availability of cargo capacity with shippers daily. He used a handwritten register for both. Shipping companies would let him know the available spare capacity by destination and departure date. In parallel, for each destination, his office would enter client enquiries. Daily aggregation of client demand per destination would determine if a profit margin could be earned using the available capacity. 'Overs' and 'unders' on either side were negotiated with both the clients and the shipping companies, and a solution was usually found before the vessel sailed.

All cargo was stored in his warehouse, clearly stating the vessel's name, the scheduled date of departure, the destination and the loading bay number. Once all the details were marked correctly on the packages, the details were transcribed to the register. Matthew would personally supervise the loading of the ships. It was particularly important to ensure that no bookings were left unshipped. A copy of the log would be sent by teleprinter to the destination port. The clearing agent on site there would then unload the shipment. Once all the cargo was accounted for in the receiving warehouse, they would send a teleprinter confirmation back to headquarters. A local delivery company would deliver the goods to the end customer.

If there was any return cargo, the same visit would be a collection trip. The sailing ship's manifest would be updated when stocked at either warehouse, receiving or despatching. Matthew Stephens was the only company that could provide a tracking service for the cargo at the end of every day. This service required excellent teleprinter and communication links with agents in various parts of the world, and all his interlocutors saw the value added in such an offering. It was a strong selling point. Trust was good, but there had to be a value proposition in business.

Matthew thought, 'One day, we will have machines and gadgets to do all this for us, but for now, we must use our heads and hands.' This approach, although tedious, ensured that any cargo loss could be followed up and, in the instance of loss or theft, could be claimed through insurance quickly. His clients were happy that they no longer had to write off undelivered shipments as a normal aspect of business. They consolidated their other business through him as well. The reputation for service and reliability was an asset that would gain a share of a market gushing with post-war trade.

Matthew would always endeavour to find shipping space for cargo when a customer expressed a sense of urgency. In the market, there were other bespoke services for the customers. There was a demand for animals to be shipped across seas, horses being the most common. There was also a special wildlife division that specialised in animal shipping for zoos. The company had sent prime Irish purebreds for stud farms in distant corners, Australian alligators for zoos and safari parks, elephants, snakes, and dolphins. Matthew thought that business was a bizarre phenomenon. Once an initial breakthrough was made, communicated widely through advertising, public relations or word of mouth, new and repeat orders keep flowing in on a tide of goodwill and reputation.

Car dealers often wanted to accompany the merchandise, especially if it involved a high-value customised product destined for a Maharajah or a Sultan. The latter received a new Rolls-Royce or a Bentley every other month. The Sultan of Georgetown in Malay made do with a stretch limousine every few months from the same factories. War had annihilated the livelihood of millions, but the upper crust thickened their skins, made money and went about acquiring the pleasures of their choice. Even their managers were allowed to partake in worldly indulgence—accommodation berths with catering facilities needed to be booked. Matthew did not take long to understand why so many family men would accompany a car to a client thousands of miles away. The accommodation came with offerings of female company. He knew the shippers who offered comfortable and discreet accommodation on their ships. He called them floating brothels. His own company had strict instructions that any arrangements for individuals accompanying premium cargo were between them and the shipping company. Matthew Stephens and Co. should not be involved. They would only book the shipment. The only service was getting goods from A to B. Any staff member in breach of the ban faced immediate dismissal, irrespective of where that person found himself. Morality was never a strong business feature, but certain red lines had to be drawn.

"Sir, the Suez Canal has been nationalised by President Nasser. It is still open for our ships, but things are moving quite quickly and may get out of hand."

"Yes, I heard, Bertram."

Mr Burroughs had just arrived but did not interrupt Matthew's rant. "The fool has nationalised the Canal. But we had it coming, I guess. I just hope Anthony Eden does not start a war; he has been obsessed with Nasser for a while now. We heard a lot of rubbish about the Suez in my previous job. We need to ensure that our carriers are not stuck in the Suez. We need to check which ships are delayed and advise our clients immediately. Contractually, we are protected but we need to find the best solution for our customers. I would hope that the Ministry of Defence arranges an escort for our vessels to pass into the Red Sea or back into the Mediterranean, whatever is quicker."

"That has been taken care of, Sir. In fact, the Egyptian ambassador to London has personally confirmed that the Egyptians are escorting our ships to safety. Notwithstanding the stressed relations between our governments, they have committed to steer our ships out of the canal into the Mediterranean."

"Yes, Bertram, I understand that we have been plotting with Israel and France to get rid of Nasser. The American ambassador assured me that they will not support any move that will alienate the Arab States. Even if there is a conflict, it will not last long. But they need to make sure that our vessels are safe." Intense diplomatic activity between Israel, Britain and France followed the nationalisation. Nasser had banned Israeli ships from accessing the canal. Britain did not want to be seen as losing hold of the Middle East, and France was fed up with Nasser's support for Algerian anti-colonialists. Exactly three months after the canal's nationalisation, Israel attacked the Sinai.

"Britain should never have followed Israel in attacking Egypt. The Americans and the Russians have moved the United Nations to get us to withdraw. I do not think the Prime Minister will survive this crisis. We are not the world power we once were. We cannot go around policing the whole world. That is America's prerogative. How ever much we dislike admitting it, there is only one superpower in the West. And it is not Britain."

"Yes, Sir, we have also been in touch with the American embassy to assure them that we have good, strong relations with President Nasser's government and will push from our side so that our government reconsiders."

This time Mr Burroughs spoke. "Good thinking, Bertram. Our problem is that these bombings will damage the canal and will take a few months to reopen. Please ask clients if fresh cargo can be sent around the Cape. From what I gather, about seventy per cent of our cargo comes through the canal. And please make sure that all freight rate adjustments include a war premium. We expect to make serious money if we sail in risky times."

"Yes, Sir, the price rise will be remarkably smooth. This is what happened during the war."

"Back at the East Asia Company, we were always worried about ships being damaged and crew getting lost during wartime. But who would have thought that a lucrative hundred-and-twenty-mile-long waterway itself would be the cause of war?"

"Yes Sir, Nasser has his domestic population to impress. This strip of water has resurrected illusions of grandeur and references to the great civilisation. But Nasser is no pharaoh. There is no divine right to power. The only way to assert it was to wrest ownership of the canal and, with it, the leadership of the Arab world. Under Nasser, Egypt has been astute. It has capitalised on its Arab status and relied on its oil imports from Saudi Arabia, rather than Libya, which was not considered dependable and which exported most of its production to the West."

But Matthew knew that regional conflicts were an inevitable consequence of the region's geopolitics in which Egypt had become such a key player. The Americans and the Russians in the United Nations General Assembly resolved the Suez conflict.

The only loser was Anthony Eden, the British Prime Minister.

The market for piecemeal shipping rapidly grew,

allowing suppliers and exporters to ship part orders instead of holding on to large stocks of finished goods. The seller was happy as he could start the execution of the export order sooner and avoid warehousing costs. The exporters started modifying their customer contracts to ensure that they could ship piecemeal. Often, exporters of even smaller quantities could club with other small shippers via the cargo consolidation services of Matthew Stephens and Co. and not have to wait to consolidate their small orders themselves. For the shipping companies, they realised that their handling charges would go up, but compared to the lost revenues of unused capacity, that was of little consequence. The buyer at the shipment's destination was content as he could receive his order and move it to his buyers quicker than if they had waited for the entire order. He would also provide warehousing at a lower cost than in England—British ingenuity at its best. The whole value chain was benefiting. This was the new 'old' way of moving freight over the high seas.

The war was behind Europe, and although the atrocities of Auschwitz had left many a life destroyed, there was reason to hope that this time round, peace would hold for good as there would be no more megalomaniacs ready to destroy humanity. It was time for reconstruction, and the global economy was in double quick time with its recovery effort, creating vast fortunes.

The Americans were playing a crucial role. The strategy had worked wonders: blitz everything and raze entire nations to the ground through relentless carpet bombing to then claim the right to reconstruct for its corporations. Heavy industry, construction, building materials, and infrastructure were sectors prospering as never before. The Brits and the Europeans tagged along and claimed their morsels. After decolonisation, Africa and Asia lost decades of economic growth and were rudderless. Corruption was the new paradigm where politics and wealth became intertwined. Politicians were striving for power not to serve but to become rich, while their countries languished. Whatever unfinished business had been left behind by the colonial powers, the British, French, Dutch and Portuguese was completed by national governments. *Vive l'indépendance.*

It was a whole new world!

Matthew asked Gwendolyn's parents for her hand in marriage. They acquiesced immediately, not that they had a choice. Matthew had been with Gwendolyn for a while, and they were all but a married couple already. Plus, they were in business together and were a successful young couple.

Mr Burroughs was invited to the wedding, and he attended the ceremony, drinks and dinner. When leaving, he approached the couple and said, "Gwendolyn, you are fortunate to be with this young man. I have always believed in his potential. You are just the partner he needs. At the rate you are going, you will both become very wealthy. Take care of Matthew and yourself."

"Yes, Sir, I will and thank you! Matthew looks upon you as a mentor. He says that people like you are exceedingly rare. You helped him when he was desperate."

"Really? What else did he tell you?"

"Only good things. He is in awe of you, Sir!"

"In that case, he doesn't know me that well." Gwendolyn looked questioningly. Mr Burroughs turned around, nodded at the people looking in his direction and left.

There was no honeymoon and they got straight back to running their business. Since Gwendolyn had left her job at the East Asia Company, she had spent all her time on their business accounts. She emphasised: "Matthew, my husband, Mr Stephens, it is great if you make profits, but you must make sure that your clients pay you on time and, in turn, you pay your suppliers on time. Cash flow makes or breaks the reputation of companies. It is basic business wisdom, but one too many overlook in the euphoria of chasing sales. We are paying a commission to our staff on shipments for which the client has not paid us yet. We should pay out only once we have the money for the shipment."

Matthew ensured his sales executives did not book business just to rack up commissions. If Matthew were to get euphoric over the growth in sales and profits, Gwendolyn would simply ask: "How many of these revenues have actually been received in your bank account?"

Gwendolyn was the reality check that neutralised irrational exuberance. She was not against success. She was against failure. There is no point racking up sales on the books if the customers do not pay on time. She explained working capital management, which was critical for a growing business. One had to ensure that customers would pay on time so that suppliers and business expenses could be paid and that profits were being cashed, not just 'booked.' They set up a recoveries department to follow up on overdue payments. While overdue payments were being investigated, the customer was red-listed, and no further shipments were allowed for the defaulting customer. Legal action would be taken when necessary. On most occasions, this would work. Any debt that was considered irrecoverable was written off as a bad debt. But one bad debt could wipe out the profit equivalent of several shipments. Paying commissions to employees and agents would be settled once the customer had paid the shipping bill entirely. Prudent credit management was the best form of insurance. The finance department ensured that all customers who asked for credit terms were subjected to a credit check and a bank reference. Market reputation was also considered. If the customer did not check out, they had to pay the shipping costs in advance.

The other important aspect Gwendolyn insisted on was prompt invoicing. Cash customers were invoiced on receiving the cash in advance, and all credit customers were invoiced as soon as the outgoing shipping manifest was completed and the ship had sailed. The odd reality of business is that one can make paper profits without making corresponding amounts of cash. Matthew knew this from his days in accountancy courses at night school, but his wife was applying the principles to their business on a daily basis. She had a simple maxim: cash flow is the lifeblood of business. When it dries up, life just withers away.

Rigorous cash flow management ensured they did not have to borrow from the banks. Not only did Matthew Stephens avoid bank overdrafts and further debt, but he also stacked up substantial cash reserves that were re-invested in growing the business even further.

Bankers and advisers quickly agreed that any business with Matthew Stephens and Co. would rely less on lending and more on presenting investment opportunities. They raised the possibility of taking the Company public, but Matthew did not want to share the ownership of what he had created. According to Gwen, their business should get rid of all its debt. He started paying back Mr Burroughs' loan. After half the loan had been repaid, Mr Burroughs asked him if the remainder of his loan could be converted into shares. How could he turn down such a request? He acceded straight away. Their business would remain closely held. Neither would sell any shares until they both agreed.

Matthew looked up from his glass of whisky. "What is going on, Mother?"

"You are living the life you deserve, Matthew."

"Mother, I wish you were still here."

"I am, Matthew. I will always be by your side."

"I don't know what I am doing or why I am doing what I am doing."

"You have become Matthew Stephens."

"But why, Mother? I still lost you."

"You will never lose me, Matthew. I will always be here. You now have what everyone covets: wealth. Just look at the silks and velvets in this room. You have come a long way from that stone floor and those bare windows. As a boy, you wanted to work at the docks. Now you own a shipping business."

"Yes, Mother, but it feels so empty. I cannot remove the past from my mind. You had an awful life, and I live in such comfort. Plus, the memory of that day keeps haunting me. I have done something awful."

"No, Matthew, there is nothing awful about saving your mother's honour."

"But I did not have to kill that man."

"Someone had to. If he had survived, there would have been other victims. Monsters do not change. Only death can stop them."

"But murder is a crime."

"Rubbish, you were not even an adult, and you had no choice."

"Hmm."

"Trust your mother. One can never do wrong in taking care of one's mother. You would do the same for your wife."

"Yes, Mother."

"Matthew, just keep doing what you are doing. You are good at it. It is your calling."

"When does it stop? Have I not become greedy?"

"No, Matthew, this is ambition. Greed is when you do not feel grateful for what you have. But you have not forgotten your humble past. "

"But why me? Isn't all this too much?"

"It is a matter of destiny, Matthew. We all drew lots when we came into this world. I picked destitution. You got wealth and influence. That is your life's purpose. Create as much wealth as you can, Matthew. And do good with it. Help others. Wealth may not make you happy, but it will still give you a lot. One day, I pray, you will find peace of mind."

Matthew put away the empty glass, switched off the light, and went to the bedroom. He murmured, "Gail Stephens is always right, always has been, always will be."

He quietly entered his bedroom.

The dim nightlight was on, and he could make out Gwendolyn's face peeking from over the edge of the quilt. He walked softly to his side of the bed and slid under the sheets. The bed was warmer nearer Gwendolyn, so he shifted towards her. She was turned, facing the other side. He just placed his hand on the curve of her hips; this soothed his conscience. It was reassuring to have a partner who was always there, someone who cared.

Matthew had been lucky with life companions. His mother had always been there. She still was. Gwen was by his side. Soon, there would be a child.

What else could one want? Such comfort is enough to lull anyone into serene slumber.

Victor on an unknown path
What comes now is hard to grasp.
My mind knows not what it hath.
Or what next I should clasp.

Yet I walk and swim.
One day, I will fly.
From all that is dark and grim
Into that vast and open sky.

Merstham

"Sir, the estate agent is here."

"Aah, please let him in, Bertram."

A diminutive, blond man with circular steel-rim spectacles peeked through the door before hesitatingly venturing into the office. "Mr Stephens, hello, Sir. I am from Hollyer and Co., James Hollyer."

"Please take a seat. So, what do you have to offer, Mr Hollyer?"

"Sir, I have been in touch with your office. I mentioned that the Heydon property may become available."

"Yes, yes. Is it?"

"You do understand that it is not Broadlands."

"Yes, although that would have been nicer."

"Sir, it is a well-appointed family property in Surrey with substantial grounds that I have discussed with your office."

"Yes, I know. It is the one in Merstham. I was in Reigate a couple of weekends ago, and we drove on through Merstham, a small town but an impressive property. It is of interest if my wife approves."

"Sir, I can take the ladyship to visit if you allow it."

"She is unwell right now. But in a few days, she should be able to make the long drive to Surrey."

Gwendolyn realised what real wealth could buy when she

visited the house that would be their new home. The Georgian mansion, outhouses, and expansive landscaped gardens were like the setting of a movie. Inside, the vast reception area with its marble flooring led to rooms on either side. There was silk wallpaper, off which Flemish tapestries hung from shining brass rails. Burgundy velvet drapes were drawn to make way for an ebullient sun. The gilded frames around mirrors the size of walls stood out as they reflected, deflected and dispersed the light throughout the room. Chandeliers dropped crystal baubles from ornate gilded arms. Walking through to the other rooms, she saw an evident pattern; the walls were either burgundy or dark green. The interplay of a bright sun, silk, gilded mirrors and crystal chandeliers came together to cajole the senses like no other house had. A subtle perfume of cinnamon and vanilla oil was floating in the air to complete the sensory overload. The house had been prepared for a viewing that should clinch the deal. Hollyer and Co. had left no stone unturned to ensure that Matthew Stephens and his wife would not be unimpressed. Such transactions came around rarely and would catapult Hollyers even higher. Their London-centric business needed to diversify out of the confines of Mayfair and Belgravia.

Hollyers were aware that the business elite was raking it in, and with their wealth, they wanted a more balanced life between the city and the countryside. They were looking to emulate royalty and the aristocracy. Matthew knew that he was part of the trend. He also knew that bridging the divide between established nobility and new tycoons was a cumbersome, if not impossible, endeavour, especially in a strictly stratified society that perpetuated itself in England and, more generally, in Europe.

It was no coincidence that businessmen like Matthew were better placed to finance the upkeep of estates than incumbents. A residence in Surrey or Berkshire was becoming the norm. Any firm that could clinch a Matthew Stephens transaction would instantly become the 'go to' estate agent.

"Ma'am, the property comes fully appointed. All the furnishings you find here come with the house. If there is anything you do not want, we can arrange for it to be removed. We can also arrange for any structural changes you deem necessary. We will put the best craftsmen at your disposal."

"We just need to make the house safe for a toddler. We are expecting a baby and we must think forward. We cannot have crystal and porcelain within reach, and we will need to ensure that winters do not creep into these vast interiors. The only change I would insist upon is that the study adjacent to the master bedroom be switched with the baby's room. We want our child to grow up next to us."

For Matthew, the imminent arrival of Gail Stephens' grandchild and the purchase of this immense mansion in Surrey posed a dilemma. "I want our child to grow up with my mother's values. The wealth of values is more important than the value of wealth. But we have all this money now. So why not be comfortable? I am sure Mother would have supported us."

The move was smooth. They continued living in London while the mansion, which they rechristened "Abode", was being readied for their arrival. The estate staff was informed of their day-to-day needs. The London staff was kept in London to keep the house going for times when Matthew would find it easier to stay there than be driven all the way to Merstham.

The government was constructing express roads up north, and maybe they would do something in the southeast as well. Matthew thought that the commute would be a lot quicker then. Gwendolyn had decided to base herself with her child in Surrey with a conscious decision to avoid social engagements in the city. She also wanted to get her hands dirty in the grounds of their vast property. There was ample land and acres of pasture to wander about. She and Matthew would walk around the perimeter of their grounds in a clockwise direction and come back in to slump into the comfortable armchairs in front of the fireplace.

A far cry from the granary where Matthew had spent his youth.

He was deep in thought. 'Life was about progressing and moving to bigger and better circumstances, but not without acknowledging one's humble beginnings. Destitution was a challenge many were born into, but one from which few could work their way out. All philosophies and religions preached acceptance and destiny. But very few preached self-reliance. Hard work and unwavering commitment shaped one's fortunes. But even these were not enough by themselves. One needed the magic ingredient: luck. That was the blessing bestowed on very few. It certainly played a role in getting me from A to B.'

Estate living did not come easily to a family with few needs. But a vast property offered calm and comfort. Without the clutter of London's hectic life and its swarms of people, the expanse provided the intimacy they needed. When Matthew and Gwendolyn were together, there was little need for the rest of the world; whether they lived in a silk cocoon or a nest of dry twigs was irrelevant.

Gwendolyn instructed her gardening team of experts to help with the planting and the upkeep of the grounds. Running the estate was a full-time occupation, one that she enjoyed and one for which she was immensely grateful. A house manager oversaw the kitchen staff, the gardeners and the cleaning staff. The governess was the direct responsibility of the mistress of the house. Matthew had established a home office that was equipped with a secretary. An office manager shuttled back and forth between the London office and the Abode. There was also a fleet of cars and chauffeurs. They decided to close many rooms and lounges and reduce cleaning staff. No such reductions were contemplated for the garden. There were immense grounds to cover and keep in pristine condition.

Matthew maintained a disciplined life. He lived by the adage of eating moderately, sleeping early and limiting himself to one whisky after dinner. He would leave early morning when he worked at the head office. If his appointments kept him at the office later than the evening, he would finish his working day and either stay in London or get driven to Surrey, where he would work from home the following day. With telephones, teleprinters and an office courier who would be driven back and forth, the transition between the locations was seamless. Matthew liked being at the helm of his ship. There was a competent team of responsible managers throughout the firm's network. However, they could only manage standard situations, not geopolitical skirmishes or nascent explosives still scattered in the seas his vessels plied.

The tone from the top needed to be one of care and total commitment, but Matthew delegated his functions as the business grew. Not every decision needed to be made at the highest level. If there were clear strategic and profitability goals, it was up to his organisation to deliver. The internal maxim was: stay loyal and stay focussed. The external motto was: always there, everywhere.

"Madam is not well, Sir. It may be time."

"But she just went up to rest. Is the nurse not with her?" He looked up questioningly.

"Yes, Sir, she is. Madam's waters have broken. I have arranged for the car to drive you and Madam to the maternity ward."

The contractions were quite strong and remained so throughout the drive. The medical staff was waiting at the hospital entrance. Gwendolyn was assisted onto a wheelchair and led away to the delivery room. Matthew realised he was still in his pyjama and nightgown, just having a nightcap after his dinner with Gwendolyn. She had felt discomfort and had gone to her room, and now they were here. "Bah, no one will notice."

Within a quarter of an hour, one house staff walked in with a change and shoes. Matthew was led into an empty room where he changed into corduroys, shoes, a twill check shirt and a navy pullover. He then headed off towards the room where Gwendolyn would be. A nurse was standing outside the room.

"Sorry, Sir, you will have to wait here. We have brought you an armchair. Would you like tea or a little snack?"

"No, thank you. How is it going?"

"The gynaecologist has examined her, and she is quite dilated. She got here just in time. We will let you know as soon as there is something."

Matthew Stephens set himself into the armchair, anxious.

"Do not worry, Matthew. It will all be fine." Matthew looked around questioningly but then surmised that his mother provided comfort from wherever she was. He closed his eyes and pushed himself back into the armchair. Parenthood beckoned. Gwen and the baby should come out healthy.

Before long, the door opened.

"Congratulations, Mr Stephens. You have a beautiful baby girl. She and her mother are both fine. You can see them if you like."

Gwen was smiling at the little new-born they had placed on her chest.

"Darling, Gwen, are you OK?"

"Yes, Matthew, isn't she cute?"

The room lights were quite dim, but he could see the deep blue eyes looking at him. "Hello, beautiful. Welcome." His voice tapered off into a sob. Tears squeezed through his moist eyes as he bent over to kiss her. Then he kissed his wife. "Thank you, Gwen. This is so wonderful. Thank you."

Matthew turned around and thanked everyone in the room.

They smiled. Matthew Stephens. Here he was, like any other new father. But that gorgeous little bundle of joy would not be like any other daughter. She would be Matthew Stephens' daughter.

The girl was registered as Sally Stephens before she was taken to Abode. Gwendolyn quickly learnt how to nurse her little gem. But that did not prevent little Sally from keeping her parents awake.

Matthew would trundle down to his office downstairs in a daze. His soporific state prevented him from getting any work done. So, he would go upstairs, have a long shower and after a quick breakfast, leave for London. The car was his sleeping chamber until Sally started sleeping through the night.

More generally, he would divert his focus from business to the well-being of his little family. He had been blessed with everything he had ever hoped for, and this was the cherry on the cake, but it was up to him to ensure that such normal aspirations were not sacrificed at the altar of ambition.

Mr Burroughs and Matthew met for lunch each Tuesday at Les Pêcheurs on South Audley Street in Mayfair for a weekly catch-up; Mr Burroughs would have the sole meunière and a glass of crisp Chablis while Matthew would always have *la lotte au Safran* with still water. Both avoided heavy lunches as that would affect the mental agility needed to keep up with each other. The duo aimed for the stratosphere and resisting the stodge on the ground had become a habit. There was no society gossip, no chitchat, just business, problems and solutions. The compatibility was uncanny. Often, they would have the same response to a problem. Intellectual incest reached a point where they started completing each other's sentences. The engine of growth and expansion was fuelled by calibrated doses of enthusiasm, optimism, opportunism, realism, caution, and outrageous daring. Business twins from different mothers!

Business cycles were approached ruthlessly. When there was an upturn, market shares were increased by aggressive pricing. When there was a downturn, acquiring struggling competitors was fair game. Banks were willing to provide limitless acquisition financing, but the terms had to be such that the acquired business could finance the acquisition within five years. This meant low financing rates from the banks, low acquisition prices and ruthlessly rapid restructuring to cut costs.

There was a special task force whose job it was to cut all superfluous staff and increase per employee productivity. Matthew had one requirement, though. Anyone who had a family and was being laid off had to be placed with a suitable job in another organisation, even if this meant that an out-placement consultant needed to be remunerated. No one should be deprived of the chance of making a livelihood. The task force was also responsible for the integration and assimilation of the acquired business as well as appointing fresh staff. The task force was highly rewarded for identifying and unleashing efficiencies that resulted in incremental profits.

Her father came to kiss her in bed, mornings and evenings. Sometimes, Sally was awake, and she would give her father a big hug. When her father left for London, she was still asleep. On Friday afternoon, her father would be home for a late lunch, spending all his time with Sally and Gwendolyn until Sunday night. They would let the governess, Rosalind, take Saturday afternoon and Sunday off. It worked well.

Under Rosalind's watchful eyes, Sally had become remarkably familiar with the nooks and alleys of the estate. Gwendolyn was happy that Sally respected and loved Rosalind. Initially, she was concerned that Sally could get spoilt with someone at her disposal all the time, but Rosalind was a seasoned child manager and was gentle and firm at the same time. She would listen to everything Sally had to say and would respond in an acknowledging manner.

She would ask Sally for her opinions. "What do you think about having pets? Is it important to be nice to your friends?" She would also teach Sally the names of flowers, introduce her to the notions of French and arrange little games in which Gwendolyn, Sally and she could all take part. Rosalind was in awe of Matthew Stephens and would get nervous in his presence. Gwendolyn was aware of this and tried to involve Rosalind when they were both with Sally. Matthew played along. Rosalind was good for Sally. So, they had to be good for Rosalind.

Rosalind taught Sally the names of flowers in English and French when in the garden. Sally would repeat the French word and start giggling. It was a game that she enjoyed.

She realised that many flowers had the same name in both languages. But when it came to grass and soil, there was no link; the French equivalents had to be repeated before they registered.

When weather permitted, Rosalind would leave mother and daughter alone in the garden. Sally would be wearing her junior Wellies and a small, waxed jacket. Her blonde locks fell like baubles over her blue eyes. Her chubby little hands would toil away with the tiny red and yellow garden tools she had received from her parents. Her favourite patch was a bump of mud where she found little resistance when digging in with her little yellow trowel.

"Do you want to help Mummy dig a square plant bed here?"

"Yes, Mummy. Should we put some water first?"

"Try without the water, Sally? You are a strong girl. If it is too hard, then we can add water." Water was a bad idea. Last time they had watered a patch, the housekeeper had had to spend an hour cleaning up the trail of little muddy boot prints all along the length of the parquet in the entrance hall.

Gwendolyn was rarely cross with her daughter. There was no reason to be. Sally presented a pure innocence that she and Matthew had never experienced before. Gwendolyn had lived a more 'normal' youth than Matthew, but nothing had prepared her for all this wealth and influence, granted that they had become part of a world where nothing was as it seemed. Yet, here was the ultimate truth of existence: a child simply happy to be there with them, bringing joy by just being present, asking for nothing but cuddles and kisses in return.

When it rained, Sally would still be taken for a stroll under the protection of a raincoat and a wide-brimmed hat. A mini-Lady if ever there was one. Rosalind had argued that

Sally needed to be at ease with the weather of her land. But she would be taken back in if it got too wet. On the other hand, Gwendolyn would stay outdoors, getting her Wellingtons stuck into the slush until she had executed her chosen task. She loved the smell of wet soil and damp grass. The splash of raindrops on puddles only added to the pleasure of being out. The garden staff would stay around in case she needed a helping hand. But Gwendolyn was stubborn in her determination. She would work the earth alone, uproot plants that had given up, plant fresh flowers and shrubs and tap in the soil before getting off her haunches.

Her return indoors was predictable; she would remove her boots in the small reception room just next to the main entrance, take off her waterproof overalls, dry her hands and face with a towel, change into a pair of warm, dry socks, and put on laced ankle-high boots. When she got to the fireplace, a hot cup of tea with ginger biscuits awaited her. If Sally were awake, Rosalind would bring her to her mother to join her on the rug at the foot of the sofa, and they would play snakes and ladders. The fresh air, followed by the warmth from the fireplace, culminated in a most pleasurable fatigue. Gwendolyn would accompany Sally to her room and often skip dinner in favour of a comfortable bed. The Surrey air is invigorating but exhausting.

Occasionally, a friend would be invited to play with Sally. As she was still to start school, the friends would be girls who were looked after by Rosalind's circle of friends. The governesses had quite a network and visiting each other while accompanying their charge achieved social contact for both. The governesses were great with each other's 'child'. The travails of riches prevented these children from having many friends. Here, life was very bespoke, and children were brought up to learn at home until it was time to go to a preparatory school to eventually land up in an exclusive school with ample playgrounds, personalised teaching and pastoral care. Sally liked to go around and visit Rosalind's friends and meet other girls in their houses. The Abode was a magnificent home, but there were no children. For the parents of the girls she visited, it was an opportunity to establish a link, however tenuous, with Matthew Stephens. Some would even boast at the office: "Oh yes, our daughter and Sally are friends. She was over the other day. Sally, oh, that's Matthew Stephens' daughter."

Matthew had had his London office renovated in mahogany, rosewood and leather. He hung a framed portrait of his mother that had been painted from one of her few photographs. He insisted on the pink in her cheeks. "She had rose lips and pink cheeks, a lot pinker than mine."

There was a large meeting table that could accommodate up to eight people. From time to time, he would use caterers to host a business lunch. Mostly, it was used for management meetings. He also gave directions that senior staff could use the table as additional working space for internal meetings when he was out of the office.

No one was to ever smoke or drink in the building. The workplace needed to be focussed, and staff should be capable of self-control when conducting business. There was no scope for disobedience. These were the boss's orders.

Strict discipline did not detract from the caring nature of the man in charge. Matthew invested in the welfare of his staff. He contracted local doctors to check up on his employees every six months. All sick leave was fully paid if the doctor prescribed it. There would be no cost to the staff for any treatment. And it did not stop there.

Stephens Vale was a modern integrated housing scheme that found its way into the lives of staff with families. The

Lever and Cadbury brothers had started company townships in the previous century for factory staff. But Stephens Vale was for all levels of staff and was designed by a renowned Swiss architect who aimed to offer privacy while building a closely knit community with its own amenities. A school was set up for both boys and girls. Teachers were recruited from the top independent schools. Pedagogical advisers were brought in from Finland. Rugby and football pitches, cricket grounds and athletic tracks were provided for students with professional coaches. The only eligibility requirements were two years of employment in an office, clerical or management job, or four years at the docks or on a ship. When some parts of the media criticised him for an Orwellian plan, he had a quite simple retort: "Why should the social elite be able to develop a more rounded personality and the working-class students be denied the chance to develop their talents? This was not about controlling their lives but rewarding their families with life chances."

The rent was capped at twenty per cent of the employee's take-home pay. Distinct types of accommodation were provided to correspond to the position and staff earnings. The dockworkers were equipped with residential halls where accommodation was more basic but where there were large communal areas. Communal life was encouraged for physical labourers, and more individual housing for office workers. Matthew did not intend to perpetuate a class system but wanted employees to enjoy social comfort.

Matthew's property management company would conduct all repairs and maintenance work. Any damage would be promptly assessed and put right. If it were due to misuse by the occupier, it would be deducted from the salary. If it were a development fault, it would be put right, free of cost to the occupier. This created the right incentive system and ensured the properties remained in good condition.

Such largesse was not without sanctions. Betrayal was punished. Matthew exercised zero tolerance for anyone who abused his trust. When he realised there had been a leak of details of contracts with certain key agents on back commissions, he traced the leak to the managers in charge and dismissed them immediately. The same applied to deckhands who had appropriated merchandise. The staff members and their families were evicted from their Stephens Vale house. Treacherous acts would not go unpunished at Matthew Stephens and Co.

Work and prosper but stay honest and loyal!

Exceptionally, Gwendolyn decided to accompany Matthew to the office in London to discuss the new candidates they wished to recruit from.

"Gwendolyn, the business is growing very quickly. We need to make sure that we can manage this growth. We really need the right people in place, people who are good and who we can trust. Many capable candidates are applying to work for us. When we are strong, we can avail ourselves of opportunities. When we are weak, we are bystanders. I do not want to be a bystander."

"No, Matthew, we will never be bystanders. We should be able to cherry-pick our staff. Matthew Stephens is an aspirational place for professionals, but Matthew, I may like you when you are weak."

Matthew approached her and grabbed her by the waist; "Really? I am very weak right now." Gwendolyn took his hand and led him to the couch. She pushed him onto it, raised her skirt and sat on him, pulling his mouth to hers.

"Oh, Gwendolyn, this is delicious."

"It seems that you are regaining your strength quite

quickly." She relished her influence on him and felt a spasm of desire. She moved her panties sideways to make way for Matthew. The sighs of ecstasy were held within, but the containment within the office premises only amplified the sensorial.

"That was hardly a sign of weakness, Matthew; should we finish our discussion on recruitment?"

"To hell with recruitment; all I want is a repeat."

"Spontaneity is the essence of existence. A repeat will be overindulgent."

"OK. So, for now, recruitment matters will get all my attention."

"Hehe; now that will be really ninny-like."

"I'll show you what ninny-like is." He pulled her back to the couch he was sitting on and knelt over to kiss her neck, moving his hands under her skirt and feeling the smoothness of her firm hips. Gwendolyn giggled before succumbing to a sigh of yearning. Matthew no longer felt weak. But then he had something to tell her that could no longer wait:

"Gwendolyn, I am buying a ship."

"What?" She moved away to hear what he had to say. This man was outrageous. His mind was always working on the next step, each more daring than the previous one. This was no step. This was a leap.

"I think we should buy a ship, not to compete with other shippers but to provide additional capacity, especially for India and Southeast Asia. Now that the war has ended, we have many demands for Bombay and Singapore that we cannot meet. I do not like to depend on shipping companies when the cargo is being booked with us. What do you think? So far, we have been dealing more with outbound business. If we had our own ship, we could use agents in those countries to fill up our return voyage."

"I do not think that we depend on the shipping companies. It seems like the other way around. We do not have to own ships. Why do you want to become a shipping magnate now?"

"But it is the business we are in."

"Not every shipping consolidator goes on to buy a ship. A ship costs a lot to buy, run and maintain."

"Alright, I will give you the documentation and projections. You can check it. We had received a proposal from our bank's Tokyo office. The Japanese are making exceptionally good ships, and they extend many options for financing."

"Matthew, you realise that we already have a big business and that you are a very rich man."

"Yes, yes, but this is not about money or wealth. It is about seizing the opportunity."

"It's becoming an obsession with you."

"I see it more as intoxication."

"Intoxication causes addiction."

"I am already addicted. I just want to grab what I can."

"That is exactly what you were doing moments ago. So, you are not such a ninny."

"I am when it comes to you, darling."

He moved towards her. She stood still. He took her hands in his, kissed them and put them on his shoulder before he moved closer, holding her waist. He kissed her neck. Her arms pulled at his shoulders. She bent her neck back. Matthew undid her blouse and kissed her neck, moving down to the chasm between her breasts. His hand moved down to between her thighs until he felt her shudder. She walked back, pulling him along until the back of her legs hit the desk. Matthew lifted her onto the desk and, in an accomplished move, moved her skirt up while pushing closer to her. Gwendolyn gushed as she felt him inside. "Oh, Matthew."

He pushed her back onto the desk. The exquisite rhythm of love had them both breathing heavily and sighing at each other. Gwendolyn pushed herself even harder towards her man. The crescendo drummed up the senses until they reached the precipice of anticipation, in tandem, where they remained for that flash of a moment before exploding.

As they drifted back into consciousness, Gwendolyn got off the desk and let her skirt fall back to her shins.

"This is not what an office is for."

"No, but you and I are both here, and so is this desk."

"And I thought I was going to go through a list of candidates with you."

"You did, but hard work has to be rewarded."

"A bit vain, aren't you, Mr Stephens?"

"A bit vain for a ninny, I guess."

"Let's ask Patrick to get the car started."

"Yes. I will call the security guard. He will pass the message to Patrick."

Life was certainly looking up. Everything was good. Prosperity and riches were accumulating at a staggering rate. Gwendolyn and he made for a great relationship. Their sexual desires were satisfied.

Matthew often wondered why fortune was smiling on someone so insignificant. Why had his mother endured solitude, insult and ill health as a way of life? Was this compensation for the misery of the past? Why was there no happy medium in our 'all or nothing' existence?

His fear was all this could disappear in the wink of an eye.

Why him? Was he that deserving? He knew he was greedy and always wanted more and then more again.

Whether it was success or sex, yes, they were linked. But what about Gwendolyn? She was not an object he possessed. Does she really have the same desires as him? Why had he never tried to find out? He had always been loyal to her, but he was a man driven by boundless greed and a relentless sexual appetite. He should have told her about the ship.

Matthew's mind was like a monkey jumping from one branch to the next. But the monkey came to a sudden halt. Quite unannounced, that life-defining incident flashed back into his mind. William felt pain and sadness both in the same breath. Anxiety took hold of him as he sat down to catch his breath.

"You all right, Matthew? You are very pale."

"Yes, Gwen. I have started getting these sporadic drops in blood pressure. I was advised to drink water and increase my salt intake. The doctor assured me that low blood pressure is a good thing."

Matthew Stephens and Co. grew further. It bought a cargo ship and named it *Gailforce*. The vessel plied the oceans from Immingham on the East Coast of England to Singapore.

"Why Immingham and not London?" Gwendolyn had asked.

"Because that's where they are going to commission an oil terminal, just next to the refineries."

"But we don't have oil tankers, Matthew."

"No, not yet. For now, the port is being used for coal exports and iron ore imports."

"But we just ship manufactured goods."

"We will continue with that from here in London. Immingham is the future, darling. So, *Gailforce* will sail from there. This way, we get to know the local market and build a track record. This will allow us to bid jointly with a bulk specialist when the next tenders come out for coal shipments."

"But tenders take years."

"No, Gwendolyn, the tenders will be put out in June next year and decided before the end of the year. We need that time to establish ourselves in Immingham. Tenders are awarded for a five-year period on specified routes. If we win, we will get whatever we need to grow our market share in the shipping of crude oil and whatever raw materials are needed to reconstruct after the destruction of the war."

"Since when have you been working on this, Matthew? First, there is the ship, and now there is Immingham. I thought we were a team."

"We are, Gwendolyn, and this is why I am sharing this with you."

"That is very arrogant. Do you not trust me?"

"Of course, I trust you. It is something that materialised in passing from just being at the office. This agent from Immingham contacted the office only last month when I was looking at the idea of another ship. You are right. I should have mentioned it to you, but I did routine checks before deciding. I am now in discussion with an Immingham-based shipper who is having problems with his insurers and bankers. He needs more collateral for the banks to renew his financing. They consider him high-risk. I will provide that guarantee and take a share of his Company, with an option to buy him out. The opportunity just screamed me in the face. Please forgive me if I did not consult you."

"Well, I am sure you are right in your decisions. But how can you trust your information on the tenders?"

"I have vetted this myself. You will be astonished at how easy it is to buy information. I learnt this from the office of the business and energy secretary. The government needs our help to get the economy going again. We are lucky to have good business links with them, having shipped all those supplies everywhere. In any case, ministers and politicians are for sale, Gwendolyn."

"Maybe, but you don't have to go and buy them all."

"You are right, of course. But big business and politics are intertwined. Neither can exist without the other."

"So, are you saying everyone is corrupt, Matthew? And you, are you corrupt as well?"

Matthew moved towards her. "Corruption is a matter of perception. I am a businessman. If I must sign cheques for a political cause, I do it. Any payment we make is legal. What is more? They are tax-deductible. The entire system is rigged to look after everyone's interests. I was lucky enough to realise this quite early."

"Does all this make you happy?"

"Happy? I am not sure. It is more that I am grateful. These opportunities just arrive on my desk without my even having to go looking for them. It is as if my environment is set up to perpetuate success. But you know, Gwen? Such success only gets me worried. When things go too well, I start feeling that something terrible will happen, or I am reminded of the past. My demons emerge and gnaw at my insides like everyone else."

"What demons, Matthew?"

"Oh, just my youth, Mother and the life we had."

"But you were a great son, Matthew. You did all you could."

"Yes, that's true."

"Is there something you want to tell me? Something that is bothering you?"

"No, Gwen, why should it? Sometimes, the past catches up with me. I must admit that I am bitter about the life I had as a child and the fact that my mother had such a pitiful existence. I feel sad because my father abandoned me even before I was born. Sometimes, I feel guilty about my success. My mind keeps telling me that I do not deserve all this, and I do not deserve you. I am a lonesome animal lost in the savannah of humanity, justifying my existence through one business success after another. It is all happening so quickly as if to erase my past altogether. But I want to hold on to that pain. It is the only thing that keeps it real."

"The past is the past and must stay there. We cannot live our lives worrying about what has already happened."

"Yes, we just have to live with it."

"What's wrong, Matthew?"

"Nothing, Gwen. What could be wrong? Everything is going fine. Isn't it?"

"You are missing your mother. Do not forget that she will always be with you. Always."

"Yes, you are right, Gwen. Thanks. I would like a drink."

"Another one?"

"Yes, please."

"Glenfarclas?"

"Of course, thanks."

As their ships laden with cargo plied the world's shipping lanes, the cash registers of the business kept ringing. The accounts that were updated weekly revealed hefty profits. The cash flow was in sync. Matthew did not want to take money out of the business; he only took a salary or a dividend that ensured he could live comfortably. It was important to create a strong capital base that would hold the business in good stead if there were to be any unexpected downturn. It would not be smooth sailing all the time. So far, life had been like a wave. It had started from a trough; it had risen and was still growing.

Matthew was poised well at base camp to prepare for the assault towards the summit. He consulted Mr Burroughs, who listened. "Matthew, it is exceedingly difficult to manage growth. One is tempted by so many opportunities, but one has to remain disciplined. You have taken a lot of market share recently from shippers. It is time to offer the clients both bulk and piecemeal services. I think that your idea to set up in Immingham was genius. But to grow in bulk shipping, you should look to acquire or merge with a sizeable bulk carrier. You already have the staff and systems in place. What you need is a substantial bolt-on specialised in bulk. This will allow you to get into natural resources more substantially. You will need more bulk handling capacity at the ports, but if you make the right acquisition, all the additional infrastructure will already be in place."

"But such an acquisition could be too big a move. Where will I get such money?"

"Matthew, there is always financing available for good business opportunities. Why don't you do some homework on the companies that would make a good fit with our operations, preferably one that is hurting because of your piecemeal approach and then let us take it from there?

"Sir, we do not compete with bulk carriers. Our bulk operations are tiny. At most, we handle some coal but not massive amounts. Otherwise, we ship finished goods and heavy machinery. The main advantage a potential partner would see with us is the high profitability generated by the bespoke nature of our services. Bulk does not have that potential. Like the cargo they transport, the prices they can charge have also been commoditised. There are a handful of companies, however, that would allow us to scale up the business."

"Do you have someone in mind?"

"Robson Overseas, Sir."

"Are you sure?"

"Yes, Sir. Their staff have approached us for opportunities. I know that they are struggling to use their capacity. And I also understand there is disagreement amongst the Robson family on whether they should keep going."

"Oh, in that case, please look for another one. We cannot afford to waste time on family feuds. In situations like that, doing a transaction with all will prove very costly in terms of time. There is no screaming urgency; think about it. Make a list and, by elimination, come up with the name of the best fit for Matthew Stephens and Co., and yes, something with one owner. You could also consider a target with its feet in both bulk and break bulk, piecemeal shipping, for instance, your ex-employers. The target must be well run and a business that would benefit from a deal with Matthew Stephens and Co."

Later that evening with Gwendolyn, Matthew could not contain his excitement. "Mr Burroughs is really something."

"Why do you say that?"

"He wants me to expand our business."

"But the business is growing quite fast already."

"Yes, but we are growing in what we do. He wants me to think bigger. He wants us to do something with one of the big bulk carriers."

"What? You mean something like East Asia Company?"

"What did you say? Yes, yes, of course, something like East Asia Company. God, why did I not think of it myself?"

"Does it matter?"

"No, no, of course not, but it is so obvious."

"But Matthew."

"True, we worked there. I remember the business well. Now, would that not be crazy?"

Mr Burroughs liked the idea. The war was over, and colonial trade could not be taken for granted. The colonies were either independent or heading towards independence. Although Britain had managed it well, there was no guarantee that companies like the East Asia Company would thrive in a post-colonial world.

Clever ideas brought along their basket of fortuitous circumstances. The British government was privatising a large swathe of its investments to reduce its accumulated colossal wartime and reconstruction debt. Although America was investing in British debt, the government was still amidst nationalist fervour and remained averse to letting its "empire era" relics fall into American hands. A UK-based consortium headed by Samuel Burroughs, major British banks and Matthew Stephens and Co., a homegrown shipping company, was considered the ideal buyer. The East Asia Company would ply the world's oceans, flying the Union Jack. The business already had direct lines to the government and its various departments: Maritime, Trade and the Foreign and Commonwealth Office. But this was deeper.

Such a confluence of opportune timing, government backing, bank support, and the leadership of a business luminary was an epoch-defining rarity. Here was a beacon of British enterprise and daring in a post-war paradigm.

This transformational move catapulted Matthew Stephens and Co. into the big league alongside the Greeks and the Americans.

Newspapers and magazines wanted to run features. Photographers, journalists and television clamoured for exclusives. But Matthew Stephens was not going to make a public spectacle. He was playing very high stakes but wanted to retain a low profile. He employed a team of bodyguards to keep the world at bay; the government provided him with a VIP escort for journeys to the airports and government offices.

When the Honours List proposals were presented to the Prime Minister, Matthew Stephens' name was almost at the top of the list in recognition of his exceptional achievements at such a young age. He politely declined. *I am honoured indeed, but to continue my work, I do not want to create any distinction between my staff, my customers and myself.*

Social elevation was a valid aspiration, especially in an England where class divisions were rampant and deeply engrained in daily life. The accent one speaks defines social standing, career prospects and life chances.

A former street urchin needed to stick to his roots. Success was a mirage that should never be taken for granted. When running a shipping business, collecting badges, names, and titles was of no consequence. The reputation that he was building in the business world was testimony enough. He had to ensure he had not bitten off more than he could chew.

1970

Mr Burroughs

"Gwendolyn!" Matthew shouted as soon as he had let himself in through the front door.

"Matthew? You are home? I am here in the kitchen."

Matthew was out of breath.

"What is the matter? Have you been running?"

"Yes. I tried calling you but then thought it better to come here myself."

"Matthew?"

"Mr Burroughs has been arrested."

"What! Why?"

"I do not know. Greg Wickes from Cargo was at his place giving him the weekly update when the police came in and announced that he was being arrested for links with slavery."

"What? Mr Burroughs? Isn't slavery illegal?"

"Yes, of course, it is. It has been for over a hundred years. Mr Burroughs brought in workers from India and sold them to his friends as domestic servants and sex slaves. I had picked up rumours but had never paid any attention."

Gwendolyn's mind flashed back. 'So, this was what he had meant about him not being all good. How could a man who was so generous and supportive be involved in trading humans?'

Matthew's contemporaries were a mixed bag: hardworking businessmen looking after their families and employees, the owner-managers. Then, there were the inheritor owners who had left the business to professional managers. Some of them were honourable men. Others were alcoholic brothel dwellers. Many had cheated on their wives and fathered bastards. Debauchery was commonplace, as were inhuman acts. Business had an ugly underbelly. Success brought out the fiend within, an evil genie that darts out of the belly button like a spitting serpent. The sense of impunity was stronger when amongst fellow hyenas, a pack of jeering predators. Contrition had no place amidst collective misdemeanour. An unshakeable bond of malice took hold of shippers, manufacturers, traders, bankers, politicians and media tycoons. Sexual deviance plunged to depths of depravity that would make the devil blink. The latest trend was sex parties where a prostitute would be drugged, collectively tortured and, at the end of the ordeal, stabbed in her vagina. Alcohol and drugs were limitless, fuelling the raucous hysteria that resonated through the walls of Belgravia and Mayfair.

Matthew thought this was where cowards got their courage.

But Samuel Burroughs? The same man who had helped him through his moments of despair? Who had behaved most honourably at the time? Mr Burroughs had mentioned India, but that was the tea trade, not the slave trade. So, was everyone flawed? Did no one else have a Gail Stephens to provide a moral compass that guided decisions in life?

Mr Burroughs had used inherited wealth as a gateway to power, recognition and influence. Shouldn't he have used it responsibly for a better society and world? On the face of it, he had. The man was a monument of philanthropy. Many a medical institution and education centre had been set up through his generosity. He still paid for various charitable dispensaries in London. Even in Matthew's case, Mr Burroughs had given him money when he most needed it. It was unfathomable why someone with such a standing would get involved with something as sordid.

Wealth could neither guarantee morality nor inoculate against misdeeds, just as it could not prevent death, replace a loved one or bring peace of mind.

"Gwen, I will go and see Mr Burroughs."

"But is he not in jail?"

"No, he is being kept at the police station until the police and the Royal Prosecutor can establish the severity of his offence."

"Is slavery not punishable?"

"Yes, it is a criminal offence; if convicted, Mr Burroughs will go to prison for a long time."

"What if he is guilty, Matthew?"

"That is not an issue for me. I owe everything to that man. If I can help in any way, I will."

'Offering help' implied deploying resources at a scale unparalleled in anything Matthew had done so far. Freeing a man from prosecution for a serious offence to which he had confessed was not something for which the legal system had been designed. But all systems have weak spots.

Matthew Stephens and Co. would not have existed had it not been for this man. Nor would Mother have survived that illness in the days when they had nothing. Existence cannot be about judging people who have shown their generosity when it most matters.

"He has always believed in you, Matthew. It is now your turn to believe in him. We must establish our own rights and wrongs."

"You are right, Gwendolyn. We have all done despicable things, but we do them for a reason."

The Station Officer, alerted by the Police Commissioner, received Matthew Stephens. He led him to the interview room, where two chairs had been set up on either side of a wooden table. "Mr Stephens. This room is a bit modest but should allow you to converse without being disturbed."

"Thank you. I will wait here while you bring Mr Burroughs."

The man walked in with an escort. He looked tired, but then his mouth widened into a smile.

"Hello Matthew, thank you for coming to the constabulary. As you can see, I am not doing badly." Matthew looked around the room and signalled to the jail sentry to leave, which he did immediately. Once there was some privacy, Mr Burroughs asked Matthew how business was.

"It is fine, Mr Burroughs. Your investment has grown manifold, but that is not why I am here. I have come to ask how I may help to get you out of this predicament."

"The only way a guilty man can be redeemed is incarceration."

"Sir, I have no idea what you did and why you did it, but we are both here now, and we need to get you out of this."

"A crime is a crime, Matthew."

"We all have our crosses to bear, Sir, but wealth and influence must come in handy at some stage."

"Thank you, Matthew, for not forsaking me."

"Sir, any prosecution can be successful only if the Prosecutor has been a stickler for due procedure."

"Matthew, I have confessed. It was a long time coming. I should have known better. I have to make peace with my misdeeds."

"Sir, you must believe you have also done a lot of good. That weighs in your favour, no matter what."

"Unlike you, Matthew, I chose to attend many a soirée with all the society bigwigs. My wife and I inherited our wealth and believed our calling was to conform to society. I was a member of numerous gentlemen's clubs. I rarely dined at home. Every evening was an occasion for drinking and depravity at one of these hallowed premises. Sometimes, the gatherings were harmless drinking, but at others, there were drugs and prostitutes. I never objected. Who was I to challenge established traditions? Then, one evening, we had boys. Although there was reserve initially, a whiff of opium and many servings of whisky banished hesitation into oblivion."

"Sir, why are you telling me all this? I do not need to know. I will defend you come what may."

"That is exactly why you need to know. Boys started featuring regularly in these soirées; many were young, teenagers even. One evening, given my business interests, I was asked if I could procure exotic material. I did not say no, and that was taken as a yes. Of course, arranging for boys to come to Britain was quite easy for me. But for immigration reasons, they had to be adults. So, these boys were young men: eighteen or more. There was shock and consternation when these youngsters realised they were not here to work in my tea business but in another kind of venture. But they were trapped. They had all been brought over by me, and, if they wanted to live here, they would have to do whatever was necessary.

"Going home was allowed, but they all chose the shame of sexual slavery against the even greater shame of returning to villages in India with nothing to show. Once the venture took form, we ensured they were financially compensated.

The pride of regularly sending substantial sums of money back home to their families erased their misgivings.

But it did not just stay there. The real problem started when I accepted a financial offer from a retired general to 'sell' one of the young tea growers to him. I had knowingly become a dealer of sex slaves. It is still difficult to contemplate, what with all the wealth I already had. I willingly subscribed to London's social circle of privilege. Despite all the members' vows of secrecy, my wife caught wind of this. I assured her that I was not attracted to either young men or, for that matter, any man. I do not think it really mattered to her. She was very much a part of the same social circles and immorality where excess was the only driver of existence. Money was pouring into society's coffers, what with the boom of the post-war years. Debauchery and excess had become the norm."

"But, Sir, I came to you for help as a mere boy. You neither took advantage of me nor am I aware of any misdemeanour directed at my mother."

"Yes, Matthew, you came to me before I became an addict. You came home to me; my home was a sanctuary I could not desecrate.

"Opium was not all. We also had cannabis, marijuana and amphetamines. Suppliers offered the latest concoction at the steepest prices, but no one cared. I must say that I was surprised when I discovered Mrs Burroughs smoking cigarettes with much more than tobacco. The wicked bat was flying higher than a kite."

Matthew smiled. Mr Burroughs had not lost his sense of humour even when relating the direst story he had ever narrated.

"I do not deserve redemption through our system. Nor does any other social warlord. Matthew Stephens is the only clean act in town. And so he shall remain. You had a remarkable mother, and you have an extraordinary wife. You can afford to be bolder and go where no one else dares because your cupboard has no skeletons. But do it only if it meets the threshold of the values that your mother and wife inculcated."

"I will continue to bear that in mind, Sir. On the matter of redemption, Mr Burroughs, it is not redemption you will gain through this system, but freedom to do deeds that will truly redeem. I am where I am in business because of you. You are my mentor. My support is unconditional. I will never judge you, but if I can get you out of here, I would like you to join me in a worthy cause. You gave me the opportunity to avoid servitude. Together, we can offer many desperate beings the opportunity of dignity."

"Matthew, it will not be that easy. The Burroughs name has taken quite a hit."

"Mr Burroughs, wealth is wealth. All our peers have skeletons and secrets. And in a way, they would be desperately hoping that this does not stick lest this affair cast aspersions of their own involvement. Society can be very unforgiving to the man on the street but remarkably lenient and forgiving of its pillars. In the top echelons of society, few can grudge someone else's attempt at salvation. The only thing that matters in this morally deprived society is the wealth one has amassed. In your case, that mountain is massive."

"I am grateful that you even care, Matthew."

"Mr Burroughs, whatever you may have done and how ever much it may be against my own convictions, I am morally bound to you."

"No one owes anyone anything, Matthew. This is just your way of thinking. I did what I did because it felt right at the time. I do not have deep-rooted beliefs of right and wrong. I see myself as a wind vane, hostage to each new gust. People like me have strong finances, but our behaviour is driven by the most basic of predilections. Behind the veneer of wealth and sophistication, I am nothing. And even that veneer has suffered a scathing blow."

"No, Mr Burroughs. There is no scathing blow; there is paranoia in London that the net will spread wider and trap more of your contemporaries. The tension in social circles is palpable. These are times when everyone has something to hide, so there is little pleasure in a peer's downfall. So, you do not have to worry about anyone. Everyone is hoping that you come out of this whole—even our government.

"I would take things step by step. The first stage is your acquittal. Once that is out of the way, we can see how we address any collateral damage."

"With Matthew Stephens by my side, I probably stand a chance."

"Matthew Stephens was 'a nobody' who got lucky because of Mr Burroughs. You can count on him."

Mr Burroughs had never had a son of his own, and the first day they had met, a sentiment had ignited in him. What had attracted his attention was Matthew's bravery in just coming and asking for help to look after his mother. There was an innocent nobility about it. He had not come for a handout. He was not looking for pity. He was offering work in exchange for pay. This spirit of self-reliance and independence was rare amongst the adult population. Yet this young man had developed it before any facial hair had appeared.

Singapore Sling

"Sir, one of our ships has sunk."

"What? Which one, where?"

"Sir, it is the *Singapore Sling*. It went down near the Gulf of Oman."

Matthew knew the ship well. It was a dry cargo bulk carrier that he had bought from a Japanese shipyard. The vessel had a British crew.

"Is that not the vessel captained by that Morgan chap? Was the vessel not seaworthy?"

"Yes, Sir, it was Stewart Morgan's ship. He has perished. There was an explosion in the hull. An Iranian-owned oil tanker sent out messages when they saw the smoke. By the time one of the Royal Navy's boats got to the site, the ship was headed into the water."

"And the crew?

"Sir, they were mainly from England, directly employed by us; all gone."

"Is this in the news?"

"Not yet, Sir."

"OK, Bertram. Get me the Ministry of Defence. Also, please ask our Personnel Director to contact the families of each sailor and ask him to convey my condolences immediately. Please send in our Press Officer."

Matthew thought, 'This is the first time I have lost a ship. And all those people, their families.'

The press release read: *British Cargo ship sinks in the Arabian Sea south of Oman with all staff and cargo. Matthew Stephens and Co., the ship's owners, express their deep sorrow for the lives lost. Matthew Stephens, the Chairman: "I am deeply shocked by this horrific accident. My heart goes out to the families of those who lost their lives. We are all part of the same family and grieve in solidarity for our collective loss.*

"We will investigate and determine what went wrong and will offer all the help necessary to family members as well as to our own staff who are stunned by this calamity."

How could this have happened? These were the people who had created Matthew Stephens and Co., yet they are gone. And I do not even know the cause.

"Sir, there is a call from Number 10."

"Please take a message. I do not want to talk."

A Crisis Room was set up at the head office. Matthew authorised the immediate disbursement of five years' salary to the families of the deceased. This was not divulged to the press. There would be no cheap publicity out of a major catastrophe.

He secured an agreement with the Ministry of Defence to retrieve the bodies of all the sailors, whether British or of other nationalities, and send them to their families. The Foreign Office put Matthew in touch with the Sultan of Oman's private office and emphasised the need for immediate assistance. Oman was more than obliging and provided their own ship and helicopters to recover bodies from the sea to Oman for embalming before being flown off in refrigerated coffins. The Omani custom of burial within twenty-four hours after death did not apply as the staff were not Muslim; the British government had explained that the quick return of bodies to their families was the main priority.

Matthew's thoughts were scattered. 'These people create my wealth; they leave their families for weeks on end and risk their lives. We pay them well but do not expect them to die. The worst thing is that their families are depleted. Some will lose everything: a father, husband, brother, son. For me, there is pain, but perversely, there would be no financial loss to Matthew Stephens and Co. between comprehensive insurance and tax deductibility of any compensation to the families of the departed. But it was the human cost that is incalculable. How does one even begin to consider or measure the grief of the surviving widow, the orphan son or daughter, the grieving parents, and the hapless siblings? Death in any form was a difficult burden to bear. Add to that the suddenness of death in the most unexpected of circumstances. Lives are lost to illness or war, not at sea on one of my vessels.'

All the ships in the fleet, wherever they were, were ordered to sail to the nearest shipyard to get a full check-up. Safety advisers were flown out to every ship to ensure that emergency procedures were well-known. Finally, every sea-faring staff member was allowed to work at an office, temporarily or permanently, if they did not feel like being on water.

The Company held a memorial service in London. Matthew attended it.

It remained unclear what had happened to the ship. There may have been some structural damage, but that could not be responsible for a ship sinking in calm waters so quickly. There was no sign of any lateral missile penetration, which could have provided some indication. The theory that had the most credence was that the boat had encountered a naval magnetic mine that was still active. It had sensed the ship and exploded, sending up a huge columnar jet that had crashed on the vessel with devastating effect. These mines had been deployed during the last war and were still lurking around in the waters. One had found its unintended mark on his ship.

The Ministry of Defence and the Royal Navy started mine-clearing operations on all his routes. Matthew waited for the 'all clear' before any ship navigated those paths again.

For him, business was not about only goods and merchandise. It was about people who made it all possible. There was nothing in business bigger than its collective beating heart. Every nerve ending and pulse was integral to the pumping mass. Damage to any component, however isolated, compromised the functioning of the whole.

Any scar took time to heal and required the passage of time. With patience and perseverance, heal it would.

Jeremy Pickett, Mr Burroughs' lawyer, was being interviewed on the radio.

"How do you feel, Mr Pickett? Acquitting a man accused of slave trading must seem pyrrhic."

"Angela, I am a lawyer, and my role is to defend my client. In the eyes of the law, may I remind everyone that an accused person is innocent until proven guilty. And acquitted when his innocence is proven."

"Yes, but surely it is for lawyers to uphold the law."

"Proving someone's innocence is upholding the law. The law lays out clear principles and procedures. I have worked within our legal system and have strictly adhered to the law. I know that many were looking forward to the fall of Samuel Burroughs. But that does not make him guilty. The law protects him as much as anyone else. The fact he has been acquitted is proof that our legal system works. I have no further comment."

"But Mr Pickett."

"Sorry, I have no further comment."

The slave trading entity had turned out to be an employment agency specialising in recruiting young staff from overseas who had all received a medical examination in their country of origin, India, and had been brought aboard ships belonging to a very reputable shipping company. This same company had given them employment contracts and had recently made them eligible for performance bonuses. They had all been eligible for company housing and free medical care. Their arrival in Britain had been recognised officially, and they were all provided immigration approvals to work in the shipping company.

The slavery assertion was dismissed as malign electioneering by socialists where politically motivated prosecutors decided to target a man of considerable fortune.

This was Britain, not revolutionary France. Here, the rich do not get sent to the guillotine. This was the land where successful people thrived, and, in turn, they contributed to the politicians and their parties.

Jeremy Pickett was richly rewarded and was guaranteed a substantial chunk of all future litigation business of Matthew Stephens and Co. Samuel Burroughs was made non-executive Chairman of the Company in which he held a considerable interest. London's business elite was given back its missing member, scratched but intact. There was relief all around. The gentlemen's clubs had received a stark reminder of the evil they propagated and the disgrace they would be snared into. They all feared the unravelling of their web of societal misdeeds and would have to be incredibly careful and vigilant. With the acquittal, their collective paranoia switched instantly to awe of Matthew Stephens.

The Burroughs' judgement was met with a sigh of relief, triumph even. Even the stock market rose on the news. The City of London could not afford a scandal when reaping the rewards of post-war recovery.

Memory was not a strong attribute amongst multi-millionaires, especially if it clashed with convenience and opportunism. Morality was a figure of speech that wound its way through circumstances and the needs of society. It was a trait that changed its cloak between the day at the office and the evening at the club. Matthew Stephens did not consider himself a moral man, but he had his set of rights and wrongs. Mr Burroughs was his benefactor, and even if he had killed someone in cold blood, Matthew would have stood by him.

Getting to know him over the years had made Matthew understand how important and influential Mr Burroughs was. On a personal level, though, the score was settled. Burroughs had resurrected Matthew's mother when they were helpless, and he had revived his mentor's position.

Project Hansdown

"Sir, do you remember Project Hansdown?"

"Of course, I do, Bertram. I have been talking to the banks to see how we can finance such a big acquisition; Hans Shipping runs a fleet of over three hundred freighters, half on the Singapore route. If one of us were to disappear on that route, the survivor would still be able to service the cargo but almost double the tariffs. What is the matter?

"Sir, Hans Shipping is in advanced negotiations with Carter Lines of America. In fact, they have signed a Memorandum of Understanding granting each other exclusivity."

"What? Are you sure?"

"Yes, Sir. Our lawyers got wind of it and have checked it out."

"But Carter has no business here. Please arrange a meeting with Henry today, if he is in London."

"Yes, Sir."

Henry, Andrew, Nigel and Simon were all directors at their family firm. Henry Rutherall was the oldest brother and, along with his brothers, had navigated the course of his shipping line with astute acumen. He had ensured that all piecemeal business would be handled through Matthew Stephens. But he had never signed any engagement on exclusivity were Hans to change ownership.

"Matthew, I am not surprised you have learnt about Carter's offer. Little passes through these waters without your blessing."

"Henry, why did you not come to me? You know that Carter is part of the Haverston empire. How can we allow them in our territory?"

"There is no *our* territory or *their* territory, Matthew. We are all fair game in this jungle."

"But you are a privately held company."

"Yes, but a company with three other shareholders collectively owning seventy-five per cent. Moreover, if I do not agree with them, they can squeeze me out. They have pre-emptive rights on my twenty-five per cent. Plus, the price is quite compelling."

"Of course, it is. They would get a large chunk of the UK–Singapore route. That will put them on the world map. Thank you for taking the time to meet me. I know what I must do."

Bertram opened the door to the Bentley that was waiting for Matthew Stephens.

"Bertram, I want to see Roger Barclay today. Also, please arrange a trip to New York with a flight out tomorrow evening. I want to meet David Haverston."

"Yes, Sir, I will call Mr Haverston's office this evening and ask for an urgent meeting. Would it be all right for dinner tomorrow? I could book you on the afternoon Concorde."

"Yes, but I would like to fly back tomorrow night. It is Sally's birthday the day after tomorrow."

"Yes, of course. I will make the arrangements."

Matthew Stephens did not like the Concorde. It hurt his ears. But this was urgent. Carter should not be allowed to set up shop in his home ground. 'Let's hope that Roger Barclay can put together financing to buy Carter from David.'

"Matthew, hi. How are you?"

"David, it is good to see you. It has been a while since our drinking days at St James's."

"I love that place. So quaint and charming. But I understand you are here to discuss Carter and Hans. You do understand that the family is no longer involved in the day-to-day affairs of Haverston Oil offshoots."

"But they do listen to you, David."

"Yes, if I have something to say."

"David, I am willing to buy Carter and Hans at a handsome premium if you get control of Hans. Plus, I can offer your oil company a twenty per cent discount on shipping between Europe, the Middle East and Asia for the next ten years."

"Carter has not closed with Hans."

"I would be grateful if you could close as soon as possible so we can arrange a back-to-back."

"Kill two birds with one stone? Clever indeed."

"But at the price of almost three birds."

"I may have them listening to what I have to say. Are you staying for dinner?"

"No, David, sorry. It is my daughter's birthday tomorrow. So, I will get a bite on the plane back."

"I understand, Matthew. Please give her a birthday hug from me."

Sally spent her early years in the company of her mother and her governess. Gwendolyn had reduced her presence at the office and spent more time at the estate. Rosalind was doing an excellent job, but Matthew was always stuck with some project or the other, and although his focus on the family has never been affected, there were only so many hours in a day.

Matthew was back in time from his travels and made it a point to be around the entire day. Sally's birthday was celebrated with the handful of girls she had met through Rosalind. Once the cake had been cut and the girls had finished their slice, they heard knocking at the door. It was Jeff, the gardener, "Sorry to disturb you, Sir, but there is a present for Ms Sally. If you follow me."

Matthew looked at the girls and signalled to them to follow him. Matthew and his entourage followed Jeff as if he were the Pied Piper. Jeff led them to the barn gate. He asked everyone to wait as he disappeared behind the gate. A few moments later, the gate opened wider, and Jeff came out with a chestnut brown Shetland pony with a white ribbon around its neck, "Happy birthday Miss." Sally looked at the pony and smiled, her eyes wet. She looked at her father while her friends were giggling away.

"What would you like to call him, Miss?"

"Brownie!"

"What a good name. Brownie, it is!" The two bonded instantly. Brownie was docile and took in all the caresses and stroking of his admirers, who were in awe.

He was set up in the barn in an enclosure with hay, pellets and carrots. Sally would visit him each morning and every evening. Rosalind found a riding instructor who would come and teach Sally how to look after Brownie and instruct her through basic equestrian drills. Sally and Brownie learnt to get to know each other and soon started going through the grounds unsupervised.

Sally started school. Rosalind advised, "Sally needs to get exposure to ordinary children. This will hold her in good stead eventually in the real world. Most parents believe that insulating their children from the world is beneficial. It is not. It only weakens them and leaves them unprepared for life." Matthew and Gwendolyn needed no convincing. It was decided. Her education would combine private teaching at home and schooling at the local primary. Her Governess was asked to engage a native-speaking French assistant to deepen Sally's second language. It was a unique upbringing that straddled two parallel universes. But it worked.

When everything was set, and the idea of a sibling for Sally emerged, Gwendolyn felt acute muscular pain and deep fatigue. "Sorry, Matthew, my body hurts, and I feel really tired."

"It is quite all right, Gwen. I take you for granted. I should not." He kissed her on her shoulder and then turned to the other side. Gwendolyn followed him, putting her arm around him. "No, Matthew, we can make love."

Matthew did not need persuasion but sensed that Gwendolyn was less responsive than she normally would have been, even in the absence of light. He withdrew and lay beside her. "Gwen, you do not have to do something that makes you uncomfortable. I may have a high sexual appetite, but I am your husband and partner. I would rather that you avoid any suffering for my sake."

"No, Matthew, I am not suffering. I love to make love to you. You know that. It is just that all this gardening is tiring. I enjoy it, but my body is not keeping up."

"Gardening is very demanding, and we have quite some acreage here. You should rely more on the gardeners. Also, you are a mother now. And that is a job in itself. Do you think that you may be pregnant?"

"No, Matthew, I am very regular, and it is not that type of fatigue. Let us not worry about it. Let us get some sleep. Unless you want to finish off, of course?"

"My lovely Gwen let us get some sleep. We will do this another time when we are both up to it." He pecked her on her forehead and lay beside his wife, her left arm and leg on him.

Neither Gwendolyn nor Matthew suspected that anything was amiss. There were no fevers, no inflammation, just fatigue and bodily pain. The doctor examined her and advised her to alternate physically strenuous activity with rest. He prescribed some sedatives and mild painkillers in case she felt pain.

She looked at her hand while her husband sat across. "Matthew, it is strange, but I seem unable to close my fist. Plus, I have had occasional spasms of pain in my hips. I am not sure what it is. I will just take some painkillers."

Matthew did not take his wife's predicament lightly and made a doctor's appointment. The doctor arranged for her to be booked into a clinic to conduct certain tests.

The doctor conducted further investigations and a biopsy of muscle tissue. A blood test revealed creatine kinase, an enzyme associated with muscle damage. Once all the results were in, the doctor diagnosed that a degeneration of her muscles was causing her spasms and pains. The condition would need regular supervision, and it was decided that there would be checks every three months.

On the way back from the clinic, she was still in discomfort, a feeling of worry that prevented any casual utterance to lighten the mood. There was an air of resignation that this thing would be with them for longer, whatever it may be.

By the time they got back to the Abode, they had assimilated the news but, at the same time, decided to confront whatever would come. As if through telepathy, their hands had moved towards each other until their fingers intertwined in a firm clasp. This time round, Gwendolyn felt no pain.

Monitoring her condition over six months revealed that the progress of the disease was slow. The origins of her illness were genetic, although Gwendolyn did not recall any problems with either of her parents. The doctor explained that the progression of the disease was unique to each affected person. It was impossible to predict when things could take a turn for the worse. Not much was known about this condition as it was often misdiagnosed. Based on case histories collected by the medical profession, facial, hand and shoulder muscle deterioration would be followed by a weaker heart and feeble lungs. So far, Gwendolyn's condition had not deteriorated beyond the spasms; there was weakness occasionally, but even that would pass.

Sally realised that her mother was unwell and tried not to add to her mother's worries. She was tender with her and showed absolute obedience to anything her mother suggested. She would stay with her governess, Rosalind, and make sure that her work at school was diligently completed without anyone having to remind her. Rosalind had experience with children with ailing parents, and she kept a close eye on Sally while de-dramatising the situation. "Sally dear, you are doing well. This is good for your mother to see. We do not want her to worry about anything. She needs all her energy to get better. We can both spend time with her. You could garden while she watches you with pride. You are lovely, Sally, and your mummy loves you a lot."

"Rosalind, I love Mummy a lot as well. I also love Papa, and I love you a lot. Is it all right to love so many people?"

"Of course, it is Sally; the more, the better. You know I love you a lot too, don't you?"

Sally's company, Rosalind's presence, Matthew's attention, and all the household staff provided an environment conducive to care, weighing into the common cause of preserving her faculties.

Matthew told the doctor, "She is doing well, and none of the symptoms you mentioned have presented themselves. Do you think that she is healing?"

"Mr Stephens, that is great news. You are all providing excellent care. The main resilience is, however, coming from Mrs Stephens herself. Her inner strength and resolve are keeping this at bay. She seems to value being a wife and mother more than being a patient." He dampened Matthew's optimism, though,

"Mr Stephens, I apologise for tempering your positive feelings, but there is no reversal of muscular dystrophy. Her condition may remain very stable for a period but could change without warning; It is a one-way street. She will continue to lose muscular mass. In the medium term, neural and cognitive deterioration would occur. She may have difficulty breathing and suffer pain, but that is not for now. We can administer steroids to alleviate symptoms, but I would do that very selectively."

"How serious is this doctor? Is it life-threatening?"

"It can be, but at a much later stage. The problem is that we cannot predict when that will be. If the pain intensifies, we can prescribe something stronger to alleviate the discomfort. The important thing is to be vigilant, but she needs to keep her confidence in determining her own limits. As Mrs Stephens is strong-willed, she will push herself; she should be allowed her freedom in this regard; she does not need to be cajoled and preserved in cotton wool.

"You may think you are making her more comfortable, but you will weaken her. Her muscles need to be used, and the blood needs to oxygenate her all the time. Also, please keep her engaged in day-to-day life. She needs physical as well as mental activity. It may sound inappropriate, but she must live as normally as possible. If the disease progresses, she will feel the limits that will come along with that."

"We will keep her engaged in everyday life. I may also seek her advice for my business dealings. She always took it upon herself to rein in my exuberance. But she has been less involved since Sally came into her life. But I will do this from home. I do not think I will ask her to come to the office."

"You have the right idea, Mr Stephens. The drive to London would not provide the quality time she needs. She needs stimulation, not stress. For most, London is an anxiety-filled proposition; why inflict it on someone fragile? I would recommend a home-based life with frequent gardening and outdoor walks that allow her a pause when it gets too strenuous. Patients do well when they are kept in their routines. That is the only way they do not feel handicapped and feel normalcy from day-to-day.

"She will also need a metallic body brace for support and comfort. The brace will need adjusting depending on where the degeneration of muscles is acute. On a personal front, you will have to be careful and attentive, nothing that a good understanding within the couple cannot sort out. She may feel inadequate as a wife, but it is up to you to provide reassurance."

Matthew Stephens understood that their life had changed and they would now have to live an adapted existence.

"Even if she puts on a brave face in her daily routine, do not underestimate the pain she feels. Her neurones are amplifying pain sensation many times the normal levels."

The best short-term remedy was to keep up her physical activity if she regularly rested. Regular massages to keep the muscles toned were also recommended. Heeding the doctor's advice, the Stephens drew up a daily routine combining activity and rest. The idea of siblings for Sally was abandoned.

Gwendolyn was given the Company's latest financial statements to keep her mentally engaged. She quizzed Matthew about the numbers. Matthew surprised himself when he could answer most queries satisfactorily. Gwendolyn could only remark, "Matthew, my absence from work has done you and the Company considerable good. You have exceptionally good cash flow in the business, and everything seems tightly controlled."

"Gwen, you had drilled these precepts quite profoundly into my mind; you should not sound so surprised that I took every word you uttered seriously. You can be as involved as you desire, Gwendolyn. We can collaborate with each other here in this house. We can walk through the lawns when you get bored or fed up. All this is so much more pleasant than being at the office."

Such interactions between husband and wife, co-workers again, became the new normal. It worked for both. The main advantage of the situation was Gwendolyn's realism concerning her condition. Whenever needed, she would leave him and head out to lie in the garden or the bedroom.

After dinner, Matthew moved to the lounge, sat in a winged armchair, investigated the glass of whisky in his hand, and wondered if destiny was paying a special visit to bring things into equilibrium. The vessel of his existence had finally hit choppy seas. Life is not going to get easier or better. The wave was past its crest. He would just have to become stronger. But Gwendolyn had been his biggest strength. How could he be strong in the face of her weakening?

Focussing on her daily routine was the most rational of remedies against anxiety and worry for both husband and wife. It would focus the mind away from the fear gnawing at their insides.

Although the planting and pruning were kept up, all socialising stopped. Matthew cut down on travel and reduced the days he spent at the office and the hours he spent working at home. Bertram could take care of most things. He was diligent and dependable. He was also the person who Matthew wanted to grow into a more senior role. While Bertram held the reins, he spent time with his precious wife. No attempt would be forsaken at preserving the tranquillity felt by man and woman. Togetherness was their tonic. The doctor soon pronounced that the balanced lifestyle was stabilising the condition. He asked Matthew to seek counselling for himself to process his helplessness. Unexpectedly, Matthew did not resist.

"How do you feel, Mr Stephens? Are you anxious?"

"Yes, Mr Chalmers. I am anxious. I want to be able to save my wife, but I know I cannot. I need to be there for her."

"But you are. You always have been."

"Not the way I should be. I still indulge myself in meaningless money-making schemes. I spend more time with my wife and daughter, but even when I am with them, I am so distracted. I have put everything in place, but my mind is not focussed on her."

"That is your life, Mr Stephens. I imagine that Mrs Stephens would also want you to continue your business activities. Moreover, people depend on you."

"Yes, they do. But I do not want to lose my wife."

"Mr Stephens, your wife is still alive. She is ill but she is getting the best medical care and has the love of her husband and daughter."

"Yes, she does, but that does not prevent her limbs from curving inwards and mobility causing her pain. She is courageous. Always has been. I hope our love will hold her in good stead while we let the doctors and medicine deal with the spasms."

"Yes, Mr Stephens."

"Pease call me Matthew. I am just a concerned husband here."

"Yes, Matthew, you are right. You must focus on what you can do and let the doctors manage their responsibility. Also, please make the most of your time together. You are obviously very close, which is invaluable."

The next time Gwendolyn suffered an excruciating spasm, Matthew comforted her by explaining that it would pass. Pass it would, but the next episode was a matter of days.

Gwendolyn was moved to another room so the nurse could be with her round the clock and administer morphine if needed. Sally knew there was a problem when her mother voiced a feeble moan. She would look at the nurse by her mother's side. The nurse would smile hesitantly, and Sally would go to her father. "Daddy, Mother is not well again. Please come." Matthew would take Sally's hand, and they would walk to Gwendolyn's room. Matthew would lift Sally and place her next to Gwendolyn on the bed. Sally would hold her mother's hand, and Matthew would move his hand from her forehead to hold his wife and daughter's hands together.

The more frequent recurrence of these crises necessitated a new brace made of lighter, more pliable aluminium. It would offer resistance without being rigid. It supported curvature but would return to its original form while providing Gwendolyn with a more natural gait.

The brace, along with massage, exercise and the devotion of her husband and daughter, propped her up. But she still worried.

"Matthew!"

"Yes, Gwendolyn!"

"I am sorry, Matthew!"

"Why should you be sorry?"

"Because I can't be your wife."

"You are my wife, Gwendolyn, and always will be."

"You know what I mean."

"Yes, I do. But you and I are husband and wife. We are also parents to Sally. What more could we ask for?"

"But you have needs."

"My only need is your well-being, darling. The fact that I was an insatiable animal in the past bears no meaning for the present."

"You know, I will completely understand if..."

"Please stop, Gwendolyn; I only ever desired you. Now, I desire your well-being. We play with the cards life deals us. Let us not forget that we have both lived a fulfilling life. I never want you to raise this matter ever again."

No fulfilling life escapes turbulence. Their fortune grew relentlessly even as Gwendolyn's health deteriorated. The wave was not crashing but was being pulled into a trough. Matthew recognised the equilibrium where the good and the bad cancelled each other out. In his view, success was associated with joy only in our shallow thinking; in the zero-sum game of life, when something succeeded, something else failed.

From a father's perspective, Sally had had a very privileged, albeit worry-filled childhood. She had not been able to enjoy a normal family life with healthy parents. Instead, she had to grow very quickly, like Matthew himself. He had not been around much, but Sally had taken that in her stride. The circumstances and the environment were quite different, but the preoccupations were the same. How could both father and daughter have had to live through the same ordeal? Was it fair to expect Sally to go through the travails of her parents just because he had had no choice in the matter? The obvious distinction was that he had been born into destitution and Sally into riches. In retrospection, though, the cards that life had dealt each of them were not dissimilar. Money and wealth offered only marginal reprieve when coping with life's realities, such as health, worry and vulnerability.

The oscillations of existence were perplexing indeed.

Was the Stephens family cursed?

As if to explain, Gail Stephens' presence made its apparition. No words were exchanged, but Matthew understood. The train was running, and he could do little to derail his destiny. He would just give it all away one day, but he had to carry on for now.

As far as Sally was concerned, she would just have to tread her own path through life; a good launch is no guarantee for smooth navigation. There would be difficulties along the way, but she would have to chart her own course.

The river flows.
Through its sinuous path
It hastens, it slows, it gathers, it grows.
Sweeping what comes along its way.
As it heads towards its final bay.

1975

Ling Hai

"Yes, Bertram? What is wrong?"

"Sir, we have trouble brewing on our routes to Hong Kong. Ling Hai, a Hong Kong-based carrier, is dropping freight rates on all routes from the South China Seas to the Mediterranean. By as much as seventy per cent."

"How is that possible? They will perish."

"Ling Hai is not just a shipping company. It owns a large chunk of Hong Kong and Macao. And has controlling interests in all sorts of businesses. It is flush with cash and has decided to expand its shipping business westwards. They are already a major shipper in the South China Seas and enjoy the patronage of the Chinese and British governments. I have spoken to the Trade Secretary and the Foreign Secretary, who discussed our concerns with the Governor of Hong Kong. They advised us to seek an arrangement with Ling Hai."

"What? Why?"

"Ling Hai has unlimited financing. It is a conglomerate that accounts for a large chunk of the Hong Kong business of international British banks. Our government will not go against the wishes of bankers."

"Of course, they will not. So, what are our options?"

"We do not have many. Either we can come to an agreement on market shares in favour of better freight rates for both sides or…"

"We attack their home market. Are the other shippers in the region for sale?"

"They are all hurting because of Ling Hai's predatory practices. They see this as very unfair."

"It is good business, Bertram. They will get market share and start raising prices when they reach more scale. In the meantime, the competition would have perished. But not this time."

"So, do we continue to sail on all their routes?"

"Course we do, and we go ten per cent lower on their freight rates."

"But, Sir, that would be financially untenable."

"We have built up quite a war chest. So please wait for our new prices to kick in and then start sounding out the other shippers. It is time to go to war. And while you are at it, please register a holding company in Hong Kong with a solid capital base. Let us be clear about our intentions. This Company will be called 'Consolidated South China Seas or CSCS shipping.'"

"Yes, Sir, but there may be a third option."

"I am listening."

"You could prevail on our customers to stay with us."

"We would appear weak and vulnerable. They will stick with us only if we can give them the best freight rates in the market. Otherwise, it will be bad business on their part. In business, one cannot expect favours."

"Of course, Sir."

The price competition in freight had a perversely positive effect on trade volumes. Lower freight allowed suppliers to ship cheaper and offer deliveries from stock at warehouses in the destination country. The warehouse business received a positive jolt, and more capacity was being added within a ten-mile radius of the docks. Small shippers exited the business by selling their vessels and crew to Ling Hai. When Matthew discovered he was regularly outbid for such assets, he knew that Ling Hai was a worthy opponent. This was not going to be easy.

But then, war never was. Protagonists often overestimate their power and capability and underestimate their opponents. They had prepared for aggression and attacks but had still found themselves unarmed in the face of a sophisticated offensive.

Matthew knew this would need a change in tactics and that he would need to dig in for a longer period.

"Hello Matthew, I have been looking forward to our lunch."

"Likewise, Mr Burroughs. In fact, I need your advice."

"I know."

"What do you know?"

"Ling Hai contacted me indirectly to convey a message. I have known the business's history since the booming days of the opium trade; the Ling family amassed a fortune in the opium trade from India to China over centuries. Ironically, it was being conducted under the protection of the East Asia Company. Opium made in India was exported to border traders with China and from China to the West. The 19th century saw the British government's complicity as this was one way of addressing the increased trade imbalance with China. But the addiction of its population needed a solution, and China called upon British India to cut supplies.

"By the time the two countries had come to an agreement

at the beginning of the twentieth century to curtail cultivation and effectively snuff out the cause of addiction to opium in China, the Ling Group had already invested in businesses in Hong Kong and Macau. In Macao, they invested in casinos, but in Hong Kong, they invested a large part of their gains in developing property that is now amongst the most expensive real estate in the world. Not only do they have huge valuation gains on their property portfolio, they also receive substantial rents through the residential and commercial markets.

"This generated further flows, and as property development in Hong Kong has a geographical constraint, they started high-rise construction. And they flourished. The Group is close to the UK and Portuguese governments, both having participated in opium export to China. Kung Ling grew up in a patriarchal environment but somehow managed to leave Hong Kong for an education in the West."

Mr Burroughs took a sip of his Chablis and then picked up the fork and knife, working his way through the sole meunière. Matthew was hungry for information and let his monkfish in saffron sauce rest on his plate. He sipped his water before enquiring, "Can we meet him, this Kung Ling chap?

"Kung Ling is no chap but a chapesse. She is the founder's daughter; she read literature and art history at Cambridge and then qualified in International Trade and Finance at the University of Pennsylvania. She could have stayed in the US but did not enjoy the general discrimination the Chinese and other Asians faced in their day-to-day life; she had already tasted it in England but expected more acceptance in the US. Alas, they are worse than us.

"Kung saw her future in the East, especially as China was putting together a high-paced industrial strategy into place. Kung Ling had grown up amidst the family's booming real estate business, but she felt that more could be done because of the unique position of Hong Kong in the world.

"She decided to go back and work with her father. She believed Chinese entrepreneurs were bigger risk-takers and better at generating cash flow. There was much to return to Hong Kong for. Kung Ling proved her mettle in the patriarchal system and, within years, was appointed vice-chair. She was attracted to the shipping business because it potentially offered a natural extension to her attachment to England and the States. The fact that the company was producing excellent profits propelled it to the forefront of the Ling Empire and allowed Kung Ling to define shipping as a core business.

"It is difficult to be in business in Hong Kong and not have a link with global shipping. You know that very well. The banks there are very well versed with ship financing. I have never met her; most men feel inferior in matters of both intellect and business acumen. She is claimed to have a photographic memory which lasts."

"Mr Burroughs, she could be dangerous if not managed properly. I will propose a truce under certain conditions. But she may still come after our shares, individually or collectively."

"Yes, you are right. They wanted me to sell my holdings in your company to them; I said they were your holdings, and I was just a custodian, but we need to be prepared as she will not give up. We must prepare for a formidable adversary as well as a potential ally. Please consider that her mind will always be a step ahead of yours. For me, it is like a duel of two great minds. I will relish this game of chess."

The waiter appeared as if he had detected that their discussion had ended. Matthew nodded; this was sign enough for him to clear the plates and wish them a good afternoon. The bill would be sent to Matthew's office as usual. As they stepped out, the chauffeurs were lined up in their respective Bentleys.

"Good morning, Ms Ling. Welcome to London. I am Bertram Powell, Matthew Stephens' personal adviser."

"Good morning, Mr Powell. Thank you for receiving me on the tarmac."

"Our offices have been in touch. We will drive you straight to your hotel."

Bertram held on to his stoic gentlemanliness by not gasping at the beautiful, elegant lady who showed no signs of her red-eye overnighter from New York. He opened the door for her and her personal assistant before walking over to the other side and sitting in the passenger seat in the front. The rest of her entourage were guided to a second car. A luggage porter loaded the bags in the respective vehicles.

The gleaming Bentleys made their way to the Special Exit gate, which slid open as they neared. The Ling Hai emblazoned Cessna Citation 500, and its crew and passengers had been cleared before arrival by the Foreign Office and the Home Office.

On the drive from the airport, there had been no attempt at a conversation on either side. The itinerary had been chalked out carefully, and Ms Ling was obviously familiar with London. The stocky concierge at the Dorchester opened the door of the car. Miss Ling looked back at him and smiled. "Hello William, how are you?"

"Very well, Ma'am. It is so good to see you again. We have been waiting for you. I will have your bags taken up to your suite. The weather is exactly right for your walk in the park. But your long flight may require you to rest."

"Hmm, it was not that bad. This time, I am coming in from the west."

"Ah, very well then. I hope you enjoy your stay with us. If you need anything, please let me know."

William nodded respectfully at Bertram, a nod that was neither a hello nor a goodbye but a respectful acknowledgement of familiarity. As Ms Ling bade farewell to Bertram and thanked the chauffer, the concierge held the car door for Bertram. Bertram nodded respectfully at Ms Ling, got into the car and was driven back onto Park Lane.

She was due to meet Matthew the following morning.

"Sir, Ms Ling is here."

"Very well, Bertram, please show her in."

She was beautiful. She had lovely translucent skin on fine features, and the elegance and brightness of a bespoke red Chanel suit accentuated her slim waist and slender, sleek legs.

She wore a jasmine-scented perfume that was pleasantly subtle. There was no jewellery except an unfussy Cartier watch with a burgundy leather strap. She smiled with her eyes and mouth and held out her hand. "Mr Stephens. Thank you very much for agreeing to meet me."

'Not only is she beautiful, but she also has a lovely voice.' Matthew was sharply dressed in a white Sea Island cotton shirt and a three-piece Savile Row suit. "It is an honour to have you here, Miss Ling."

She was so young, probably not even forty. Once seated on the comfortable sofas, a trolley laden with pastries and choice teas from Fortnum and Mason was wheeled in. "This is very kind of you, but I have just had breakfast."

"So, have I. Just a cup of tea then?"

The trolley was wheeled out of the office as the two settled in to face each other. "Ms Ling, I understand that you read at Cambridge and Wharton. So, your beauty is matched by your intellect and business acumen. I just went to night school and learnt some accounting. I had a very modest upbringing."

"Thank you, Mr Stephens; that is charming of you. I would not have expected otherwise, of course. I was lucky that my family let me leave Hong Kong to pursue my studies. Chinese families reserve such opportunities for their sons rather than their daughters. The downside is that I have spent the last few years trying to become that son."

"You are running a remarkable business. You have built your credentials in a wealthy and influential family."

"Yes, Sir, but your achievements are a salute to the human spirit, an inspiration for the entire world. I had a fortunate upbringing, but I am no self-made tycoon everyone fears and respects simultaneously."

"Self-made is just a euphemism for a poor background. I was the bastard son of a single woman who cleaned houses to make a living."

"All the more remarkable, Sir. You have shown what heights one can reach without all the baggage."

"Oh, I had baggage. Of course, it was not Oxbridge or the Ivy League kind, but baggage, nevertheless. It still is. In London, I remain the perennial outsider. I have wealth and power, but being considered as landed gentry is another thing here."

"Do you care? Does it matter?"

"It does and it does not; business does not care about all this, but society is very insecure. It is much easier to bask in the glory of one's entitlement than be threatened by an 'arriviste' who comes from the grime of inner London."

"You cannot do anything about envious people who covet every element of your massive achievements. I was also an outsider when I went to the universities you mentioned. In Hong Kong, it was quite the reverse and, in a way, quite perverse. The less well-off behave with unmerited deference towards me."

"You are so right, Miss Ling. We are both outsiders in our own ways. But who cares? I never imagined exposing myself to a potential adversary."

"We are not adversaries, Mr Stephens; we are potential partners."

"Oh, that is worth exploring, indeed. Isn't Hong Kong just fascinating? It is organised chaos at its best. I love its energy. The British are lucky to have it for a few more years. But you want to spread your wings wider than Hong Kong. I understand that you have plans for Marseilles, Antwerp and Immingham."

"Mr Stephens, shipping is a global business, as you have demonstrated admirably. We are just a modest business still trying to find its feet. But yes, we do have plans for Europe. Not just for cargo between Asia and Europe but also for transhipments to the Americas. But then you know all this."

"The more the merrier, Ms Ling. We can all co-exist. For that, we will need to co-operate."

"Yes, Mr Stephens. Co-operation would be more meaningful once we reach a critical size with a healthy market share. Right now, we are minnows compared to you. Lions do not share their meal with lesser animals."

"Minnows and lesser animals do not have the piranha power you command; we must find a way that works for both sides. I believe in a healthy market where everyone earns a fair return."

"At this point in time, our Board is driven solely by market share."

"Predatory pricing is a terrific way to get market share, but it is not sustainable. Your group has vast cash flows from your property business, and your cost base is lower than most others. So, I gather it may be more sustainable for you."

"The very fact that you are giving me your time here this morning bears testimony to our survival."

She was good. She complimented as she threatened. He needed to up his game.

"Ms Ling, like I said, it is an honour for me to receive you. And you are right. This would not be happening had you not pursued your strategy. But to move things forward, we need to stabilise the freight rates. This will give both more profit. Regarding your European aspirations, we could set up a joint venture for certain ports and routes and share in the spoils."

"That sounds very constructive, Mr Stephens, but there must be something else."

She was sharp, this Ms Ling.

"Yes, there is. All transhipments from Europe to the Americas will be done exclusively by Matthew Stephens and Co. But you will continue to ply the transpacific routes to the West Coast of the Americas. We can discuss it if you would like us to join you on those routes at some stage. But for now, my main concerns are the Asia–Europe and the Europe–Americas routes."

Ms Ling was thinking, 'Matthew Stephens is something. He is telling me what to do and what not to do. He almost has a nonchalance in his manner.'

"That is interesting indeed, Mr Stephens. But the Europe–America routes are where we see the future. In fact, I was in New York for a couple of days."

"Yet you decided to see me in London on your way home. It is an immense pleasure, of course, but you realised that the Americans are quite happy working with us and will not cross us. That is the way this trade works here. We accept newcomers who come at their own risk, but we do not cross each other. Shipping is not the only trade that works on these principles. I am sure your Board back home will consider such an arrangement quite a coup. I can have this all sketched into a sort of Memorandum of Understanding, and if you and your Board are happy with it, I will come over to Hong Kong with Mr Burroughs, and we will sign it."

"What if they do not agree? They were of mind to acquire a stake in your business."

"Yes, I know, but neither Mr Burroughs nor I are sellers. We love shipping far too much."

"Very well then, I will wait for your draft proposal. Thank you very much for your time, Mr Stephens." She got up and held her hand out. Matthew pushed on the armrest to raise himself, and looking into her perfect almond-shaped eyes, he took her soft hand in both of his. "Like I said, the pleasure is entirely mine." He walked alongside and had to just nudge the door before a valet on the other side opened it. Bertram smiled, looked at Matthew and said, "I will walk Madam down, Sir."

The two protagonists smiled, nodding at each other as Ms Ling turned to follow Bertram, walking away from Matthew Stephens.

Matthew returned to his desk and asked to be put through to Mr Burroughs.

It was time for an unscheduled lunch.

"Hello, Matthew. Is this seat taken?"

"It will be now, Sir; Ms Ling is a charming lady. And my, is she beautiful? I will send her a Memorandum of Understanding, but before I do that, I need to ask you something."

"Yes, Matthew?"

"How much of your holding did they want to buy?"

"All of it."

"I thought as much."

"They are a cash-rich group."

Matthew was silent momentarily and thought, 'Was Mr Burroughs being straight? Will he sell him out? Was he being paranoid?'

"They are your shares. Would you sell, Mr Burroughs?"

"Why do you ask?"

"I just feel that they will return to make you an offer. They are yours to sell, of course."

"Yes, Matthew, they are mine to sell. But as long as you keep growing the business as you are, I do not wish to sell. Of course, I cannot give you a lifetime commitment, nor should I."

"I believe Ms Ling will make you a big offer."

"Interesting, I will hear her out and let you know. That I will do. And if I ever decide to sell, I will let you know before acting on it."

"That would be great, thank you, Mr Burroughs. This lady has impressed me, and I want to take her very seriously."

"And so you should. You do sound smitten, though. She is beautiful."

That she was, that she was.

Matthew felt disarmed for the first time in his life and made his way back to the office. Miss Ling had touched a nerve he did not know he possessed. His standing in the business world had presented many impressive individuals, and the places he frequented were full of attractive women. But this Miss Ling was a combination that he had never encountered before.

And then, out of nowhere, he realised he was not alone.

"Matthew, how are things?"

"Well, you know, Mother."

"Banish all ill thoughts from your mind, Matthew. You are a married man with a lovely wife and a beautiful daughter. That is your world. We do not pursue other relationships while we have a family of our own."

"Of course, Mother, Ms Ling appeals to me on various levels. But so did Gwendolyn. She still does."

"Gwendolyn is your wife, Matthew. That is sacred. You would not have been where you are without her. Plus, she needs you more than ever. So, be a caring and loving husband. And then there is Sally. I know you do not mean to neglect her, but she needs you a lot more now that her mother has this affliction. Yet you are caught up in this spiral of business deal after business deal."

"Yes, Mother. You are right. And thank you for keeping my head screwed on right and providing shelter from being *led into temptation.*"

The Minister for Trade and Industry did not believe that giving exclusivity to Matthew Stephens and Co. on Asia to England routes was feasible, especially as this would cause diplomatic rifts with the Greek, Portuguese, Norwegian, Danish, Dutch and Belgian Governments. The solution should be in the hands of shipping companies. The business of government was not business. But the Royal Navy could escort his large oil tankers between Arabia's Red Sea, the Persian Gulf and Britain. And for a strategic resource such as petroleum, the government could prioritise the use of the super tankers his company already possessed. The Ling Group would not be offered this cover as they were neither in the Middle East nor in the oil tanker business.

Matthew had one of his instinctive inspirations. 'I should enlarge my super tanker fleet and use Japanese and Korean shipbuilders so their production capacity is saturated for some time.

'I also must check the consequences of Mr Burroughs selling his shares to Miss Ling. I need to get hold of that lawyer chap. If he tells me he is conflicted, then he is already advising Mr Burroughs.'

Jeremy Pickett was on the line. "Mr Stephens, Sir. How can I be of service, Sir?"

"Oh, hello, I need to draft a Memorandum of Understanding with a Hong Kong-based company."

"What is the name of the company, Sir?"

"Do you have any clients in Hong Kong?"

"Sir, I am sure that the network of law firms we are part of has clients there."

"Mr Pickett, I will need you to work on it, not someone from your network."

"Of course, I understand, Sir."

"But I will need to ensure you are not conflicted."

"Of course, Sir. If by any chance you are referring to the Group, I think you may be. I have already told them through our network that we are retained Counsel for Matthew Stephens and Co."

"Has anyone here approached you?"

"Sir, I am not allowed to tell you, but I can assure you that we will not be conflicted on anything that pertains to you. The Law Society has well-established guidelines for conflicts of interest, real or potential. Plus, we earn considerable fees from you, Sir."

"Thank you, Jeremy. Loyalty and trust come before everything else for me. Bertram will be in touch with you."

"Always at your service. Have a fine day, Sir."

Matthew directed Bertram to take this forward. "Any Memorandum of Understanding will take rounds of negotiation. Nevertheless, please remain very alert. We need to keep a tab on the Ling Group. Feel free to use our government and banks for this."

"Of course, Sir. I was just wondering if we should contemplate a counteroffer. They do not need the money, but it will signify strength."

"Yes, that may be an idea. We can also offer something related to our Asia-Pacific business. I was thinking of our lucrative dry cargo business out of Australia. That business is a cash cow that will keep giving for years. Asia cannot get enough coal, and Australia cannot stop producing. The Lings may suspect a problem, but once they have done their due diligence, they will realise that we can be partners in parts of the world and competitors elsewhere. We should grow wherever we are present, either through aggressive or through conciliatory means."

"Yes, Sir. I will try to get contractual variations drawn up. I do not think we should mention this to Stuart Waring, our area Director, yet."

"You are right. He may feel threatened and look elsewhere before we get anywhere. On the other hand, if we can get Ms Ling into our fold, I think we can do without him."

"Sir, he has been key in growing our Asia-Pacific business. We need to take care of him, whatever the scenario. Plus, he is a very well-connected Australian."

"You are right, Bertram. I was being a bit hasty there."

Bertram nodded and left the office. As soon as the door closed behind him, the visage of Ms Ling flashed into his eyes. That is some woman. But why was he developing a soft spot for her? Was it her beauty, demeanour, intelligence, or business acumen?

"Yes, Mother?"

"Matthew, this is not what you should be obsessing about. Your wife is not well, and she is all that matters. Do not get distracted from the right path."

"Yes, Mother, I know. But why has this woman made such an impact?"

"It is the timing of her appearance. You have very few challengers in your business. When one appears in a package such as Ms Ling, it is obvious that you are in awe. You are human, and you are a man. You are not physically engaged with your wife, and here is an attractive possibility. Gwendolyn is the only person you should be with. She is your wife. She is your life. Abandon all distractions and reject all temptation. I know you are a man, but you are my son."

"Yes, you are right! Thank you for keeping me on the right path."

The Peninsula's lounge overlooked the bay that was already heaving.

"Would you like some more tea, Mr Stephens?"

"No, thank you. I will have some when Ms Ling is here. Bertram?"

"No, Matthew, thank you. Ms Ling is here."

A vision in flared, white, satin trousers and a matching blouse with a yellow, linen-tailored jacket walked towards them.

"Mr Stephens, Mr Powell. Welcome to Hong Kong."

She was accompanied by her legal counsel, Jacob Brown.

Fresh beverages were served.

"I trust that we can speak freely in this corner of the lobby."

"Yes, Mr Stephens, the hotel staff will ensure we are left in peace."

"Excellent! Please allow me to begin. Am I right in

understanding that the Hysung conglomerate wants to buy you out? And that your shareholders are not opposed to the idea? Add to that the economic difficulties of China, the current turbulence in the Hong Kong property market, and the dominoes all stack up at the precipice. I assume you want either a better offer from us that compensates your shareholders or a substantial share in a joint venture with our own Asia-Pacific business?"

"Yes, Matthew, that is exactly right. Personally, I am not keen on selling to anybody."

"And you see me as the lesser evil? I will take that as a compliment. The Koreans are indeed very cash-rich, and what better way to expand than to add to their massive shipbuilding business? I met their new Managing Director in a London club last month. I seem to recall that he has an Ivy League background and is a bit of a playboy. He is remarkably young and wants to make his mark. Not unlike yourself."

"I am neither young nor a playboy, Matthew."

"Nor am I. We will need to look at the figures and see what we can do. We could consider a controlling interest but not by buying out the selling shareholders. We would consider injecting additional capital as well as our Australian business. In addition to our Australian business, we would also consider putting in our local business in the region. The business would, however, stop shipping to Europe and cease all transhipments between Europe and the US. We will keep the current management in place, and I will be an executive Director as will Bertram. Your uncle will be Chairman."

"You have thought this through, but our shareholders may favour a cash deal and exit altogether."

"Ms Ling, I am offering you to not only keep your job but also to be at the helm of a much larger business."

"Of course, I understand. But this is not just about me. It

is about our business and its owners. The sellers would like to maximise their proceeds, and the stayers, who are in the majority, want to expand in Europe and America."

"They can expand in America on the transpacific routes. In fact, with Australia, you will rule the Pacific. But Europe and East Coast America are a non-starter for us."

"What about a higher bid?"

"I am sorry, I do not want to get into a bidding war with the young Ivy Leaguer. His youth gives him a huge ego. If he succeeds in acquiring your business, I will compete against him as with any other."

"Well noted, Matthew. I will take all this back to the company and let us see where we go. How long would it take to set this up if I get a positive inkling?"

"Bertram?"

"Ms Ling, we can draw up a draft Memorandum of Understanding and have it sent to you by lunchtime. The figures will only be added once we have done due diligence. We can sign tomorrow if the broad lines are acceptable to you."

"Excellent! In any case, you are our guests this evening. So, we will be meeting later. Thank you for your time, gentlemen."

The stretch limousine that came to fetch them at the hotel was received by a flurry of door attendants from the hotel. The concierge himself held the car door open for Mr Stephens. The air conditioning in the car made it almost chilly. "Asians, Americans and Sheikhs love their air conditioning."

Hua Ling Towers were imposing glass and steel skyscrapers overlooking Kowloon Bay. Ms Ling herself was at the entrance to receive them. She took them into the lobby and led them to the high-speed elevator that whisked them to the top floor. As they stepped out, they found themselves in a marble, glass and silk lobby not unlike that of the Peninsula Hotel. Across from the elevator hung a large tapestry that represented Confucius. There were silk hangings with ships ploughing through rice fields.

As they turned the corner into the main reception area, there stood a gathering of smartly suited gentlemen; these were the board members. They all turned in their direction and bowed. Ms Ling made the introductions. The Chairman, Hua Ling, was seated in an imposing throne-like chair. With the help of his attendants, he got up and greeted Matthew. "Mr Stephens. This is an honour indeed. Welcome!"

"The honour is entirely mine, Sir. Getting here was a long trip but meeting you in person makes it a pleasure."

On cue, drinks started making their rounds through the gathering. Everyone was smiling.

"Ting, ting."

Everyone looked in the direction of the noise. Ms Ling smiled, a glass of champagne in one hand. "On behalf of the Hua Ling group, we welcome you to our headquarters. Our chairman, my uncle, is delighted to meet you. I take this opportunity to confirm the board's unanimous interest in pursuing the terms of your draft Memorandum of Understanding, and we look forward to signing it tomorrow before you fly back to London. We hope you will return to Hong Kong at the end of successful negotiations to inaugurate our joint offices. Here is to our joint venture."

Matthew responded with a big smile. "Here, here. May I propose our new joint venture be named 'Ling and Stephens.' After meeting Mr Hua Ling today, it is the only name of which I can think."

"Here, here."

The financial press greeted the deal with enthusiasm. The Hong Kong and Singapore Asians had continued their onslaught on global shipping. The fact that Matthew Stephens had sponsored this deal had not been the focus of the coverage. Matthew's idea of proposing the name Ling and Stephens had proven to be a clever idea. The Scandinavians and Greeks would have baulked in envy had it been yet another coup by their 'English nemesis.'

At seventeen, Sally's childhood blonde hair was darker, her eyes were a deeper blue, and her face had chiselled its way through to a delicate collage of subtle cheekbones, small nose and lush lips. Her features were a perfect combination of chromosomes. She had her father's handsome features and her mother's femininity. Her straight back and equestrian poise added a noble elegance to her presence.

Her looks were only matched by her character. Forged by adversity amidst riches, Sally presented an admirable juxtaposition of strength and simplicity grounded in the basics of right and wrong. Sally cared for her mother, not in any overt nursing sort of way, but by just being a daughter who was always around, a daughter who would fetch the odd something or bring a cup of tea and often engage in the banal conversations that mother and daughter so often got into. Sally ran the house with her mother and looked after her alongside the nursing staff. The maturity that came from adversity had made its mark.

For Sally, it was natural for a daughter to help her mother. What was difficult for her to fathom, though, was how nurses could be so devoted to patients. They were neither blood relatives nor were there any big salaries in caring for patients. A nurse's compassion came from a sense of purpose, a compulsion to care, to bring comfort to someone who is ailing, to smile, to encourage: the noblest of professions. Being a doctor must be equally rewarding, but it did not offer a relationship that surpasses medicine, a kinship closer than family, or selflessness that puts the patient above everything else.

Should she not become a nurse herself?

Gwendolyn found it an interesting idea. It was a wise option. Their daughter was not very different from them in her independent-mindedness. Matthew would share Sally's perspective. Despite the massive business they had built, her husband had never intended a gilded cage for their daughter. Wealth came with constraints, and Sally did not want to be bound by social norms. There had never been plans to force their daughter into any direction; she would find her way in life. Of course, there would be mistakes and lessons for their daughter. There would be heartaches, and there would be pain. There were no shortcuts in life. Sally Stephens would just have to assume her own mantle as a viable human being.

Sally on her part knew that for cynics, it was easy for the super-wealthy to have ideological aspirations. Nursing, however, was no easy career option. It was not just about comforting and holding the patient's hand but also about the nitty-gritty of dealing with failing bodies and shattered dreams, with flailing tempers, unpleasant sights, repulsive odours, bruises and bodily discharge. Nursing required full commitment to the patient while maintaining detachment. The human mind was not naturally conditioned for this dichotomy. So, education and training bridged the gap. The duty of compassion without the bindings of relationships had to be formally taught.

For Matthew, there was a beauty about it, the beauty of empathy. Such service had no price. Sally's indifference to wealth was perplexing but merited respect. The parsimony

Sally demonstrated in her day-to-day life was unusual, but one could only feel sheer admiration. Here was one rich kid who would not need the crutches of wealth to get through life.

When the moment approached for her to apply to the Nursing College in London, Sally's main concern was that she would be putting miles between her ailing mother and herself. Gwendolyn dismissed any such reservations:

"Darling, who knows? I may be around for decades! Life is all about pursuing your aspirations and just getting on with it. One cannot live one's life with *what-ifs*. You must follow your calling. In any case, it is not as if you are moving oceans away. London is just up the road. The Florence Nightingale Faculty is the world's best, and if you earn a place there, what is there to think about?

"Oh yes, last night your father asked when we should look at houses. He mentioned a townhouse in Cadogan Square, close to Sloane Square. It comes with staff. Or would you rather be around Grosvenor Square?"

"Mother, if I get a place at the Nursing College, I will be offered a room at their Hall of Residence. I do not want a serviced house or anything that sets me apart from other students. How can I ever make true friends if I live in Belgravia or Chelsea?"

"Oh. But Sally, you are Matthew Stephens' daughter. Are you not proud?"

"Of course, I am, Mother. More than pride, I feel gratitude. But I must live away from this world of wealth and privilege. You have given me an exceptional education and a set of values which I want to put to good use. I want to live the life of Sally Stephens. Just as you lived your life. And just as father lived his. Before you became so wealthy."

Neither Gwendolyn nor Matthew had expected their

daughter to elect for a room at the College Hostel. What was the point of having all this wealth if one's child was to return to where one had started? Wasn't the whole idea of wealth creation to be able to offer a better life to your children? Yet, their only child was looking for a simple life in the same city where they had started their own modest youth. They had hoped that she would live the comfortable life that all parents wish for their daughters. But as she approached adulthood, those expectations dissipated rapidly; it was the detached attitude she had displayed towards her privileges. She had not come around to conforming to her status in society. Even her social peers were puzzled by this. Sally's father had more wealth than all their families put together. Instead, this attractive but unglamorous girl was aspiring to become a nurse.

Sally got admission to the school of her choice and was offered a room at the Hall of Residence, but where she was concerned, it was not just the accommodation that needed to be standard. She was determined to dress down: no more expensive tweeds, silks or Egyptian cotton, just everyday clothes from everyday shops. Her mother looked at Matthew and sighed in resignation: "Girls her age should be taking care of themselves. Putting off eligible men is not a trait I want her to excel in. It is fine helping others, but that should not come at the cost of neglecting oneself."

Matthew smiled and could only dismiss his wife's remarks. "Rubbish darling, Sally should wear whatever she wants. Our daughter has caught on quickly to the fact that all this material mishmash is meaningless. Simplicity is the only truth." He then looked straight at his wife. "Look at us, Gwen. We started with nothing. And before us, my mother did not even have enough to buy us a square meal, let alone the medicine she desperately needed. You and I worked normal jobs and then got lucky; fortune smiled on us, and we became rich. But then I lost my mother, and you became ill. These things balance out, you know. And Samuel Burroughs? His pandering to society only got him into trouble. It took him a lifetime to grasp existence's true meaning.

"We do good or terrible things and then are left with our just pickings. Everything gets squared off while we are still here. Nothing goes unrewarded or unpunished. Sally wants to do good, and I hope that she will get her rewards, whatever they are. She has grasped all this quicker than most: conforming to society's mandate is a futile pursuit."

Gwendolyn smiled at the affirmation her husband had so emphatically made in front of their daughter. "But one cannot live in a social vacuum, you know. And are you not being hypocritical, given the vast wealth you have amassed? You wear the finest suits and drink the rarest whiskies. It is easy to dismiss one's fortune once one has it."

"You are right, of course, but wealth is not just suits and whiskies to me. Wealth is power and influence."

"And you work for even more."

"Yes, I am addicted to business, not wealth. We all respond to our calling. If Sally wants to care for people, who are we to stop her?"

Sally's quest for simplicity kept growing. Matthew could have bought her a fully serviced house in Belgravia had she shown an inclination, but Sally had preferred the communion with student life in halls of residence. Matthew Stephens gave in as he always had. He could not remember the last time he had persuaded his daughter to do anything 'conventional.' Wealth was not a positive for her, or at least not a means through which she wanted to be appreciated and liked.

"Father, wealth is what you have spent your life creating. Has it made you happy? Did you always want to be so rich?" Sally's voice was a variation of the tone of his own mother's sound. It was younger and crisper. Gail Stephens must have sounded like this when she was a young girl.

Sally was remarkably precocious. And, of course, she would be a fine woman irrespective of how she dressed. But for now, he had to answer her questions.

"Sally, I am happy for the people I have in my life, but I lost my mother, and now my wife's health is a worry. So overall, happiness is a relative concept for me. No, I did not want to be rich. I just did not want to be poor. I never grew up with a sense of entitlement; how could I? We were destitute. But I had a sense of purpose. When I saw what my mother had to endure, I became paranoid about poverty. This paranoia forged my future. It still does."

"Still? Are you serious?"

"Yes, Sally. I am petrified of destitution. Not for myself anymore but for those who confront it daily. Poverty damages in ways that only a poor person can describe, not knowing whether there would be a next meal, fearing illness because doctors and medicines cost money, despairing each time a creditor came knocking at the door, protecting one's mother from predators, worrying for your own safety every day. Very few can withstand its wrath. My mother stood firm, like an anchor in a turbulent ocean. But I felt sad that she had such a miserable life. I did not want that for us. I had to extricate us from our misery. I want others to be able to do the same. I want to help. Of course, there is a lot of poverty, and I cannot help everyone, but I can make a start."

"Father, I have only seen you surrounded by riches, so it is difficult to imagine how closely you experienced poverty yourself. I would very much like to be part of any project you undertake to address poverty. Father, did someone help you?"

"Of course, Sally. Life is a puzzle of 'improbables.' When

I was desperate, I met a benefactor who helped me, Mr Burroughs. You know him well. When I got the opportunity, I helped him back. Success plays with me in strange ways.

"As for our riches, wealth creates more wealth. And with all this comes immense power. But to what effect? My mother is no more. My wife is unwell. My daughter does not care about any of this."

"Yes, Father, I do care about all this. I just do not want to be defined by it. I care for you and Mother, which is all that matters. I will always be your only child. You will always be my parents. But I do have to trace my own path in life, however modest it may turn out to be."

The persuasive powers of Mathew Stephens crumbled in the presence of his young daughter. Sally had developed a sense of conviction and humility that was rare. Steadfast in her beliefs, there was little that a middle-aged father could do in the face of such purity and determination. Not a God-fearing man, Matthew felt something hitherto unrecognisable in her, something he could only relate to as a bystander. Although divinity had never manifested in his life directly, he believed it had played a role in moulding his daughter. By some quirk of fate, his daughter was simple, honest, trusting, caring and sensitive. These were all qualities she shared with the other women in his life: his mother and wife. But neither of them had been born into riches like his daughter.

He wondered what sort of a man someone like Sally would eventually share her life with. Would he be caring, loving and supportive, or someone like his father who had not bothered to stay on?

The radio was tuned in to BBC World Service: "The Organization of Arab Petroleum Exporting Countries

(OAPEC) have declared an embargo of sales to Western countries. This has led to a spike in oil prices and huge worldwide stock market declines. This development is also expected to have major repercussions for the shipping industry transporting the oil."

Matthew bit into his buttered slice of toast and put it back in the tray before picking up his cup of hot, strong tea. 'So, it has happened. The Arab countries have decided to punish the United States for supporting Israel in the Yom Kippur war.' He picked up the phone. "Good morning, Bertram. Could we meet at the office in half an hour? We may need to contact the Foreign Office, the Trade Secretary, as well as the energy minister. I also think we should talk to the Norwegians. Yes, I am just going to have another slice of toast, and then I will be on my way."

Bertram held open the door to his office. They both went in and sat at either side of the large paperless desk.

"Sir, the Norwegian shippers are in tatters. They have all overinvested in ultra-large crude carriers. In fact, there is still a massive order backlog with their shipbuilders. They will not survive this."

"Yes, Bertram, if this embargo holds, the Norwegians will be wiped out. We will also suffer. Unless!"

"Unless what, Sir?"

"Bertram, we need to become the in-house shippers for North Sea Oil. As the stock market was weak, I built up positions in the companies exploring, extracting and refining there. Once the dust settles, our ultra-large crude carriers will ply the seas. Also, we will lease Norwegian ships. Please call the big shippers in Norway, or better still, let it go from the Norwegian embassy, which can offer this as a rescue to their shippers. I have picked up that they will set up a state support system for their most important industry. It is not certain how long the Norwegians will provide support. Investing all their oil-generated resources in bailing out an industry with surplus capacity will be silly. Also, please activate the cancellation clause on our orders for oil tankers, even if it means losing our advance payments. There will be plenty of desperate, empty vessels for us to call on. We will give these empty vessels enough cargo if we carry oil ourselves. The government needs to support us this time, as they said they could do nothing on the Ling case. I expect Norway and Britain will become best friends until this crisis is resolved."

Norway set up the Guarantee Institute to help with the losses of one of its most successful sectors. This was a bottomless endeavour and proved untenable as there was acute overcapacity in the tanker market and much of this excess emanated from Norway. Matthew Stephens and Co became a major shareholder in three of the largest oil and gas exploration UK companies in the North Sea. The Norwegians also held rights to large reserves. Matthew had offered Norway to charter their tankers in exchange for being allowed to hold shares in Norway's Statoil. But as the government was committed to sole ownership, Matthew had to look at alternatives like Maze Petroleum and Norway Energy. Here, he leveraged the UK government to avoid any pushback from Norway on its strategic assets.

Shipping had not been plain sailing, but at least he knew the business. This time, though, he had to get out of his comfort zone; it was a matter of doubling or quitting. Here, he was now throwing himself deeper into the political waters of petroleum. Are the stakes just going to keep getting higher? Not only did he need these shareholdings, but he also needed to keep sailing on the eastern routes. He thought, 'I had been just an accountant in a shipping company. How have I become someone with a stake in geopolitics?'

The high oil prices created havoc in the Western world but did not change the overall stance on the Middle East. Israeli influence in the US, UK and France would continue while the same governments walked a fine line in diplomacy with Saudi Arabia, Iraq and Iran. Energy dependency and social conscience were at opposite ends of the morality spectrum, and this was set to continue. But all oil producers needed someone to carry their crude across the oceans. And there were few alternatives to Matthew Stephens and Co. The manoeuvres worked. He became the in-house tanker provider for British and European oil companies. Matthew Stephens and Co. could sail without reducing the cruising speed of his tankers as he was getting his own fuel needs at in-house prices. The higher fuel prices for his competitors had obliged them to reduce their cruising speeds to reduce their consumption.

Sally settled at Nightingale's without much ado. The classes were at the Waterloo campus, as was her accommodation. She embraced student accommodation as if it were special. For a young, attractive girl who was a natural candidate for SW1, it was ironic that she had chosen SE1. London's societal divide could not be starker than in these two neighbouring postcodes. More generally, one could draw a dividing line from north to south through London, and it would be amply obvious that the western half was either rich or middle-class and the east was either working-class or abjectly poor.

Sally's camouflaged life lent itself to familiarisation and comfort in her new surroundings. The proximity of Waterloo station allowed her to take a train to visit her parents. She could have asked her father's chauffeur to pick her up, but that would have been unbecoming of young Ms Stephens. Sally made friends at the Nursing College, and occasionally, she would go out with them for a drink and a modest meal in an inexpensive restaurant. She loved to take the bus and ride on the upper deck. She also liked the Underground. It was quick, convenient and affordable for a student. But most of all, she enjoyed walking in London.

When going out, her friends and she would cross the river over to Charing Cross and walk around Soho and Covent Garden before they would huddle in an affordable restaurant. Liz, one of her co-students, suggested they try this Thai place near Goodge Street. It was not really a restaurant.

Sally had allowed herself a small student's allowance. So, she suggested to her friends that the following month would be better. The other girls chimed in with relief and gratitude. A meal could cost more than five pounds per person.

The food at the Thai Kitchen turned out to be delicious and reasonably priced. Sally decided that she would return there with her parents one evening. It was a bit basic for her father, but she knew her parents would like the place. Her father had travelled often to Asia and might like tasting the same food here in London.

Thai Kitchen

Sally insisted that the Bentley dropped them off a block before the restaurant. She preferred to arrive at the restaurant walking with her parents.

From the outside, nothing was inviting apart from Oriental-styled English lettering in navy blue over a white background that spelt out: 'The Thai Kitchen.' There were whiffs of exotic cooking being pushed out by the extractor fan.

Once inside, the fragrance of Thai cooking was overwhelming and got the taste buds working. Matthew recognised the pungent, salty smell of fish sauce and felt himself transported to the street food along the banks of the 'Chaopraya' when he heard the sizzle of vegetables hitting hot oil.

As they stepped into the establishment, Matthew, Gwendolyn and Sally Stephens were met by the owners, a middle-aged couple; they both bowed to welcome their clients and nodded a smile of familiarity towards Sally. There were three tables in a room that appeared more like a kitchen in someone's house. A boy of around eight or nine peeped from behind a counter. Sally asked her parents to sit at the table next to the counter. "They are from Thailand. As you may have gathered, this is not a 'normal' restaurant; it is more like a meal in their house. I came here with college friends. The food is exotic and a touch spicy. Father, I thought you might want to try this place as you had travelled to that part of the world."

Matthew laughed in delight. "How lovely. They have created a little corner of Thailand in the heart of London!"

The Stephens were the only clients when they arrived. And so it remained for the rest of the evening. Sally's father started talking to the Thai owner about a hotel in Bangkok. It turned out that the Thai gentleman had worked there himself in guest relations. Matthew asked him to grab a chair and join them at the table. Hesitantly, he did as he was told but stayed at the edge of the table at a distance from Matthew to not encroach on his clients' space. He explained that his family had arrived in England via Calcutta. A wealthy Indian trader, Mr Banerjee, had offered him a position in one of his hotels in Calcutta. Mr Banerjee's primary business was not hotels but trading textiles. Staff were transferred between his businesses regularly. This exposed them to different trades while allowing the owner to redeploy staff according to seasonal demands on the business. The textile business traded in jute, silk and cotton and generated substantial cash flows; the hotels were trophy properties in the Park Street and Chowringhee areas of Central Calcutta. Two years as hotel general manager in India had led to a posting in the London branch of the Calcutta-based trading firm. Textile trading was different to the hotel business and he had had to learn quickly.

Matthew was keen to listen, as were Gwendolyn and Sally. It was great to learn about someone's life story.

Things had been going well for Sarawut and his wife, Natcha; their son, Jo, was born in London and was soon to attend a local state school. They had been worried about his integration at school. Other children had called him 'slitty eyes' or 'brown sauce,' but things had settled down, and he had friends. Life was good in London, and the family was happy. But then, Mr Banerjee's trading business was affected by the British government's trade policy. The trading operations in India, along with other Asian countries, had fallen victim to trade quotas and price restrictions imposed by Great Britain.

Consequently, the volumes being shipped from the region to England dropped drastically. Moreover, the governments in Asia were aiming for more self-reliance and retaliated so that imported goods would be more expensive than local products. Reduced business had meant cost cuts throughout the organisation. By Indian standards, the London operation was too expensive; using agents in London was cheaper than using one's own establishment. The London branch booked losses, and the decision to shut it down became unavoidable. His bosses in India were aware of their Thai officer's family, and they had kindly offered him relocation and a decent position back in Calcutta. There was nothing they could offer him in London. This immediately implied that the family had to either decide to return to Calcutta or home to Thailand or stay put and fend for themselves in London. They agreed on the latter.

"So, you opened this restaurant?" This time, it was Gwendolyn who expressed her curiosity.

"With our savings, we opened a small grocery store. Most of it was local English fare, but we stocked shelves with Thai products, most of which were either canned or bottled. Although some perishable foodstuffs were being brought in by air and sea in refrigerated containers, the landed price of the fresh produce was too high to make it a viable proposition for a small grocery store in the Goodge Street area. So, we adapted recipes to local produce. Our regular customers became curious and started trying Thai products. In response to requests for recipes and tips, we started cooking classes to educate our clients on using ingredients. The transition from the cooking classes to the restaurant was slow. Not all dishes could work for the English palates. We worked on a menu that would accommodate the whims of Londoners. We then applied for a restaurant permit to start something that felt like a greasy spoon and had only three tables for four people each. This would be the smallest of small restaurants in central London!"

Given that Sarawut and Natcha ran the shop during the day and a restaurant in the evening, they worked long hours. To keep the overheads manageable, they did not employ any staff. There was no extra accommodation cost, as their residence was a flat above the shop.

Since they started, they had not advertised; they had no budget for it. Their cookery 'students' became their clients, and things had just moved on. Their customers came by word of mouth. There was no liquor licence, but customers could buy their drinks at the off-licence across the road and bring in their bottles. Sometimes, they had capacity evenings; there was no one on others. The food was cooked fresh. They minimised wastage by storing small meat and fish portions in a freezer. Sarawut had learnt about food storage and waste management at the hotels he had worked in. They had learnt that the frozen produce could be directly used in sizzling oil. They ensured they were extra careful and vigilant, and there had been no accidents.

In this unusual grocery store setting, the house lady cooked while the man and son cared for the tables and the customers. When Sally's father heard of this arrangement, he laughed. "What a smart man you are. Did you hear that?

The wife does all the work, and he keeps us happy with his stories. My compliments to your wife; the food here is delicious."

Sally's father spoke about visits to Thailand, India and Cambodia. He expressed amazement that Thailand had managed to resist colonisation all along. Was having military rule any better? The discussion between the Thai gentleman and Sally's father meandered its way through politics, tourism and the state of the Thai economy.

"Exchanging views on one of my favourite parts of the world is a real pleasure. And you have brought a small piece of Thailand to us in London. We need more ventures like this in this city. I am fed up with the rubbish we are served in restaurants here. Here is my card. Drop by one of these days. I may be able to work something out."

"Sir, that is very kind. In fact, I am not here just for my family. I am also here because of my younger brother. He worked in a tea plantation in Darjeeling and was brought over to London for a job by the plantation owner, a highly respected Englishman. Once here, it turned out to be a trap, and he was given dishonourable tasks. He wrote to me that he was sorry and was really ashamed. When we came here, we were told that he had committed suicide."

"Sarawut, that is a very sad story. Do you know who this employer was?"

"Yes, Sir, he is a very wealthy man called Samuel Burroughs. I understand that he is untouchable. Even the British justice system cannot touch him."

"Hmm."

"I am sorry to bring this up. I will leave you to finish your meal in peace."

"Not at all Sarawut. Your story has been a fascinating revelation. Thank you for sharing it."

"What a delightful meal, Sally; your mother and I enjoyed that thoroughly. Keep us informed of other such discoveries, won't you?"

"I am afraid I do not know too many other places. We can always come back here if I do not find anything else. And father, I am sorry that he mentioned Mr Burroughs. I hope that does not spoil your evening."

"Not at all, Sally. I am not surprised at what he said. Sarawut and his wife are lovely people. And thank you for this lovely evening."

Matthew Stephens looked at Sally, beaming in the delight of her company. There were no words to express his pride in the strength of her simplicity. His daughter could have gone the way of any of the other wealthy girls, ones who remained enclosed in their own environment, trapped within the hollowness of high society and whose only means of self-appreciation was to spend daddy's money on gaudy clothes, vulgar trinkets and overpriced restaurants and clubs: a bunch of good-for-nothing wasters.

Gail Stephens had never cared that she was poor. Sally Stephens did not care that she was rich. Yes, that is where it came from. The memory of his mother gushed into his thoughts; a smile broke out as moisture found its way into his eyes.

Mother was right when she had said that she would never leave him. If only she had come to him when he decided to rescue Mr Burroughs.

Matthew knew that he fulfilled a significant role in global trade, especially in the massive flows in the oil and gas sectors. Oil companies were always under pressure to invest heavily in exploration, extraction and refining. It was thus financially convenient to have someone else invest in ships. Companies would use the Suez Canal route with its high clearance charges or the cheaper Cape of Good Hope route, depending on the oil price. Stephens and Co. had fleets operating through both routes and offered the big oil companies the chance to respond to customer demands and delivery schedules by switching course when needed.

He believed that oil had become a staple commodity for the energy-hungry world. The shipping of crude had quite a few players already: the Greeks, the Hong Kong-based liners and the American juggernauts. The tankers had reached monstrous sizes, some resembled aircraft carriers, only longer. Moreover, the Middle East was volatile. Shipping relied on a constant level of demand and supply through the years. Occasionally, volatility was set off by tinderbox politics. Oil producers had equipped themselves by increasing or reducing production through cartel agreements.

Shippers did not have the same flexibility as oil producers. Shipping fleets were long-term investments. For more growth, there was a need to diversify.

South Africa shipped a lot of natural resources to the north. Matthew started buying shares in South Africa Resources, the country's largest iron ore producer. Once he had purchased a ten per cent stake, he nominated a Board member. In parallel, Matthew Stephens leased purpose-built dry bulk carriers and got them kitted out with conveyor belts, chutes and bucket belt uploaders. By the time the ships were ready to sail, South Africa Resources issued a new tender for carriers to transport iron ore from the port of Saldanha in Saldanha Bay, north of Cape Town, to the EMO terminal in Rotterdam from where the raw material was transported to the rest of the Netherlands, Germany and Austria by rail.

The tender was priced low enough to secure the deal to reduce oil dependence and catapult the shipping business even higher.

By then, Matthew Stephens had offices and agents in over a hundred countries.

Gwendolyn sipped at her tea and said, "Matthew, isn't it strange that you have grown much bigger than the company where we had our first jobs and met?"

"It's all because of you being by my side."

"No, Matthew, you were always very bright and ambitious. I just happened to be around."

"You remember that time you called me a ninny?"

"Yes, of course."

"Well, I had promised myself that I would never be considered a ninny again. Not by you, not by anyone."

"I was foolish then but very fond of you."

"Yes, Gwendolyn, ours was a destiny made in heaven. Sometimes, I am scared that it has all gone too well. No one deserves so much, so much love and so much wealth. It is like winning the lottery every morning and falling in love every evening."

"That is wonderful, Matthew. So, you are not the hard-hearted, ruthless man everyone thinks you are."

"I was a nobody who you made a somebody, Gwendolyn. The media needs something to focus on. When they do not have access to the individual, they construct an image based on suppositions. I do not think that they are far from the truth in so far as my business tactics are concerned. They are also right in considering me as an outsider. I guess that I am. Money is not a passport to society, especially not when the landed gentry envies you."

"Matthew, did that Thai restaurant owner ever contact you? The one whose brother had committed suicide?"

"Err, no. I guess he found out that I had a hand in the acquittal of Mr Burroughs and concluded that I was as evil as everyone else."

"Do you regret your support to Mr Burroughs?"

"Sometimes, yes. That evening at the restaurant. I almost felt that I had been an accomplice."

"You had no choice, Matthew. You were morally bound."

"I think I did it more out of self-interest. I needed stability in our shareholding and strangely needed to demonstrate my power by taking on the system."

"We do what we have to do, Matthew."

"Sir, there is a man here to see you."

"Who is it, Bertram? Is he in my diary?"

"No, Sir, he is waiting in the reception area. He says he is your father. He speaks with an American accent."

"My father? Please show him in."

It was him! He was modestly dressed, but he had a clean shirt on. His hair was thin and neatly combed back. The eyes were a deep blue, and although this was a man in his eighties, he stood straight when he held out his hand. "Hello, Matthew." Matthew did not take his hand. Instead, he walked towards the settee in the corner and indicated that the man should follow him.

"What is your name?"

"Peter Grayson. I am your father. I was the man who left Gail behind. I was a coward. But I am your father."

"How do I know?"

"Matthew, you just have to look at me. Of course, I paint a shabby picture in this office of yours. But if that is not enough, here is a picture of your mother and me."

There was no mistaking that this was the man who had abandoned them.

"So why did you leave?"

"I was young. I had no job and no money. I lived off Gail. She brought the bread home. I wanted to do something, but there was little work. I felt worthless. America gave me hope. I got this offer to work in New York. They were recruiting English-speaking labourers for their roads and factories. I had no experience, but they took me on because I was young and able-bodied. They were looking for single men as they only wanted to pay for a single-person, one-way transit. I was selfish and took the opportunity and left. Gail was a strong woman, and I was sure she would be OK. Even though she was with child."

"Well, she was not OK. Life was very difficult for her. She was very poor. We were very poor. And she had very poor health."

"Did she ever tell you anything about me?"

"Apart from you abandoning us? No."

"You must really hate me, Matthew."

"I certainly did. But life has compensated me adequately. Apart from the fact that Mother is no more."

"Yes, I know. I went around where she used to live. They told me about you. Matthew Stephens 'this' and Matthew Stephens 'that.' You are a big man and very successful."

"What do you want, Mr Grayson?"

"I am your father."

"No, you are not. I had only one parent, and she is no more."

"I can understand your feelings, but we are the same blood."

"That did not seem to matter to you when you left. So why should it matter to me now? In any case, I do not need a father. It is too late."

"Too late to have a father?"

"Too late to make amends."

"But I have no one: no family, no friends. I never met anyone like Gail again."

"And you never met your son. Besides, I have a family of my own and do not need any more relatives."

"How is your family?"

"Mr Grayson, it is none of your business. The only reason I agreed to meet you was curiosity. I have always wondered what sort of man can abandon his vulnerable, pregnant wife.

"We will not meet again. Mr Grayson, Matthew Stephens does not forgive, and he does not forget."

"But Matthew," his voice faded as his eyes were close to tears.

Matthew rang the buzzer.

"Could you please show Mr Grayson out?"

"I deserve to suffer, Matthew, but I am proud of you."

"There is nothing that you should be proud of. People like you need to come to terms with their shame. Goodbye."

Peter Grayson slouched as he walked out of his son's sumptuous office. Blood was not thicker than water. Fatherhood was about caring, not about abandoning. He had learnt the hard way, the undeserving father of a deserving son.

Bertram was beckoned. "Just one thing. Grayson is indeed the man who abandoned my mother. It was the first time we laid eyes on each other. I do not want any contact with him. Nor do I want him boasting or shouting that he is related to me. Please keep a tab on him. If, for some reason, he ends up on the street, make sure that he is fed and housed."

"Yes, Sir, I will see to that. It is not my place, but I hope meeting him was not too difficult."

"Difficult, no; intriguing, yes. A relationship must be cultivated. One cannot just bail out and opt in later."

"Of course, Sir," Bertram nodded respectfully and backed out of the office.

"Oh, Bertram, one of these days, I want to discuss a

new project with you. Nothing that is business-related but something very close to my heart."

"Of course, Sir, whenever you wish."

"I need to know what support the government offers teenage orphans who have to fend for themselves."

"Of course, Sir, I will make calls to the offices of the Minister of Social Affairs and the Mayor's office."

Bertram walked in. "Sir, I have just got off the line to the American Ambassador. He explained that President Carter and Omar Torrijos, the Panamanian leader, had signed a Treaty to grant the Panamanians free control of the Canal as long as the canal remained neutral. The actual handover could take another ten years, but at least this way, the Panamanians would calm down, and the local protests against America would stop."

"It is good to know Bertram. Please thank the Ambassador. I hope that there is no repeat of Suez. Where the US is concerned, shipping between the East Coast and West Coast already has serious competition from the railroads.

"Strangely, these canals are put into place with such pomp and celebration, but then they all succumb to the power-hungry despots who rule the lands through which they flow."

"Yes, Sir. We will need to shift to the railroad as well. But dry cargo from Chile and Peru will still need to be shipped to the East Coast of the US. They will not want to haul anything by train through so many countries."

"I had met with the Chilean miner Antofagasta's owners in New York last year. I recall them mentioning that they have their own Chilean railroad operations and ports. Let us stay in touch with them to ensure we keep pressure on the Americans and the Panamanians to keep the canal open. Please speak to the Peruvian ambassador as well."

"Of course, Sir. Will there be anything else?"

"Yes, you may recall my mention of a new project a few months ago."

"Of course, Sir. I have spoken with the Minister and the Mayor and have some useful information."

"Very well. Please set up a meeting for us to get started."

"Mr Stephens, Sir, I understand your flight back to London is tomorrow. As we have finished the negotiations on the shipping of bulk cement, would you like me to show you around this evening?"

"Yes, Sonam. That would be very nice."

"That is great, Sir. I will take you to the Chatuchak market. They say that it is one of a kind. It is a bit ordinary for you, Sir, but we can go for tea at your hotel if it gets too mundane. Sir, would you like to do something this evening?"

"I'd like to get some sleep."

"Sir, please don't take this wrong, but would you like some company?"

"What did you have in mind?"

"Anything you wish, Sir. Bangkok offers many possibilities."

"Yes, I know, Sonam. But I am not looking for a prostitute or a rent boy."

"I am so sorry, Sir."

"No, I understand. This must be a standard expectation for many of your visitors. After all, the sin capital of the East has its own followers. I understand that there are still some opium dens operating within the premises of some hotels."

"Not in a hotel like yours, Sir. The Peninsula is one of our most respectable landmarks."

"You are right. I might have a drink at the hotel's bar on the shores of the Chaopraya. You are most welcome to join, of course."

"That is very kind, Sir."

"But if you would like to return to your wife and daughter, then I would rather you do that."

"Are you sure, Sir?"

"Yes, Sonam, of course."

"Thank you, Sir."

"Spend all the time you can with your family. We all spend too much time on our careers and business. What we do not realise is that a career can never replace the lost time one could have spent with one's family."

"Thank you, Sir. Good night."

Matthew was reconciling his sense of adventure in business to his lack of interest in the fringe benefits of travel and wealth: 'I have everything because I have shunned all sorts of perversion.'

The bar at the Peninsula was not very busy. A waiter showed him to a riverside table and left to fetch a drink.

"The malt whisky you ordered, Sir."

"Thank you."

Cradling his glass, Matthew looked out onto the shimmering surface of the grand river. And then the shimmering lights started moving as if all by themselves. There was no steamer. The water surface was still, but the lights moved as if to rearrange themselves. Matthew took another sip. The specks of light arranged themselves on the water's surface to form an image.

"Mother?" He had silently uttered the word. The mind alone had spoken.

"Matthew. Yes, it is me. How are you?"

"I'm fine, Mother, but then you should know."

"Yes. But you are missing your family."

"Yes, Mother, I am. Here I am, thousands of miles away, having a drink alone."

"Not by yourself anymore, Matthew."

"Is that why you are here? To keep me company?"

"I am always there, Matthew. You know that."

"Yes, I know, Mother, but I am glad you are here today. I have had a busy day."

"You work very hard, Matthew."

"Why, Mother? Why am I still working so hard? I already have more wealth than I could ever use."

"It is your calling, Matthew. My calling was to survive. Yours is to create wealth."

"I have a lot of wealth. In fact, I am one of the wealthiest men in the country. I have a loving family, but I am always working."

"Yes, Matthew, you have to aim for something else."

"Such as what, Mother?"

"A cause."

"So, you already know?"

"It is the right direction. Dignity is our birth right. No one should be allowed to take that away."

"How did you manage, Mother?"

"I was the target of many men, Matthew: a woman abandoned as soon as she was pregnant. And not married. Most men saw me as meat. There were scavengers circling around. But then, I had to fend them off. I learnt not to give in. And the first time I learnt that I could stave off one of those jackals, I became bold. It was only a matter of time before I was feared."

"Did you not tell my friend Buck's mother about his father's advances towards you?"

"Yes, his wife needed to know what a pig he was. And the world needed to know that Gail Stephens would not hold back from ruining the lives of those that sought to harm her."

"Vengeance. I seem to have inherited that trait."

"Do not forget and certainly do not forgive."

"But the hurt happens, and the pain remains."

"This is where your project comes in, Matthew. You could have faced a similar fate, but somehow, you fought through life, coming out unscathed. Help these kids, Matthew, even more than you do now."

"Sir, have you finished with your drink? Would you like another one?"

Matthew looked back at the waiter. "Huh? Oh no, thank you. I will head back."

Matthew walked back slowly through the manicured lawn. Just before entering the building through the door, the porter was holding out for him, he turned around and looked at the river. There was no image, just a shimmer.

"Sally, I am happy that you have started working as a nurse, especially as you coveted the noble profession so much. I am grateful that you visit us regularly. Gwendolyn and I look forward so much to your visits here."

"So do I, Father. Yes, of course. This is my home, and I miss you both when I am in London. So, I will be here a lot more than you would want. Oh yes, this morning, I saw a picture of you on the cover of *Time* magazine. The title was impressive: 'Is there nothing stopping this man?'"

"Yes, they brought that to me at the office. Those Americans. They love a rich man. But they can be unforgiving. If one of our businesses were to fail, they would put my photo next to the *Titanic* with the title: 'Is there no saving this man?'"

"But you must be proud of your riches."

"No, Sally, I am not proud of my wealth. I am a businessman who has had more luck than I am due. Of course, I am grateful for our wealth. But I am proud only of you and Gwendolyn. I regret that Gwendolyn seems to be paying the cost of our success with her health."

"You can't blame yourself for Mother's illness."

"But I do, Sally. She is withering away before my eyes. And the mighty Matthew Stephens is helpless."

"Do not worry, Mother is stable. I wanted to tell you and Mother something else, and it is best to just let you know."

"What's wrong?"

"Nothing. I have met someone in London. He is a doctor, and we both really like each other."

"A doctor? How very nice. Are you going to bring him over one day?"

"No, Father. That will not be possible. The thing is that he does not know I am Matthew Stephens' daughter."

"Why?"

"Because I do not want to be some entitled, rich girl. He thinks I am a nurse, and I want him to love me for who I am."

"But, Sally, you are my daughter. Are you ashamed of me?"

"No, not at all, but I want to love someone who loves me for me."

"But one day, he will find out."

"Yes, but until then, I am just Sally Stephens, the nurse."

"And I thought I was twisted."

"Please, Father; I think I know what I am doing."

"Yes, but I hope he is nice to you."

"Yes, Father. He loves me."

"Great, that is all that matters. The rest is all humbug."

There was a calculated innocence about her plan. Wealth can be a barrier to true emotional engagement. But poverty had never helped his mother find true love either. So maybe real, respectful love is a rare privilege he and his wife had been bestowed with. May Sally also find it.

Sanctuary

"Yes, Bertram? What information do we have?"

"It is quite sobering, Sir. In England, almost half a million teenagers fend for themselves. Half of them are orphans, and the others have left home early. Some sleep rough while others are in shelters. The government funds the shelter scheme, but some corrupt people work there. Many youngsters are mistreated, prostituted and even asked to work for criminals."

"This does not come as a shock. Children continue to be born into poverty. The family cocoon does not work, and they feel they can fend for themselves sooner or later. There are jackals prowling everywhere. It is a jungle out there."

"Sir, it is not just the children. Often, parents have marital problems, financial worries, alcoholism, and depression and prefer that their offspring leave home. Some cases are worse. These concern emotionally damaged youngsters whom their family members have abused. These children are the most vulnerable. They know that they are being asked to do something wrong. They feel guilty as if they were to blame."

"Bertram, it is an evil world we live in. These innocent children are betrayed by their own families. Poverty-stricken parents willingly sacrifice their youngsters for a price to pitiless predators. Some of them are sold off to rich men as sex slaves and objects of entertainment. Some are tortured, and many are humiliated. A few of my peers indulge in these callous practices. For them, there are no moral bounds, no human constraints. All that matters is deviant pleasure."

"Yes, Sir!"

"No, Bertram, no! We must put this right. What is the point of having all this wealth and power if we live in cahoots with such animals!"

"What would you rather have, Sir?"

"Rather than have them all castrated? I want to set up a centre for these homeless youngsters, where they can be received, lodged, fed, educated and taught self-confidence."

"You mean like a boarding school?"

"Yes, a bit like that, but with the facilities in London. Do you know Westminster School?"

"Yes, of course, but that is an elite school."

"That is exactly my point. Why should our misfortunate youngsters not be given a similar chance? They may not have the academic baggage or social skills of the rich. But they have faced adversity. And adversity forges character."

"Sir, we have a couple of properties in London that may suit such a venture."

"Bertram, it is not a venture. It is a mission. Don't you see the difference? I am fed up with ventures. I no longer want to deal with meaningless crises over which we have no impact: Canal closures, submersible explosives, wheeling dealing all over the world. For what? How much wealth do I really need? What I need is a mission, a purpose. I need to bring some meaning to this existence.

"Did you say a couple of properties? That would only be the start. Please acquire more suitable buildings. Once you have ten in London, start looking at other cities. Use the

Social Services statistics to locate the regions with the most acute cases."

"Yes, Sir, and how do you propose that we finance this mission? Should I take it from the business? It will be tax-deductible, of course."

"Bertram, our buildings should be assigned for a peppercorn rent to the mission. All running costs should be taken from my dividends. I do not need tens of millions to live my life. I will also ask some of my peers to open their wallets."

"Fine, Sir, do you have a name in mind?"

"Not yet, but something like 'Sanctuary' should be OK. This should be a charity, but it should not stigmatise the young who find themselves there. I do not want anyone to think that these are society's rejections. Rather, I would consider them scholarship winners because of their exceptional potential. Maybe some can be offered positions in Matthew Stephens and Co. if we can accompany them through their youth. That is how I started in life.

"And the Sanctuary should not sound like a church. Not all these youngsters are Christians. We can instruct them on spirituality but not impose a religion. Please keep this low-key. I do not want this to be a publicity stunt."

"Of course, Sir. I shall discuss this with people of trust and come back to you with some concrete ideas."

"Please set up a slot in my diary when you want to discuss the next steps."

He made his way to the car and felt positive when exiting the office building. Once they had reached Hammersmith, he looked out of the car that was driving him home. As soon as they were on the motorway out of London, there were pink and blue shades in the sky with faint puffs of cloud. Mother was smiling.

"Matthew, I am so pleased. You have found your calling. There is much still to do, but you have embarked on the ultimate path. Do not allow any distractions."

Mother approved. She would always be a moral compass, supporting him when he did the right thing and pulling him up if he strayed. She had stuck by her word and remained the only constant through the vicissitudes of existence.

"Thank you, Bertram. You have done well in choosing the Finsbury Park and Battersea properties. Such warehouse buildings are easily converted to whatever we need. I like the idea of creating accommodation for teachers on the premises. Please proceed with planning permissions and conversions and start recruiting the teaching and training staff. When will we be ready to welcome our first guests?"

"Sir, if all goes to plan, within one year."

"The sooner, the better. Please get whatever extra resources you require. I also need you to run our business."

"Yes, Sir."

Impatience was a trait intrinsic to most successful people, but it must be kept in check. Otherwise, it could send subordinates into a vicious spiral of panic and stress. Bertram was Matthew's confidante, friend and his Man Friday for just about everything. He understood impatience and tried to anticipate most eventualities. But this was new territory. Sanctuary was like a business, but not really. The targeted result was not money but human well-being.

The mission was to rehabilitate the disenfranchised and equip them for a normal life without allowing society to stigmatise them as charity cases. It was not going to be easy. Building back self-esteem and dignity would be challenging for some of the youngsters.

Sanctuary would be an educational institution that

rehabilitated while teaching life skills. Bertram would have to find a good principal. The next recruit would be a physical instructor. Together, they would determine with their architect what kind of building configuration would be required; they would also have to arrange for sporting facilities and field access for games. A safety and hygiene expert would have to vet the plans before work could start.

All the buildings would be painted bright white inside. There would be hospital-type lighting and adequate heating throughout the premises. There would also be closed-circuit T.V. surveillance of common spaces.

For Matthew, this was as exciting as starting a new life. For Bertram, this would be a final rite of passage to be chosen to succeed him. He would qualify if he showed the same dedication and commitment that he had demonstrated in furthering the cause of the business.

The phone rang. "Yes?"

"It's Mrs Stephens, Sir."

"Yes, Gwendolyn. Are you OK?"

"I am, Matthew, but could you please come home?"

"Yes, Gwendolyn, I will leave shortly."

"Thank you."

Something was wrong, but Gwendolyn was OK, or so she said. If she had called him at the office, it was serious. He would have to go straight away.

Bertram said nothing when he saw Matthew walk out of his office. Any question would have been inappropriate. Nevertheless, he accompanied him down to his car, opened the door, and shut it gently, nodding to Matthew once he was seated. "Home, please, Andrew."

The chauffeur put the car in gear and guided it off the porch onto the road. Traffic would be light as it was early afternoon on a Tuesday. The journey was an uneasy passage of time that had Matthew flipping through the newspapers without reading a word. While his eyes saw the newsprint, his mind kept returning to Gwendolyn's call. He hoped that she really was OK.

As they turned into the driveway, nothing was amiss. The Abode was enjoying the afternoon sun that shone on it. The gardeners and helpers were going about their duties. When Andrew pulled up, Matthew opened the car door himself and scrambled to the entrance. The door was opened as soon as he approached the house.

"Good afternoon, Sir. Madam and Ms Stephens are both by the fireplace."

"Sally, Gwendolyn, is everything OK?"

"Please come and sit down, Matthew."

He did her bidding. Something was wrong.

"Father, I came here to say something to Mother and you face-to-face. Thank you for coming straight away."

"Sally, your mother did not say what the matter is. So, I have been imagining all sorts of things. What would you like to tell us, Sally?"

"Father, I am pregnant."

"Sally, great! Are you OK?"

"Yes, I am, Father. But Mother is very worried."

"Why are you worried, Gwendolyn?"

"Sally found out last week. She had some further tests and has been told that she is two months pregnant, still within the period where she can terminate the pregnancy."

"Terminate? Why? Sally, why did you keep this to yourself for a week? It would have lightened the burden if you had spoken to us earlier."

"I am sorry, Father, but I needed a few days to get my thoughts together before deciding to have this baby."

This was indeed serious. His lovely daughter was pregnant.

"Does your doctor know?"

"Yes, he does. He offered to end the pregnancy. He could not disappoint his parents. They have high hopes for him and that did not include having a child with a nurse out of wedlock."

"So, are you getting married?"

"No, Father, we are no longer together. He does not believe that his parents will understand."

"And what about you?"

"I told him that I understood. After all, I am just a nurse who had got herself pregnant."

"No, Sally. You are not just a nurse. You are our daughter. You are the richest heiress in England. And you did not get yourself pregnant. He got you pregnant. Why don't you fight for yourself?"

"No, there is nothing to fight about. I do not want to buy his presence if there is no true love on his side. I am just disappointed that my feelings were genuine, but his were mixed up."

"The swine. How dare he? Why don't you tell him the truth?"

"No, the truth is what has happened. He loves me. I am sure of it. But he has duties to his parents. I want to take his decision at face value and decide myself. I will never see him again, but I will keep the baby and bring him or her up as a deserving mother."

"But Sally, an unwed mother in these times. Is that wise? What will the world say?"

"Mother, I will not be the first unwed mother of our time. My priority is the baby rather than what the world thinks. I know your society will gossip and cast aspersions, but that is not a concern. I am not ashamed of loving someone. I am just disappointed. More importantly, I will try my best to make up for the absence of the child's father."

"Sally, my dear. Listening to you reminds me of the dilemma my own mother faced. You are making the same decision. Gwendolyn, of course, Sally is capable. And we are both around. About the world, do we really care? What is important is this little family we are all part of, the centre of our existence."

"Thank you, Father. I love you both and am very grateful."

"There is nothing to be grateful for. Gwendolyn and I will support you in whatever way we can. You know that already."

"Thank you. Is it OK to vacate my lodgings in London and move here for a few months? In any case, I will need to find a new job once I am ready to return."

"Of course, Sally. This way, I can see you all the time, even when your father is at the office. Now that you will be a mother, please indulge us by accepting any help we offer."

"Well, thank God that is settled. We never imagined that we would become grandparents this way. But why not? This would be great for Gwendolyn and me. And what is more? The child will be a 'Stephens' this way."

The 'Doctor' had played out history all over again. Their daughter was 'knocked up' by an unthinking usurer whose cowardly response to her genuine love had been to abandon her when she needed him most. She had loved him without reserve. But her status of 'just a nurse' had prevented him from taking the responsibility. How dare this bastard hurt his daughter and abandon her like this?

In her despair, Sally retained her lucidity and made an irrevocable decision. She was unequivocal with her parents: if they had opposed her keeping the baby, she would just go her own way. Sally's parents succumbed to the obvious: the

Sallys of this world were headstrong and would stick to their convictions, irrespective of their adversities. That is exactly what Gail Stephens had done, and Matthew had been the result.

The truth was that despite everything they possessed, Sally was all they had.

As parents, though, it was a duty to acknowledge the situation. Gwendolyn had to lay things out for her daughter even though her husband saw nothing untoward in Sally's reasoning. "Sally, you have chosen a very difficult path. It is not the wrong decision because the way things stand, there is no right or wrong decision. You must think it through and believe in it, not for us, society, but for yourself and the baby. If you stick to your beliefs, it is certainly the most important decision you will ever take. It will not be the easiest path forward, but we know you. We trust you to do the right thing. Sally do not ever forget that as a family, all we have is each other. You have been here for us, especially for me. I may not have been here today had it not been for your strength and support. Your father and I will never question your decision and will support you unconditionally.

"Moreover, your presence here will be a source of strength as we continue our battle against my illness. Imagine looking after your baby and keeping an eye on your mother. You will certainly be a busy bee."

Matthew was reminded that Gwendolyn's health was deteriorating. Sally would be a real tonic for her mother. Plus, a new baby would be fantastic.

Matthew had to try not to speak out his thoughts: 'That scoundrel. Status? Really! Why do these posh toffs see themselves as superior? They are so blind to humanity in their close circles as they wallow in the quagmire of ignorance. Wait for the day he realises what he has done.

Sally was right about wanting to be loved for who she was and not for whose daughter she was.'

Matthew reflected on how conservative England, with its abhorrent class system, had survived the war. Even in his own case, wealth had not provided social status. The aristocracy was too obsessed with keeping its "purity" intact. It did not matter that very few of these nobles had the means to manage their inheritances, estates and even their day-to-day life. Debts had piled up because the show had to go on. Having to work for a living was anathema, to be avoided at all costs.

What these aristocrats sought was rent. There were exceptions, of course. Mr Burroughs received income from his estates but was also a respected businessman. However, his proclivities had turned out anything but noble. But this 'Doctor!' Surely, education should have brought him to his senses. How could someone who had taken an oath to care for everyone unconditionally have reservations about his love just because she may not have been a doctor herself?

Sally helped at home and spent a lot of time with her mother. They would eat breakfast together and walk through the gardens with an empty wheelchair for her mother if needed. They would come back in for lunch, follow it with a siesta and then sit by the fireplace. The dinner menu would be settled with the kitchen maid. The food would be well balanced as befitting two ladies with a condition. There would always be something that would resonate with Matthew's appetite, balanced or not. The 'girls' would then giggle and groan, trying to get out of their armchairs. Sally would push at her armrests to heave herself and her bulging belly upright. Then, she would walk over to Gwendolyn to help her get up. They would then slowly make their way out again if it was dry and walk more until it was time for Matthew's return from the office.

Matthew had stopped working in the evenings, and his office time was further reduced. Bertram would take care of anything that needed doing.

Occasionally, Matthew would see them in the garden from the driveway. He would smile gratefully for his fortunes: wife, daughter and a grandchild in the belly, all here at the same time.

As Sally approached her due date, the family decided to move to their London home. Matthew and Gwendolyn wanted Sally to deliver at the St Mary's Hospital in London. Sally did not object. It would also be more practical for Matthew's work.

Any worry about their daughter's decision to have her baby disappeared with the arrival of the seven pounds of joy late one night. Sally's father whispered to Catherine as her mother cradled her in her arms: "Since the arrival of your mummy, you are the best thing that has ever happened to us." He looked at Sally: "I am very proud of you, Sally. This is marvellous."

Sally's mother was squeezing her shoulder. Mother and daughter smiled at each other through moist eyes. The arrival of a new family member was the pinnacle of joy. A certain circumspection had persisted since Sally told them about her pregnancy. Bringing up a child without a husband was a dilemma for grandparents when the future of their only daughter was at stake. But then again, life could not be planned and altered to fit a predetermined trajectory; girls were strong and capable of fending for themselves and their loved ones. Matthew needed little reminding, although to be put in front of such irony defied comprehension.

Within the confines of a hospital room, tears flowed from the eyes of the four members of the Stephens family: the newly born Catherine Stephens, her mother, Sally Stephens, Catherine's grandmother, Gwendolyn Stephens, and Catherine's grandfather, Matthew Stephens.

They would not move back to Merstham but stay on in their comfortable house in Kensington Palace Gardens, which was big enough to accommodate all of them. Grandmother, mother and daughter had vast green spaces within easy reach. The house offered privacy as well as access to Hyde Park. Sally recalled how flabbergasted she had been when they had all visited the place for a viewing a few years back. How could such houses exist in the heart of London?

Matthew and Gwendolyn had smiled at each other in the knowledge that their daughter was about to cast away her wealth complex. They knew that Sally would have managed even as a struggling single mother.

Sally's stubbornness had indeed softened. Her daughter was not going to have a father. But she would have a start in life that was rightfully hers.

Whatever belongings were needed had been brought up from Merstham. Gwendolyn's body brace was amongst such necessities. Her condition had stabilised over the past decade, and the family had learnt to live with Damocles. Matthew discovered a strange new convenience in being London-bound. Whenever the idea struck him, he would leave the office and ask to be driven home. He would drop by unannounced during the day and head straight to Catherine's room. Then, on his way out, he would see Gwendolyn.

Sally loved the attention her daughter was getting and was happy that her decision had brought so much joy to her parents. They were always there for her. Although she knew that her father had always lived a complete life as a major businessman as well as a family-centric, loving father and husband, she had only just discovered the tender, forever-doting grandfather who would drop everything just to come home and admire his baby granddaughter. Catherine would giggle in his arms, melting Matthew Stephens' heart.

They also decided that the enlarged family would enjoy complete and strict privacy. Under the purview of Matthew Stephens, the implausible became feasible. He had decided that London would offer anonymity. Bertram had ensured that a personal message was transmitted to every editor. No magazine or tabloid would run a piece on Sally Stephens' single motherhood. Even though he had acquiesced to his daughter's wishes for no media attention, he would not fall prey to the vagaries of social propriety. His daughter was a single mother, just like his own mother had been. And they would live a complete family life.

After a few weeks of self-isolation, Matthew decided there was nothing to hide. Sally did not agree and responded that it was best to stay under the radar as she did not want Catherine to become a subject of society gossip. But Matthew was not sure Sally's strategy had worked in the past. It was thus time to abandon the status quo of secrecy. What was there to be afraid of? Catherine was a matter of pride, not of shame or concealment.

For Matthew Stephens, events did not come more extraordinary than this and needed to be relished. He did not want a sudden splash in the papers, far from it. But he wanted to take his ladies to the cafeteria in the park and the tearoom at Hyde Park Corner. He wished to push the perambulator around the perimeter of the Serpentine. In any case, he was no movie star, and there was little chance for the normal public to be interested in an unassuming old man out and about with his family. The security brief around the Stephens nucleus was low-key and at a distance. They would be there but not visible.

The unlikely foursome of grandfather, grandmother, mother and granddaughter was soon seen together everywhere. The initial whispers and glances mellowed down within weeks and completely died down within a few months. This was a non-story for the media. No journalist or columnist could get this through their editors. Wealth had obliterated all gossip.

Catherine would be brought up with the help of a governess for the first two or three years, although she would only help when Sally expressly asked her to. Sally was no longer sure if depriving Catherine of everything she had enjoyed herself was worth pursuing. Parents teach values. Sally had her genes from her grandmother and parents and had learnt excellent lessons from her life in London. There would be enough to distil and transmit to her daughter.

Even though the Stephens foursome had been out and about, they never featured in magazines. Celebrity status was reserved for the temporarily famous, not for business magnates of the stature of Matthew Stephens.

Catherine would be kept away from her father at all costs. The doctor did try to contact Sally when he learnt that she had delivered a baby girl through a medical colleague at the St Mary's Hospital, but getting through the Stephens fortress was beyond him. Moreover, the last time he had called, he was delivered a message in no uncertain terms. Two men in suits had rung the doorbell of his house. He had gone to open the door, and the next moment was a hazy return to consciousness with an aching face and body, clotted blood and blurry vision. After much effort, he focussed on a piece of paper crumpled next to where he lay: *Stay away, forever.* Sally never learnt of the event. The doctor started looking for a position in the wider commonwealth. He had abandoned Matthew Stephen's daughter and now risked losing everything. He would need a new start somewhere far away. Australia or New Zealand? Once his departure from the UK was confirmed, Sally was moved to a house on Lott's

Road in London's SW10 with her daughter. This would be Sally and Catherine's home. Gwendolyn was moved back to the Abode. The girls would visit every weekend.

Catherine was brought up by her mother, grandparents, and French governess Nathalie. At age three, she started attending the local Montessori nursery, where she was registered as Catherine Stephens. Sally would walk Catherine to school each morning, and Nathalie would fetch her mid-afternoon. Catherine was quite an extrovert and quickly made friends. This continued when she was moved to an elite primary school. The mothers would drop their girls at Sally's house. When they saw the house, they were curious, but Sally and Nathalie had a standard answer. Catherine's father was not around anymore. The interested mothers took this to mean that Sally was either a window or a deserted single mother.

One of the consequences of the media restraint was that some of the mothers who had invited Catherine and Sally, even though they had made some connection between her and her father, kept it to themselves. They all realised that she was financially comfortable, but beyond that, there was little to discuss. Sally was very down-to-earth and very pleasant. Although some women pitied her, most envied her. Sally had shown courage and guts in bringing up her daughter by herself. In turn, Sally realised that her married peers were close to being single mothers themselves.

Behind the façade of married bliss often lay a cry for help and understanding. There were many victims of infidelity. Then, there were problems with alcohol and drugs. But rather than supporting each other, these very same victims gossiped about each other. As soon as one's back was turned, the others would dig in their spiteful daggers. Sally realised that she might be a hot subject herself even though she could not match the sordidness surrounding some. The most recent unfortunate target had been Claire's (frequently invited by Catherine) mother. "Her husband left her for another man. What sort of a woman pushes her husband into the arms of a man?"

While taking care of the social needs of her daughter, Sally kept her contacts at a manageable distance. She would host the occasional tea party but rarely attended the ones to which she was invited. When she had struck what she believed was the right balance, she became increasingly comfortable and quite content. She neither felt sorry for herself nor tried to blame anyone for what others may sometimes have considered a rough deal. She just took stock of what she had and was grateful for her parents and Catherine.

Once Catherine was in a reasonable routine, Sally started voluntary work as a social counsellor at the Town Hall to assist the less fortunate. Her job brought her face to face with distressed people, from pregnant youngsters to retirees, trying to cope with loneliness and neglect. Sally was a good listener but exercised empathy rather than pity. Pity was condescending and disingenuous. Helping people was about connecting with them and providing clear feedback.

She also became more comfortable with the wealth she had been born into. What is the point of rejecting or hiding the truth? Sally realised that most problems were due to social pressure, and she had experienced its consequences through her doctor. It often pushed people to do what was expected of them, even if it meant overstretching one's finances. Even the wealthy succumbed to peer pressure. It was ironic that everyone in her family had such simple tastes. Granted, they lived well, but living an ostentatious lifestyle had never been on the cards. The Abode had provided full privacy. Her father had never sought visibility or fame. This was why she could not fathom the quest for wealth by her father.

"Wealth is a product of what I do, Sally. It is my calling, just as caring for people is your calling. I live and breathe business. I have paid the price for not always being there in your childhood. But it was a senseless spiral in which I was entrenched. The adage that wealth creates more wealth is no fallacy. Business opportunities just dropped into my lap. Anyone with a half-decent proposal still comes to me.

"Wealth is handy for material comforts, and extreme wealth buys influence and privacy. It is no accident that Sally Stephens and her daughter are not victims of the paparazzi. It would have been a great story and could have given the Royal Family's own shenanigans serious competition. But that would be a serious breach of personal space.

"We cannot forget that we are a simple family that got lucky; we lost our poverty but kept our basic values. I did not even make it into London's landed gentry. However, it hurt when I was refused membership to a club in Mayfair. It was clear to me that I was being led astray by my worldly aspirations. We would never define ourselves by wealth and social status but by a sense of right and wrong. But wealth lets us settle scores with fools who deceive us, like your Doctor."

Sally's father really had an unforgiving nature and she was certain that her father had somehow taken care of him. She had made him promise that he would never pursue the father of her baby: after all, she had loved Mark and dearly so. She would never forget the moments they had spent together. Of course, it had gone wrong. Irrespective of the disappointment that she had felt at being left alone, she could not bring herself to dislike Mark, let alone hate him. It was a mockery indeed that she would have been spared the demise of their romance had she not concealed the truth about herself.

If there had been one insecurity Sally had suffered from,

it had been the fear of being loved because of her father's wealth. It was over-idealistic, given the materialism that enmeshes everyone's existence. Still, it was an ideal, simple in its innocence and remarkable in its purity: wanting to be loved by a caring doctor while just being a nurse. If she had looked upon him as an equal, so should it have been for him. She had never judged anyone because of their background, means, and societal standing. She appreciated them for their commitment to doing good. This was exactly why the profession of a nurse had appealed so much. Nurses do not discriminate.

Yet, she had paid the ultimate price for the whitest of lies. Although, in all this, she knew that she had been right. Her father's thinking was aligned with hers. He was a simple man caught up in the complexities of business and wealth creation. Even though he did not fear wealth like she did, its value to him had been limited. Her mother's health had brought that home conclusively. For the moment, spending as much time as possible with her parents in their hour of need was a duty for her and her little daughter, Catherine.

What her daughter would want to do later in life would be up to her. But for now, they would both need to be there for her parents; there was gratitude for the London house and the weekend trips to Merstham so that they could all spend time together in the proximate glow of that flickering fireplace.

"Sally, it is so nice to be here all together."

"Yes, it is true. We are together here, but I need to do more with my job as a counsellor. I started with all these aspirations to help people to be self-standing. Yet here I am, a single mother supported by my parents."

"Rubbish, darling. You help me. You help Matthew. And you serve as a counsellor. We are all grateful and count on your support and affection to keep us going. As are all the people who come to you for advice.

"Your father and I admire your strength. You have always chosen a difficult path when you could have chosen a much easier life. In doing so, you remind us that life is about much more than business, wealth and material belongings. You keep us grounded. And you give us hope. By deciding to become a nurse, you have served humanity. By keeping your baby, you made us very proud grandparents; we were already very proud parents. And you know, Sally? Your father and I do not say it to you, but inside, we are very proud of you for not using the Matthew Stephens name. Of course, our simple name helps." She giggled. "Being called Sally Haverston or Sally Rothschild may have been a slightly different proposition."

"Mother, we can choose how we live, but we cannot plan who we fall in love with. It just happens. I do not regret having been secretive about you both. A well-educated doctor from a well-off middle-class family would naturally not want to be tied down to an ordinary nurse."

"But you are no ordinary nurse."

"Yes, Mother. For an honest relationship between man and woman, I was."

"But I want to see you happy. There are lots of men who would want to be with you. Plus, I will not be around for long, you know."

"Of course you will, Mother."

While in Merstham, the spectre of tempted fate reared its ugly head and entrenched itself amongst the Stephens; Gwendolyn suffered excruciating spasms. She asked to be freed from the brace. The nurse administered painkillers, but when the pills did not alleviate her suffering, a strong dose of morphine was used. Gwendolyn suffered discreetly and one day lost consciousness. The doctor was summoned; Matthew was at home, as was Sally. The doctor nodded to the Stephens, and they followed him out of the room.

"She is really in pain. We give morphine only when she is really suffering. These episodes are getting more frequent, and her muscles and nerves are behaving very unpredictably. From here on, her quality of life will be very poor, and she will suffer great pain. Please be aware that her spinal cord is deteriorating rapidly, and her bodily functions are failing fast. Soon, her vital functions will be affected. Her days are truly numbered. It would help if you discussed how you want this to go." He paused and looked at both.

"So, Mother faces certain death, now?" Sally looked back at the doctor and her father.

The doctor did not reply and looked down.

"Doctor, what can we do to reduce her suffering?"

He looked up and softly said, "There is the final solution: assisted dying is illegal here, but it may be possible in Switzerland; alternatively, we can wait for her to get onto life support, and if there is no improvement, the system can be switched off. Of course, all this must be thought through. The immense emotional aspect and the law and medical ethics issue must be adhered to throughout the process."

Matthew and Sally looked at each other. Matthew spoke, "Let's get the process started then." Before leaving, the doctor nodded at both and said, "I will be back tomorrow morning to see if she needs to get on to a life support system. I will call the hospital to arrange for a system to be set up in her room here, in case. Good night, Sir, Madam."

Sally walked over to her father and hugged him, her eyes crying into his shoulders. Matthew had not cried since the passing away of his own mother. He put his head on

Sally's other shoulder and sank his weeping eyes deeper into their sockets. So much had happened since Gail had left, but little had changed. Every time the seas were placid, a random wave would rise and crash into the hull of his existence.

Life companions are supposed to be around for life. If one's time were to be cut short, what good could life do for the one left behind? Of course, these matters were out of his hands. Preparing for the inevitable should come naturally. But it did not.

Matthew could only reflect: 'Gwendolyn has always been by my side. We have always loved each other. What is all our wealth going to be worth if she leaves? Should I continue with business or just call it a day and spend my time doing something good?

'Irrespective of what happens, I must be grateful for the women in my life: my mother, wife, daughter and granddaughter!'

Gwendolyn's passing away received restrained reporting in the media. There was a small service in St. Katherine's in Merstham where husband and daughter said their prayers, and Catherine bid Granny goodbye after kissing her cold hand.

Her departure had been anticipated, but her disappearance hit both hard. It was one thing having a sick wife and mother alive at home. It was quite another having an empty, silent room as the closest real-life memory.

Father and daughter spent the week in Merstham, Gwendolyn's absence present everywhere. The fire was on, and Sally was sitting in her armchair, but each time she looked across, her mother's seat was empty. Her father sat on a small sofa beside the armchairs and gazed at the fire without seeing the flames. It was a vacant, glazed look that showed nothing. "Are you alright, Daddy?"

"No, I am not. I miss her. I still cannot accept that she is gone. My rock of Gibraltar has floated away, and the wind has left my sails. I feel that I do not belong here anymore. Sally? I was just wondering if it is OK for us to sell this house. It no longer feels like home."

Sally moved back into the house on Lott's Road with Catherine and Nathalie. Matthew moved to a comfortable apartment in Grosvenor Square. He gave up the homes in Merstham and Kensington Palace Gardens. Father, daughter and granddaughter would meet regularly. This would be the new family nucleus: a nucleus that had shifted from Gwendolyn to Matthew; he wondered if his obsession had been worth it. He could have spent more time with his wife when she was around rather than indulging himself in meaningless money-making schemes. He had also short-changed Sally in the time he spent with her. Showing up at birthdays and being there for the occasional crisis was not the parenting he should have cultivated, especially as she had had to deal with her mother's indisposition. How had he fallen into the trap of indifference? And for what? Wealth? How empty was that? This had to stop.

Sally noticed that her father was spending more time at his flat and regularly sent the car around to fetch them to spend time together. The Sunday walks in Hyde Park quickly evolved into a daily ritual unless it was raining heavily. Light rain was negotiated under the cover of raincoats. Catherine loved it. She particularly liked the hot chocolate her grandfather would order for her at the Dorchester. The waiter would ensure that the hot chocolate was served at a temperature ideal for little Catherine. Now and then, a person passing by would nod at her grandfather. Did everyone know him? Some of them would even smile and wave at her. She would wave back because that is what her mummy had taught her.

Matthew increasingly delegated his management responsibilities to his managers. A large part of him was withdrawing. The business he breathed was no longer delivering the oxygen it once did. Occasionally, a spark would light up. It had to do with his Sanctuary project.

"It's a very noble cause, Father."

"I am losing hope myself, but I want to provide hope for others. You are most welcome to join us if it is of interest."

"Father, I enjoy my counselling but would be very happy to join Sanctuary at the right time. I still need to hone my counselling skills." At the Town Hall, Sally was a compassionate listener, but when it came to advice, she was her father's daughter. Her message was never ambiguous: "No self-pity, please. Things happen." People must accept their own situation and stop trying to blame someone or something. One must get on with it. The tone was gentle, but the message was firm. "It is very difficult indeed, but you must accept the situation and take it upon yourself to deal with it. One has to decide for oneself and then live with the decisions taken. It is futile to look for an easy way out because there never are any soft options."

Although each case was different, there was a common thread running through the grievances of most of her visitors, something she had never really had to worry about herself: the lack of money. She realised that to bring about real change, there would need to be a financial aspect to the assistance she could provide. She persuaded her father to establish a Charitable Trust called Horizons and fund it adequately for the problems she had encountered: unemployment, self-employment, single motherhood, temporary accommodation, skills training and help with bills.

Under a system of referrals conceived with her father, Sally examined each case during her counselling and decided if some financial assistance was warranted. She did not want free riders; she kept the selection process personalised and subjected individuals to a thorough screening. Sally was the only person who could refer cases to the Trust. No other volunteer at the Town Hall could do this. The Town Hall did not raise an eyebrow; they were pragmatic. They knew whose daughter Sally was and had no problem with her running her own little aid programme under its auspices. Sally sometimes discussed the referrals with her father. He always said, "Sally, everyone deserves a chance. But we cannot help everyone. So, we must ensure we can help someone who merits it. Yes, this does mean that you will have to reject a few. But being helpful to someone is not about being nice; it is about being helpful. If, for whatever reason, the person does not qualify for financial support, the help you can offer is an explanation of why that person did not qualify and what else they could be doing to address their problems."

She knew what her father was getting at. Charity must be deployed judiciously. Whether she could give them money or not, she should not forget her job as a counsellor.

Sally Matthews, who never believed she had any of her father's traits, realised otherwise. In her case, though, the acumen was not to create wealth but to distribute it. She developed a keen sense of philanthropy. The way she went about it was logical. She rounded up a few like-minded people. She left the Town Hall and set up an office, more like a Day Centre, to meet people in a building her father owned. People would be received by her 'welcome' staff member. They would sit together for tea and then agree on the right adviser. A more thorough advisory session with a 'case manager' would be organised as a follow-up, and an action plan would be drawn up that would be monitored by the 'case manager.' Weekly updates were provided during meetings chaired by Sally, and she would decide to choose certain cases to meet the 'client' herself.

As the workload increased, she had to make sure that the interests of her own daughter were not sacrificed; as it was, Catherine would have to cope with life without ever knowing her father. Losing her mother to a cause would be inexcusable.

Father and daughter decided that Horizons would be merged with Sanctuary. This would reduce her involvement with the social work and devote more time to bringing up her daughter. Her organisation, 'Horizons,' was already well run, and the fact that Sally was less involved in the day-to-day practical details allowed an objective perspective.

Sally stayed single. There were many suitors, and she remained sexually active, but love was a sentiment to which she could no longer relate. Her emotional needs were met by looking after her father and raising her daughter. One major heartbreak was enough to avoid the snare of romance forever. Wealth had prevented any material hardship. She acknowledged that things might have been a lot different had she not been the daughter of Matthew Stephens. The fact that she was the heiress to the Stephens fortune was inescapable; if one could do some good out of it all, why not? What is the point of starting from scratch and barely managing to do any real good? It would be selfish in a perverted sort of way.

But should Catherine not be imbued with the same values as her mother's? Once she was a bit older, Catherine could also live a life of discretion. Perhaps Catherine would succeed in pure love where she herself had not. Life can be lived in modesty and simplicity. Looking back at those early days in London, those two maxims had been her life compass. Of course, it had meant declining the early invitations from social peers who had also moved away from home around the same time. While her school and Surrey friends were putting up anchor in London's smarter postcodes, SW in the main, she had embarked upon a frugal existence with a second-hand bicycle and a room in the Nursing College's Hall of Residence in SE1. Catherine could do something along those lines if she wanted.

As Matthew Stephens' daughter, being blasé about wealth and possessions was easy. The scourge of wealth was difficult to fathom for most, but for Sally, riches were not conducive to a normal life, trust and confidence in others. Worse, wealth had not protected her mother against ill health.

Nevertheless, the Stephens' riches allowed her to do good work and confront social problems. There were families with abuse, violence, alcoholism, disability, disease and depression. Horizons excelled in offering tailor-made support through its network of specialists. Many professionals provided free services. Moreover, Horizons had been subsumed into Sanctuary. Together, they were managed efficiently with excellent internal control mechanisms in place. The government would never have been able to run such a project; corruption would have eroded any benefit to the victims. Sally became the Managing Director of the merged entity and, in consultation with her father, looked at extending its scope.

Her father had focused on neglected boys, but under Sally, Sanctuary started welcoming girls in dedicated facilities with female staff. Sally always remained calm and allowed her reflex and intuition to take over when things became difficult. Her nursing background allowed instinctive adaptation. There was a significant difference, though. As a nurse, she had not had to determine which cases needed attention and which did not.

Matthew's own mission was to help hapless boys. Under Sanctuary, there should be distinct institutions for boys on the one hand and girls and family counselling on the other. Matthew's personal focus was on High Society's disgraceful treatment of young boys, and he would remain personally engaged to ensure that perpetrators paid a heavy price. That encounter with Sarawut in the Thai Kitchen kept haunting him. Somehow, he had helped the culprit escape the crimes against Sarawut's brother. The boy had committed suicide in shame.

Matthew wanted to save the vulnerable youth. For him, insecurities crawled into innocent, impressionable minds, presenting predators with opportunities to manipulate and ravage. Society offered little prevention. So, care and support for the aftermath were even more critical than punishment for the perpetrators.

The boy was only a teenager, with a few spots on his chin but a handsome face with chunky features. There were bruises around the upper cheeks and a bleeding upper lip.

"Come here, young man. Take a seat. I understand from my people that you were beaten up. What happened, Son?"

"Yeah, I went to that Sheffield bloke's house to tell them that my mother would not be able to come and clean the house," sobs stifling his flow. He caught his breath and continued, "She is ill, my mom. Sheffield was with other men in the parlour, and I was called in. The men all smiled at each other. Sheffield told me that my mother's absence was not a problem. But he asked me to stay."

"What's your name?"

"Oliver."

"How old are you?"

"Thirteen. "

"What happened?"

"They closed the doors and asked me to sit alongside a fat bloke on the sofa. He first put one arm around my shoulder and put his other hand on my thighs." Tears streamed down to join a discharge from a leaky nose. "I looked at him, and he tried to kiss me. I moved my face away and stood up, saying, 'No fuckin way!'"

"And then?"

"Someone from behind held me while another put a wet handkerchief over my mouth and nose. It smelt very strong, like varnish."

"Did you pass out?"

"Nah, but I felt unable to move. Someone punched my face, but I did not feel it. They pushed me against the dining table and then pushed my face onto its surface." The tears came down fast and strong with loud sobs.

"It is OK. You are safe here. How did you come here?"

"After those sick fucks had finished with me, one of them who had not bum-fucked me and had even tried to stop the others, came up to me and said that I should come to you. He said that I should tell you everything, and then he put me in a taxi, gave your address to the driver and paid for the ride."

Not everyone should burn in hell.

The fact that a group of rich businessmen had sodomised him was unsurprising. Their depravity was confirmed when a physician revealed the ruptured rectum and considerable blood loss after examination. There was government support for dealing with cases such as this. However, this was not a case. This was Oliver, a thirteen-year-old boy. For an organisation that caters for fragile and damaged youngsters, this was it: a being so damaged that shame and pain had convulsed in an evil ritual of demonic proportions.

This Oliver will be rehabilitated with love and care. As would all others who came to his door. But how many more Olivers are out there? Some would be in an even worse state. The cruelty and callousness of the city's vultures was immeasurable. Alcohol and drugs extinguished all humanity and made vicious jackals of them, collectively impaling their prey in some twisted pact.

'A Home for Oliver' was set up within Horizon to institutionalise support and intensive care for maltreated and sexually abused boys, not just homeless youngsters. The Home would receive abused youngsters, give them medical attention, and offer nursing to calm down and let their distress abate before they felt well and secure enough to discuss their ordeal with psychologists and physicians. A psychiatric nurse would take notes and create a case file that would be sent to Bertram's office.

Bertram's office would seek an urgent meeting with Matthew if the psychologist put a 'VS' note on the leader page. 'S' files would be dealt with without Matthew's direct involvement. Besides Very Serious and Serious, the other categories were HL, HU and MA. Youngsters who were Homeless, Hungry and needing Medical Attention were transferred to the Medical Unit. Matthew received a weekly report from Bertram's office with the number of youngsters taken in under each category and how they were doing. Matthew would scrutinise the list from 'A Home for Oliver'; he would be personally involved in key decisions about his young guests.

When the 'patients' were ready for a supervised return into society, their names would be taken off the 'residents' list'. After an interview, Matthew Stephens had to sign all movements off the VS and S lists. Each patient had to be given the care and time needed. There were no incentives for the staff to move them off the list earlier. More buildings and staff were added when patient rooms and common facilities were getting close to capacity. Matthew Stephens and Co had a property portfolio in London. Small two- to three-storey buildings with a simple brass plaque engraved "Oliver" had appeared in London. No single building would hold more than twenty patients at any given time. This was the best way of ensuring personalised care and attention. There was no luxury but simple comfort and stringent hygiene. The idea was not to get the victims used to something that would make it difficult to return to normal life. The values that Matthew wanted to teach were cleanliness, compassion and self-belief. Young working-age youngsters were given apprenticeships in his business and supervised by qualified managers.

In parallel, he would delve into the perpetrators' whereabouts and dealings and exact the appropriate compensation. Beyond any financial compensation component, there would be an element of punishment. Social standing, however frivolous, meant a lot to these sick bastards. When things went wrong, the same 'friends' who had frolicked alongside would disappear. Not only would the perpetrators have to relinquish substantial wealth, but they would almost immediately lose their network.

Matthew's engagement had the desired effect in London. There were fewer cases of trespassing on the dignity of youngsters. Everyone feared being socially dismembered. For the organisation to have a similar impact on other cities, he would need to link up with sponsors who were local pillars of society. He would tap into his own network of the wealthy and powerful.

An urgent case had just been referred to Matthew by Bertram over the phone.

They had received a fourteen-year-old boy. His eyes stared into a terror-filled void, and his lips trembled.

When his silence eventually gave way, he blurted out that he had run away from his employer, a leading public figure. The utterance of the first sentence culminated in a gush of tears and a whimper that gasped for breath.

The abuse had become unbearable; things had become increasingly violent, and the more pain the public figure inflicted upon this young boy, the more pleasure the perpetrator derived. There were cuts, bruises and cigarette burn marks. What the boy was unable to articulate, his body gave away. The psychologist opined that shame had dissolved into a permanent state of fear after months of such abuse. The anxiety of yet more pain had become an acid that had bubbled until the day a silver candlestick found its mark deep through the public figure's forehead, nose and lip. The second strike had cracked the skull, and yet another had let bare the brain. Matthew was reminded of his own youth and Mr Strike. This boy had to be saved. The minor had been referred to 'A Home for Oliver' by the police. They realised that he was the victim and that justice would be quicker through Matthew Stephens. Making it a formal police case would distort reality and blur the lines between perpetrator and victim.

Matthew made some telephone calls and learnt that the skull injury was not fatal. There would, of course, be no charges against the boy. The story being put out was an attack by an unsuspecting burglar. Once the press and the police had been sorted out, Matthew Stephens asked for the boy to be given as much time as necessary before further psychological assessment could occur. When the facts were analysed, the therapist concluded that the adolescent initially felt humiliated. But when humans are subjected to continuous pain, their only hope is that their suffering will end. The boy had been reduced to the status of a domestic animal that no longer felt humiliation but only feared pain. After reading the analyst's report, Matthew Stephen's eyes became moist while his face reddened. He stood up, walked towards his desk, sat down again, contemplated for a moment, and sighed.

Matthew found out the perpetrator was the Chairman of GlobOil. How could someone with his influence and reputation stoop so low? He asked Bertram to call Hector Mitchell's lawyer and tell him there would be criminal charges.

Within a month, Matthew Stephens and Co. secured a five-year contract from the biggest oil company in the country to buy two super tankers of crude oil per month at thirty per cent below the going spot rate. The profit stream from this deal would be paid over to 'A Home for Oliver.' The week after, the Chairman of GlobOil submitted his resignation, citing personal reasons, and left the country for good. His Belgravia townhouse was sold, and the proceeds were contributed, in their entirety, to 'A Home for Oliver.'

Money bought social redemption if no one wealthier or more powerful held you to account. Not even the world's largest oil company Chairman could buy a reprieve that allowed him to carry on. His days in London were over, and he dare not misbehave in New Zealand, either. Matthew had eyes everywhere.

When Matthew discreetly recounted to Bertram what had happened with the Chairman of GlobOil, he realised that not everyone approved of his ways. Even Sally was not on board.

"But Father, you can't make a financial gain from the boy's misfortune."

"I can and I must. Misfortune is not a disease; it is bad luck, and revenge is the only way to sort it out. The boy could not take revenge, but I can. Legal action would not have got anywhere. I know that from experience. These people believe that they are above the law and norms of humanity. Well, now they have me to reckon with, someone who is higher in the wealth pecking order. Any financial retribution is not for me; it is for a cause. This action will only increase the resources we can put into the institution."

Matthew knew everyone had something to hide, something they did not want anyone else to get a whiff of, and something that could potentially ruin them.

Sally understood why he had felt such disdain for social standing. He had known only too well how deceptive the façade of respectability was. As someone who had never really been seen as a natural part of the nobility, her father had reached the peak of the business pyramid. His business instincts were intrinsic to everything he did. So, it was unsurprising that he had exploited the information he gathered on misdeeds to clinch many a deal.

Sally wanted to stay away from such a society. She now had a daughter who had to be protected. The only way would be to live a discreet life for as long as possible. If Catherine ever met someone who would love her for who she was rather than what she would inherit, Sally would have been a good mother.

Catherine learnt what her mother taught her. Although her schooling had been in a select primary school, by the time she had to start her secondary education, she was moved to a local school. Given the school's catchment area that included council estates, the school had no other heirs or heiresses of billionaires. Catherine was good at English at school and enjoyed whatever she learnt. Some like-minded pupils at school proposed that they set up a book club and meet each Saturday at someone's place to talk about books they were reading and exchange books so they would not have to buy them. Often, they would meet at Catherine's place.

Sally would buy cakes and biscuits for the junior literary gathering; the house was tastefully furnished but not ostentatious. This way, youngsters had no tales of fabulous furnishings to recount when they returned to their own homes. Sally would leave them by themselves while she went for a wander down Cheyne Walk. Sally was pleased that Catherine was happy and remained close to her grandfather. They should be there for him just as he was there to look after them both. But there must be limited involvement in Father's affairs, or she would neglect her daughter.

"I love reading books, Mother. I do not understand how authors can imagine stories and then write them so that we can see the characters and feel what they are feeling." All Catherine wanted was to finish her studies and work with books. She read literature at senior school and followed with a degree at the University of London.

As she grew older, Sally told her the truth, explaining why she preferred that Catherine continue her normal life. Catherine could not agree more. Her first job was as a proof-reader and copy editor at an unassuming publishing house. She would read submissions, suggest changes, and discuss the suggestions with the author. It was a meticulous job that required excellent grammar and a superb, individualised touch in dealing with egotistical authors who would consider someone giving them feedback on the plot or where to put a comma or a semi-colon an outrage.

Catherine wanted to learn more about the family business but was now content with her 'partly true' life. She had made some friends, but as she grew older, and the question of meeting men came into play, mother and daughter decided to take the practice of 'a normal existence' to another level. They agreed that if the occasion arose when Catherine would come home with someone, Sally would be the proprietor and Catherine the tenant. This was a plausible proposition, and when they tried it, there were no hitches. Sally would stay in the background or make herself scarce if she thought her daughter needed privacy.

For Sally, preserving the façade was especially important, and she was diligent in the execution of their plan. Catherine did not see any inconvenience in following her mother. Sally told her daughter about when she fell in love with her father, Mark, whose baby she had decided to keep even when he had offered to end the pregnancy. Mark was not married, nor was he someone who had intended to have a quick fling with one of the nurses. He just had very rigid ideas of society. He came from a professional upper-middle-class background, and she was just a nurse. She spoke well, but the family he came from was pretty set in their ideas. They had not sent him to Eton to marry a lowly nurse.

Catherine knew it had not worked out for her mother, but if that was why her father abandoned them, it was even more important to meet someone who would like her for who and what she truly was. In any case, it would be a strange world if the super-wealthy would only find soul mates within their own incestuous circles.

Mother and daughter continued to live in the same house and were presented to Catherine's male friends as landlady and tenant.

The "Sally and Catherine roadshow" went on for a while.

Matthew Stephens was aware of this mini drama but decided not to interfere. Was Sally still pursuing her anonymity strategy? She did not feature on the Board or Management structures of any of Matthew Stephens' companies and this provided the distance she had sought. Sanctuary was a registered charity, so people never really enquired. The press would associate Sanctuary and Horizons with Matthew, but there was more interest in his main businesses than in his charities. In any case, Matthew would not appreciate media coverage of what he was doing in his personal capacity. He also understood Sally's motivations. One could not force the reins of such a vast business empire into the hands of someone so unwilling and disinterested. How does one give someone everything when that someone does not want anything?

In business and social circles, stories were rampant about 'offsprings' bleeding their parents dry, succession battles, court cases, family litigations and shambolic cases. There was no mention of Matthew Stephens' succession.

After a few false starts, Catherine met a nice boy. He even took her to meet his parents. But then it was his turn to meet hers. Catherine realised that the lie was untenable and broke down.

Sally held her firmly to console her girl. Reality could be brutal. Had mother and daughter let things go too far? Things between Catherine and Ian were never intended to be casual. Sally had approved of Ian straight away. Despite this, they had stuck to their normal course of conduct, one of pretence. The landlady and tenant show had been played out before and had proven effective. And it had been necessary. Sally had had an illegitimate daughter with a man who had shirked his responsibilities; as 'just a nurse,' she had not been wife material.

Catherine was now in a case of history repeating itself. Even worse. She was playing a lie in collusion with her own mother. And for what? The very same reasons that her mother had. Sally had wanted to live an ordinary life of anonymity; more importantly, she had wanted to be loved for who she was and not for what she would inherit. Mother and daughter had chosen collective solitude right in the heart of the one London borough where discretion was rare. People may have been curious but mainly kept to themselves and ruminated within a selfish existence; self-obsession left little space for compassion or empathy for others. London and Paris were magnificent to chroniclers and tourists. Yet many lonely souls populated these cities, perpetuating the urban scourge of isolation. Chelsea was a village of the rich and famous, a hotpot of envy, gossip and slander. It was a complex paradigm, but Sally and Catherine enjoyed everyday life while pursuing life within their own version of depersonalisation.

Catherine

"Thank you for dinner, Ian. This is delicious. I need to tell you something, though."

"Catherine, if it has anything to do with your past, please do not worry. I am sure there will be plenty of time once we marry."

"Sorry?"

"Yes, Catherine, I have messed up in the past, but this time, I want to make the right decision. I am sorry, Catherine, I did not come prepared for this, but it is what I want. Catherine, will you be my wife?." He looked into her eyes as he held both her hands with his.

Catherine felt a knot in her belly. This was quite unexpected, and she felt a wretched cramp in her stomach. She was about to win and lose within a matter of seconds. "Ian, why you crazy man. Of course, I will. But Ian, I still need to tell you something first."

"Nothing will change my mind."

"Ian, I am not who you think I am. I am not some middle-class person living with my landlady. I am Catherine Stephens, Sally Stephens' daughter and Matthew Stephens' granddaughter. I am his only grandchild."

"What, *the* Matthew Stephens?"

"Yes, Ian."

"But why?"

"Because my mother wanted me to be loved for being just a girl."

"But you are not. Oh, my God. And the landlady you live with…"

"Yes, my mother, Sally Stephens. She was abandoned because she was not socially acceptable to my doctor father. She was just a nurse and had hidden her family links."

"So, you both are in on this."

"Yes. I am sorry."

"No, I should be sorry, Catherine. I am not in your league. I am just a lawyer."

"But you are what you said you were."

"Do you care for me, Catherine?"

"Yes Ian, I do.

"Will you still be my wife?"

"Of course, but after what I have just told you, are you sure?"

"Yes, Catherine, more than ever. I understand why being so wealthy must be intimidating, especially if your mother had such a bad experience. I have just one request, though: if you agree to be my wife, you will also agree to us living on our own earnings and not your father's millions. I only have a small flat in Putney, and you have already visited my family home. Would that be acceptable to you? Oh yes, and no society wedding or magazines, please."

"Yes, Ian, of course. And do not worry about the media. Matthew Stephens will ensure no media encroachment in our lives."

"Are you close to your grandfather?"

"Very. In fact, I would like you to meet him."

"What? Oh, of course. Gosh. This is all so unexpected."

"I am sorry, Ian."

"No, do not be. Is it OK if I tell my parents?"

"Of course, Ian. They need to know. They may not be as forgiving as you. I am sure they will know what is good for you. If they disagree about me, then I will have to accept it."

"It will be quite a shock for them, not that you hid this from everyone but that you are Matthew Stephens' granddaughter. Of course, they will approve. They want me to be happy with someone I love."

"I love you too, Ian. That is all that matters."

"Mother, I am so happy. I had always dreaded this day. And now it is all resolved. We no longer need to hide who we are. At least not from Ian."

"Oh Catherine, the world is really smiling at us. I have often questioned my decision to impose anonymity on you, but it seems to have worked out. And you will not have to face the same fate I did. I feel so vindicated in all this."

"Mother, Ian has made me promise to live on our own earnings. I am so happy. I hope I can be even half the mother you have been to me."

Complicity is a wonderful, cosy feeling when mother and daughter embrace each other, beaming with joy and pride, pride in being loved for oneself.

Matthew was informed. "You girls are both the same; I hope this has not become genetic. Otherwise, I will never have a generation of Stephens who will identify with their ancestor. I am sure my mother and wife, looking at us as we speak, are delighted. Cheers! to all my wise women who have given me everything. Catherine, I hope you have a few daughters yourself unless, of course, you want boys."

"Come, come, Father. She has only just got engaged."

"No pressure, but I don't want Matthew Stephens and Co. to die with me."

"Father, you are not going anywhere. In any case, the business is too vast to disappear."

"That's what they said of all the empires as well."

"Father, you find our attitude to love and wealth quite bizarre. But this is who we are. We are grateful for everything you do. You have done so much for so many. You need to take time off work and start thinking of a life after. When you retire, would you like to stay in England or go to France and Italy?"

"I am not thinking of retiring any time soon. But it is a good question. I enjoy living here. We are very fortunate to be in Britain. But we are arrogant. Some say we are patriots, but I say we are delusional people who live in the past and do not adapt easily to reality. And I, for one, do not relish how we have become so obsequious towards the Americans. Britain scoffs at Europe but bows before the States. When I retire, it will surely be in this part of the world.

"Britain is the most beautiful place I have known. The undulating lands of this country make my temples thump with excitement. But it is not just England. Next door, we have France and Italy, God's prototypes for paradise: glorious nature, fantastic food, culture to celebrate, beauty to behold, quality of life to envy, and languages that are sensual and musical. I could choose, of course. But not America; they are a different kind of people. So, the long-winded answer to your question is that I do not know. But I am sure I will know exactly where and how I will live by the time I retire."

"And your succession? Have you thought of that, Father? There is quite a lot at stake. Have you considered giving it all away?"

"My natural succession is undoubtedly you and Catherine. I know that neither of you wants anything. There is indeed a substantial business. But it can also have nonfamily members at the helm. On Sanctuary and Horizons, though, I would look to you."

"Thank you, Father, for sharing this with me. I promise I will not raise this ever again. As we share the happy news, I just wanted to ask some questions I had at the back of my mind."

To Matthew, his daughter was asking relevant questions, especially as this massive inheritance existed. She did not want to be burdened with its resolution. She just wanted to focus on Horizons.

Matthew's mind was in active mode. How had all this come to be? Shipping had been a passion. Shipping and oil riches had been re-invested into buying banks, a controlling interest in a consumer goods company, a pharmaceutical giant, and a major car manufacturer. Bankers had fallen over themselves vying for his time, each pitching an idea that would make even more millions. He had chosen some of the best managerial minds to head up his businesses, and his clutch of companies was not run just by English Etonians and Oxbridge-educated managers but also by Asians, Americans and Europeans. If business was international, so should the staff be.

Shipping had remained the backbone of all business interests and had benefitted from his full-time involvement. However, Bertram had been allowed to take over much of the decision-making. There were no shareholder-employees or managers. Any recognition for good performance was in a cash bonus, never shares. The only control he wished for was in ownership. This was Britain, where owners were owners and workers were workers. He was submitting to the rigidities of the British norm, but here, they aligned with his ideas of owner capitalism.

Catherine wore a tulle and satin off-shoulder gown that flowed flawlessly down her body.

The dress consultant, Madame Delahaye, had dropped everything when the call came through from Matthew Stephens. This was one grandfather who wanted the very best for his granddaughter. The dress had to be perfect, no matter how many trips to Paris it would entail. She would have to implore Hubert de Givenchy to surpass his habitual excellence. This had to be extraordinary. No, there would be no press, and no one would see it apart from those present at the wedding. But there was no scope for any compromise. The price was not even brought up.

"*Ne vous inquiétez pas, Madame Delahaye. La robe sera exquise. Je vous le promets.*"

Madame Delahaye had to ensure all the press correspondents were kept at bay. The instructions were very clear. The wedding was a closed affair at a country house in Hertfordshire. The church ceremony took place at the adjacent chapel. No press was allowed at the chapel apart from the family photographer. He was also the only photographer allowed on the grounds after the church. No guest was allowed to take photographs. This was stipulated in the invitation.

There was a cool breeze under a clear sky. Once inside the house, it was a lavish setting. A champagne cascade was set up on pristine linen alongside substantial white roses and lilies arrangements. Matthew and Sally were smiling, their eyes gleaming with elation. The guests were few and were friends of Catherine and Ian, some colleagues of Sally, Mr Burroughs and Matthew's trusted lieutenants. In attendance were also a choir from Horizons.

Catherine and Ian would honeymoon in Italy, driving around Tuscany and Lazio before boarding a boat to Sardinia. Ian had agreed to the honeymoon offered by Catherine's family, but, to him, the luxury of the arrangements rang an alarm bell, a reminder that Catherine's world would be very different.

The couple enjoyed a glass of wine in their white, silk robes as they sat on lounge chairs on the balcony that oversaw the calm sea. As the evening turned into night, they spoke about what they had enjoyed so far. Ian took a more serious tone. "Catherine! All this is lovely, and I am very grateful to your family. But!"

"I know you find this a vulgar display of wealth from my grandfather."

"Oh no, not at all. I understand he wants you to have a wonderful time; it has been fabulous. My only concern is my own complex. Even though I am very happy with my career and satisfied with my means, I could never offer you anything like this. This is a parallel universe where I do not belong."

"Ian, I do not need anything like this. I just need you. This is a rarefied environment where I would suffocate if I did not have the oxygen of your love."

"Wow, that is quite a line! Have you been rehearsing it? Sorry, Cath, that is very sweet, but you have grown up with all this."

"I grew up with the values of my mother. She loves my grandfather but does not measure herself in terms of her lineage. Moreover, Grandpa loves business but does not care much about his wealth. He just puts it down as a by-product of his business success. Neither he nor my mother will ever smother us with something we would be uncomfortable with. They know that we both earn, and what is more, we have each other."

She leaned over to kiss his cheek. Ian turned his face to catch her lips. She responded to his lips and lingered while she felt his hand and arms under the silk robe pull her towards him. His robe was open, and their skin met. The arousal was almost instant as their lips and hands explored. Catherine sat on him to feel him inside her. He raised his back to put his lips to her breast with his hands on her hips. As he gently pecked on her nipples, her thighs and hips pressed harder against him, with sighs escaping her lips. Her moist warmth sent a rush of blood to his loins, which aroused her even more, a spiral of joy and delight in the rhythm of passion. She opened her eyes:

"Ian?"

"Ian?" in a slightly louder voice.

Ian looked into her eyes.

"You OK? You just disappeared into another world."

They had not finished, but Catherine got off him and came to his side.

"Yes, I am OK."

"Are you sure? You just blanked out in the middle of our making love?"

"Oh dear!"

"What is it, Ian?"

"This has happened before. I have blanked out before, but that was years ago."

"Blanked out? You were awake. Although you were no longer looking or seeing. I wondered if you had had a heart attack."

"Do not worry, it is an electrical impulse. I had it checked out, but there was nothing. I just overheated."

"We both did, but I did not blow a fuse. Anyway, let us go to bed for a good night's sleep."

Ian had had a similar episode with a girl called Emma a few years ago and that had ended badly. The previous occurrence flashed into the mind and took over the senses. Emma's blue eyes, her mouth saying no, the smell of earth had all come back to life.

God, please let this not be happening again.

The rare occasions on which Matthew Stephens would appear in the media included the annual publication of the *Sunday Times* List. His very brief profile would always be accompanied by the categorisation of 'self-made' and business interests as 'various.'

"It does not matter how they classify me. I would have liked them to just put me down as a son, husband, father and grandfather."

Business was booming, and the family was blessed.

"Sir, Catherine's husband, Mr Parson, wants to speak to you. It is urgent."

"What is it, Bertram?"

Catherine was in intensive care at the Monroy Hospital. Matthew left the office and asked Bertram to ensure that Sally was informed and driven to the hospital.

They both arrived at the same time. Sally hugged her father as they made their way to intensive care. At the reception of the intensive care unit, a doctor met them.

"Mr Stephens, Ms Stephens. I am Dr Fairbank. I am looking after Catherine. She is in quite a critical state. We are trying to re-establish her oxygen levels." He asked them to follow him to his office.

They walked into her room. Catherine had various pipes attached to her mouth and nose. Her throat was bruised. There were sensors attached to her head. They looked at each other. Sally found her voice. "Where is Ian, her husband?"

"Ma'am, her husband has been arrested. He called Mr Stephens from the constabulary."

"Arrested? Why? What is going on?"

"Mr Parson called emergency services. Once at the scene, they called the police, and he was picked up for questioning while Catherine was driven here."

"Is Catherine all right? Is she going to make it?"

"Her vital functions are working, but her cerebral activity is impaired. We must wait and see how much damage has been caused."

Sally cried as she leaned against her father. Matthew slowly led her out of the room. "We'll wait in the sitting room if that's OK?"

"Of course, it is." A nurse accompanied them. Once they were seated, the nurse volunteered. "She is in very good hands. We will be with her all the time and will keep you informed. Would you like a glass of water or a cup of tea?"

She brought two glasses of water and then left to join Catherine.

"Daddy! I do not understand what is happening. Did Ian say something to you?"

"Catherine was asphyxiated."

"What? How? By whom?" cried Sally in despair.

"Ian was crying, but he told me that there had been an accident and that he may have strangled his wife by accident. He sounded sincere when he explained that they had gone too far while having sex. And that he may have suffered an episode. He did not go into details." Sally thought: How twisted and tragic is that? What goes on between a couple is sacrosanct and is prohibited territory for everyone else. Asking why was now futile. All that mattered was Catherine's survival.

Sally was praying desperately: God, please let her come through, and please let the brain damage be minimal. Then she looked at Matthew, "Father, let's pray for her to come out of this alright."

They waited.

The door opened, and the nurse walked in. "Please follow me."

"What's wrong, Miss?"

"Catherine has just suffered a severe seizure."

When they walked in, Catherine was trembling. The nurse asked them to wait by the door while she joined the team trying to resuscitate her. They administered electric shocks. Her body seized with the first charge, her chest rising before falling back. The monitor was still bleeping an alarm and flashing a red light. Another charge was administered. Still no change. The staff looked at each other as the monitor went into a constant low tone. Catherine went still. They took off the charge pads and bowed their heads in resignation.

Dr Fairbank walked over. "I am very sorry. Her heart went into ventricular fibrillation, impairing the blood flow to her brain, and then both cardiac and neural systems collapsed. Please stay here with her for as long as you wish. The nurses will remain with you." He bowed, turned towards the door and slowly left the room.

Matthew and Sally were holding each other's hands as they approached Catherine. Sally whimpered and squealed as she sank her head onto Catherine's hand. Matthew held Sally's shoulder tightly. The nurse brought two chairs and set them next to the bed. She then retreated towards the back of the room with her head bowed.

After a few minutes of sobbing, Sally got up and stepped back with her father to sit on the chairs. They looked at Catherine and then into each other, weeping through bloodshot eyes.

Sally and Matthew both knew that mothers were strong until they encountered the misfortune of losing a child: Primal Despair. All other pain was secondary.

Grandfathers, on the other hand, are less strong, and they must deal with the pain of their child and their own.

Matthew Stephens was overwhelmed. 'When it really matters, I am nothing.'

When leaving the hospital, Matthew asked Sally to come to Grosvenor Square. "We both need to be with each other."

Sally did not resist.

Matthew poured a large whisky each. They both took a sedative and, within an hour, stared into emptiness. No words were exchanged until they decided it was time to go to bed. Their rooms were adjacent. Within moments, fatigue, sedatives and alcohol combined forces to send them into a universe of subliminal agony.

Catherine's funeral was intimate in a small chapel adjoining the church on Eaton Square with Ian, his parents, Matthew, Sally and Bertram. Ian paid his respects. "Catherine sought love for herself and her alone. I loved her as a girlfriend, as a wife, and now I will love her as an eternal part of my being. God decided to take her away from me so suddenly that I have yet to acknowledge her absence. May the same God give her soul peace and give me the strength to suffer in silence. Thank you to Matthew and Sally for not having objected to her marrying just an ordinary chap. I will always be her husband, and she my wife."

Matthew smiled with tears in his eyes. Catherine had chosen well. How can he feel any anger towards this man? The accident had happened within the couple in their privacy.

After the burial, Sally was taken home, still under sedatives. A nurse had been engaged to keep an eye on her. Matthew told his chauffeur to go back to the office. He was going to walk back home.

Once the chauffeur had driven away, Matthew walked toward Belgrave Square. At the corner, he found the church door open. He stepped in, walked over to the bench and slid onto the spot at its edge. He looked up towards the altar, crossed his hands and whispered tearfully, "Why Catherine? Why?" and burst into tears. His head remained bowed as tears streamed down his face.

A hand was placed on his shoulder. It was a tall, matronly-looking black lady wearing a brown suit. "You all right, Brother?" He looked at her, shook his head and cried again. "I have just lost my only grandchild. She was the world for me."

"I am sorry for your loss, Brother. But you are in God's House now. He understands your pain."

"Does he? Does he now? So, what would he like me to do?"

"Cherish the memory of the departed."

"How? She was only twenty-six years old."

"You know how… You know how. God blesses you."

She took his hands, squeezed them, looked into his eyes, and smiled a soft, kind smile. The look of compassion and the warmth of her soft hands around his own filled him with a strange tingle. A surge of warmth swelled within as he saw her turn away to leave. For a fleeting moment, the church had lit up with candles everywhere.

She did not look back; as suddenly as she had appeared, she was gone. A smoky haze had settled where there had been light.

He looked at the door, no one. His head turned back when something caught his eye. There was a shiny brass plaque on the memorial stone on the floor. He got up and walked towards it. The inscription read:

VICKS, Oscar Lionel Ian eternally remembered.

1856 – 1870

Matthew thought: fourteen years. That is all this boy lived, for fourteen short years. Matthew started to walk away when something prompted him to look again at the plaque. And suddenly, the realisation came upon him:

Oscar Lionel Ian Vicks eternally remembered
O L I V E R
14 Years.

Fourteen was the age of the boy who had come to him for help. Matthew Stephens looked towards the altar and then stared up towards the cupola. He had understood. He held his head up high and walked out of the church. He headed out towards St James's Park, found a bench on the way, took out his mobile phone and gave clear instructions.

Matthew Stephens was in a hurry to do His bidding. He had come to hold his hands. Matthew reached Green Park and walked through it until he reached his office. His chauffeur was waiting in the car in the driveway. "Sorry, I needed that walk."

The death of such a man's only grandchild would normally have generated considerable media coverage. One tabloid was thinking of a salacious headline: "Billionaire's Heiress in Snuff-hush Funeral." The whiff of its first edition reached Matthew Stephen's team before the printed edition made any delivery van. There is no way the hospital could have leaked this, but the police were quite another matter. Within two hours, the editor and the journalists were served injunctions. The owners of the newspapers who lived abroad had been warned. The four-hour destruction of all traces of the sensationalised edition had been executed with ruthless precision. A revised edition was published in time for the newspaper rounds the following morning.

All that appeared in the media was a short obituary signed by Catherine's husband and her mother in *The Times*.

When freelance reporters tried contacting Ian Parson at his city law firm, they learnt he was off work for personal reasons. The public never knew about the mishap where a man had accidentally choked his wife to death while making love to her because of a neural 'short circuit.'

The chemical imbalance during Ian's lovemaking had caused him to lose awareness. On this occasion, Catherine had felt a hand move to her throat, and before she could react, a second one moved on to her mouth. Ian was still in the act while his grip on both mouth and neck tightened. By the time he had climaxed, it was too late. Matthew listened, chose to believe that Catherine was aware of the condition, brought no charges against Ian and asked him to go abroad. Having someone around who had somehow ended Catherine's life was too painful. The Rotterdam office would be a good place to start.

Ian knew that this was not an offer but a command. Getting away from the here and now while learning about the shipping and oil business as the company solicitor was an opportunity. His parents were supportive and believed that getting out could prove cathartic. He should not suffer rapacious journalists who were honing their fangs. Ironically, in a country with some of the world's best newspapers, the tabloids sensationalised with such impunity: bloodhounds, unfazed by the public interest they claimed to uphold.

Who would have thought that Ian would find himself in such a situation? Life had been so normal until that fateful day when he had proposed to Catherine. It was not her fault, but the blackout had not occurred since that episode with Emma in their younger days. Catherine and he would probably not have worked out because of his own massive complexes, but being responsible for her death was something else.

Still, he would have to pick himself up. He would grieve for the loss of a very dear wife and then get on with what remained of his existence.

"Sir, I have just heard that Mr Burroughs has passed. He had a cardiac arrest. There is a funeral this Sunday. His lawyer has called to inform us that there is a will that leaves all his shares in Matthew Stephens and Co. to you."

"Thank you, Bertram. I will say some words at the funeral. But no press, please. And Bertram, please do not call me Sir anymore. Call me Matthew. So, Mr Burroughs did not sell out to the Chinese or the Americans. He had me on tenterhooks since that lunch."

"Family and Friends of Samuel Burroughs, thank you for being here today. Mr Burroughs, that is what I have always called him, was a friend, a benefactor, and a mentor without whom nothing would have been possible for me. He was a kind man and a good human being. He ran his affairs with a rare flair. He did not take his status for granted. He considered social standing fickle. Instead, he coveted trust and reliability. He did not suffer schemers, treasured loyalty and helped the helpless. It is painful indeed to lose such wisdom. Please join me in a minute of silence in his memory."

The congregation included his wheelchair-ridden widow, members of the Royal Family, the Prime Minister and Cabinet members.

"London tycoon given closely guarded farewell." The financial press was more incisive. "Burroughs demise gives Matthew Stephens absolute control."

His bankers called within the week. Bertram took the meeting. "We have been approached to sound you out for a potential acquisition. The potential seller is based in Hong

Kong and has had contact with Mr Stephens in recent years."

"Thank you, Bertram. Please run it by Ms Ling and let her take the decision."

He should have never doubted Mr Burroughs' support. But that affair on body shopping of young boys had created negative sentiments. This was his repayment or his trust in Matthew being able to do something positive for the misfortunate youth. He had helped Matthew but destroyed many young lives during his lifetime. But in his death, he wanted to make amends, posthumous atonement!

"This makes me think we need a laser-sharp focus on A Home for Oliver. But first, Bertram, please pour us both a drink."

"Yes, Matthew, there is another personal matter, and I do not want to intrude."

"Please go ahead, Bertram."

"Miss Sally is struggling to get over her loss. I have noticed her leaving meetings in tears."

"Yes, Bertram, it runs in the family. I felt very low when Gwendolyn left. Catherine's departure was a real shock because of its suddenness, but by now, I have realised that their departures are the price I pay to keep my existence in equilibrium. Sally is very strong but losing her only child is a step too far. I understand that she is seeing a psychologist. I hope that it helps. I understand that there is medication that can help to blunt the emotions and to make things more bearable. But I should be more sensitive to her day-to-day anguish."

"Matthew, it may be an idea to suggest that she takes time off from counselling interviews and sessions for Sanctuary and get more involved at the corporate level on bigger issues."

"Bertram, you may be right, but please believe me when I tell you she is very strong. Her whole life has been about dealing with mishaps and misfortune.

"Of course, losing one's child is atrociously painful. But time will help her. As will we. On the broader involvement in corporate matters, I am counting on you to put in place able managers who can work together and keep the business going. I do not believe we should try to burden Sally more than she already is."

A Home for Oliver

"Samuel."

Matthew Stephens looked at Samuel, another young man struck down by society's sickness. What was wrong with people? Why were sick perverts running society? Most were happily married, at least on the face of it. And yet, this obsession to prey upon the helpless, the destitute. Worse, they were targeting young boys. Was every social warlord effectively a paedophile? Was sodomising young boys the only gratification they sought?

His uncle had sent Samuel to Edward Craithorne's house in Egerton Gardens. Samuel had only received one instruction: "Mr Craithorne is a very important man. You are very lucky that he is letting you serve him. Do whatever he wants with a smile."

The uncle then returned to join his friends in the cavern to continue drinking the potent ale.

"Come here, young man. Why don't you join me to watch some television?" No sooner had Samuel sat down beside the gentleman than the older man's arm went around Samuel's shoulder, nudging him closer.

Samuel said nothing.

Mr Craithorne turned sideways and put the other hand on the boy's thighs. He then opened the boy's trouser button and slid his hand in.

Samuel felt wrong but did not say anything.

His host then put his mouth on the boy's and prised it open with his tongue. Samuel closes his eyes, his breath getting deeper. The image of his uncle flashed into his mind. "The bastard's sold me out."

"No, Mr Craithorne. Stop."

"Why Samuel? What is wrong? I cannot stop now. Just see what I have got." He took Samuel's hand and guided it to his erection. Samuel withdrew his hand as if he had hit a live wire. He pushed the man away and got away from the couch. He ran towards the door, realising it was not latched, before going out into the courtyard, to the main gate and exiting the house. He ran, turning at Egerton Terrace, until he found himself on Brompton Road. Once he saw the very heavy traffic, he stopped at a crossing, waited for the lights to change and jogged across the road. Once on the other side, he slowed down to a walk. He looked back occasionally but realised that no one was chasing him. Samuel thought about what he had just experienced and suddenly felt sick. He had to pause on the side and heave when he felt the bitter phlegm rise in his throat, only to be expelled in a splatter on the wall. His memory was sharper than ever, and he felt the bristle of Mr Craithorne's moustache on his mouth; his stomach convulsed again as he wretched, spouting out even more bile. His eyes discharged tears, and his nose started to run. He walked and walked, his mind in overdrive until he reached the Thames, where he crossed the river on Albert Bridge. Once in Battersea's familiar surroundings, he made his way to the council flat his parents and he lived in.

He climbed the stairs and went through the exposed landing to the flat entrance. Before going in, he leaned over the balcony fence to look down the road to ensure no one had followed him. He went into the flat, tiptoed his way to his room and slid under his quilt without changing into his pyjamas. The vision of Mr Craithorne approaching his mouth was still implanted in his mind, but fatigue provided the relief he sought. His eyes had got heavier.

"Why didn't you hit him?"

"I was scared, and he was an important man."

"And your uncle, where is he?"

"He still lives with us. He was very annoyed because he did not get the agreed-upon money."

"Is he related to you?"

"My uncle, why yes. He is my mother's brother. He lives in Kent but stays with us while working in London."

"What does he do?"

"He is a metal forger. He comes to work at the forge shop in Hailbury Road."

"Oh yes, I know that place. Samuel, leave it with me. Tonight, you will sleep here in the guest accommodation. You will be provided with clothes to change into. Once you are washed and ready, you will join me for breakfast tomorrow morning."

"Mr Stephens, I do not have any money. What will I have to do?"

"I am not Mr Craithorne. You must get a good night's sleep. That is all."

Matthew smiled. Samuel was a dashing young boy, but destiny dealt him cruelty. Not any longer.

The following morning, Matthew walked from his office to Ed Craithorne's office. Bertram had called to alert them of the impromptu visit. A blonde lady met him at the reception and asked him to follow her to the Chairman's office.

"Matthew, why! What an honour! Please have a seat."

Matthew just walked over to his side, grabbed his jacket's

lapel, and punched him on the nose. While his head reeled back, William kneed him in the groin.

"What the fuck, Matthew! What is wrong with you?!"

"What is wrong with me? Edward, you filthy paedophile! You sick bastard! You are finished!"

Ed Craithorne realised that there was nothing he could do. There was no point in presenting an explanation or a defence. "I know I am sick, and I know that your punishment will mean my ruin. But is there any way of making amends? I will do whatever you want."

"You need to resign immediately and leave the country within the month. Your house needs to be sold, and the proceeds transferred to A Home for Oliver as a donation."

"But Matthew, please. I have spent my whole life building all this."

"Yet, you have lost it all in the blink of an eye. If you do not want your reputation publicly destroyed, go quietly now."

"How can I trust you, Matthew?"

"You cannot. Nor could any of your other peers who left everything behind."

"You were behind each of their deportations? I thought that it was just a rumour. You are one of us, and we do not betray each other."

"Goodbye, Ed! Join the other scumbags in some far-off corner of the Pacific Ocean. And do not try any tricks. I have eyes and ears everywhere."

"Yes, Matthew, I know."

"Yes, Sally, you left a message. Is everything all right?"

"Father, I have just had the results of my biopsy."

"Darling, biopsy for what?"

"I had a small lump in my left breast. So, I had it checked. The doctor has just called me. I am positive."

"Gosh, Sally! I am sorry." He could not continue.

"Do not worry, Father. I have an appointment with the oncologist tomorrow. If you want, you can come with me."

"Of course, darling. I will be there. Have courage, Sally. We will deal with this together." God, what was happening here? He had lost his wife and granddaughter, both so quickly. Oscar Wilde's Lady Bracknell came to mind. The irony brought tears to his eyes.

The oncologist was a lady. She asked them to take a seat.

"What are you going to do for my daughter?"

"Mr Stephens. For Sally…" She turned to both. "We will follow established oncology protocols. The next stage is an assessment of how much the cancer has spread. The treatment will combine precise surgical interventions, radiotherapy, and chemotherapy. It will be a long process, but we will be with you along the way. We have the most highly regarded oncology department in the country."

"Thank you, Doctor."

Sally asked, "Will I need a mastectomy?"

"Yes, Ms Stephens. We will schedule a procedure for early next week. When the surgery is completed, you can have a breast prosthetic." She looked hesitantly at Matthew and said to Sally, "Perhaps I can discuss this with you tomorrow."

Sally responded, "We can talk openly in front of my father. He is the only family I have."

Matthew looked at them and nodded. "I need to go down. I will wait in the reception." He turned and left the room.

Ensconced in an armchair, he reflected. The most famous and renowned cancer facility was Sloan Kettering in New York. He walked to the reception and asked to use the phone. "Yes, Bertram. It is me. Could you please arrange a plane for us tomorrow morning? I am taking Sally to Sloan Kettering. Please make the arrangements."

Sally did not protest. Matthew insisted that they both take sedatives to catch some sleep on the way over. "We have a long day ahead." They both woke up when the pilot announced they were starting their descent. The rest had been restorative.

Matthew's New York manager was waiting on the JFK tarmac with their chauffeured limousine. They were whisked away to the hospital. No words were exchanged until they found themselves at the institute. A doctor with rimmed glasses greeted them at the entrance. Matthew's manager nodded and quietly took his leave. "Dr Cairns, Mr Stephens and Ms Stephens will stay with you for their consultation." He left the chauffeur there and walked towards the road to wave a taxi.

Dr Cairns took them to his office and asked them to sit. "We received your test results from London last night and have processed the data in our system. I would be grateful for the original documents to press the validation button."

He scanned through the documents. "I also spoke to Dr Jennings, the oncologist you saw in London yesterday. I want to run through the details. This afternoon, we will do another scan as the tumour has grown since the previous MRI scan. For now, I suggest you go to your hotel, freshen up, and return in a couple of hours."

Dr Cairns walked them through the lobby back to the entrance where the limousine was waiting.

"Father, are you all right? You must be tired. You can get some sleep while I come back to see Dr Cairns."

"Sleep is the last thing I need. If you would rather that you see him alone, I would, of course, understand."

"Not at all. But it is going to be a long day. It is all happening so quickly."

"Sally, this is why we are here. This needs to be dealt with quickly. Once the treatment starts, we will enter a routine."

"I am sorry to take you away from your affairs in London."

"Bertram will take care of things. Right now, my only business is you."

The car pulled up at the entrance of the Waldorf Astoria. The concierge opened the car door. The hotel manager greeted them as they stepped out. "Please follow me." He led them through the luscious lobby to the elevators. There was no idle talk. Arriving at the floor, he led them to their suite. He let them in and showed them to the bedrooms that flanked the living room on either side.

"Your bags will be here soon. Please dial zero if you need anything." He nodded respectfully and made his way out.

As soon as the bags arrived, they left each other to go and freshen up. The urgency was palpable; they each had a short shower. After she had dried herself, Sally ordered sandwiches and tea. She brushed her hair and got dressed.

Matthew was also ready and asked the valet to lay the snack on the little dining table. A pensive silence followed as they partook in the assortment of sandwiches. Neither took milk or sugar with their tea. Within minutes, they were both on their way back to Dr Cairns.

"Has the tumour spread to other parts, doctor?"

"That is still unclear, but the London results point to Stage 3. We will confirm this with more scans. If confirmed, this stage will require surgery, chemotherapy and radiotherapy. We may also need hormone therapy. It is an established process, Ms Stephens. We will provide you with the best medical care available, but you and your father must remain positive and strong. We also provide psychological support throughout your stay. Depending on your progress, this could take two to three months. After that, you will be taken to our recovery resort outside the city. There will then be care and monitoring. During your stay there, it will be determined if you need more chemotherapy. If all goes well, you could be back in London in six months."

"What are my chances, Doctor? And please call me Sally."

"Sally, for your stage of cancer, your chances are fifty-fifty. So, we all have to focus on the hopeful fifty per cent. We will be your family and home here, and we will get through this together."

"Dr Cairns, I will stay in New York until Sally is well again."

"Of course, Sir. Having you here will be a real source of strength for Sally. We can arrange suitable accommodation for you."

"For now, I will stay at the hotel. Sally needs her space. She does not need my intrusive presence to distract her." He managed a small chuckle.

"As you wish, Mr Stephens."

He wanted to be there for his daughter but not breathing down her neck. She had quite a lot to deal with, and the doctors needed to work in normal conditions. They do not need a panicked father meddling.

Sally was admitted into a well-appointed private suite. Matthew remarked, "You will be comfortable here, Sally. I will stay at the hotel and come by every day. I can move and get a room here if you need me here."

"No, Father, you will be more comfortable at the hotel. Once we settle into a routine, you can go to your office. It will offer some distraction."

She thought with such a clear mind. If anyone could beat

this thing, she could. There was a knock at the door. A nurse came in with a hospital gown. "Hi Sally, we need to get ready for the scan."

Matthew took the cue and kissed his daughter on the head.

Back at the hotel, a valet accompanied him to his room. Just before leaving, Matthew requested, "Could you please bring me a bottle of whisky?"

Matthew threw his jacket on the sofa, went to the bathroom, and hit the shower twice within hours. He turned the water to full this time and stood under it, scrubbing off the day's worries. When he came back to the living room, the doorbell rang; it was the waiter.

He poured Matthew a double whisky. "Sir, will you be dining with us this evening?"

He looked at his nameplate. "Andrew, I am not hungry; I will have my drink and take a walk. Is that fancy burger place around the corner still there?"

"Indeed, it is, Sir. Would you like me to book a table for you?"

"No, that will not be necessary. I just need to get some air. It has been a long day. And the jet lag is going to hit me if I stay indoors. Thank you for the whisky. It is perfect."

"Very well, Sir. I will be on call in case you need anything. Have a pleasant evening, Sir."

The city was bustling. Of course, it was. This was New York. Just walking on the pavement was energising. He carried on until he reached a newspaper kiosk. The cover page was stuck onto the board that jutted out. The sensational headlines in huge letters read, "Dot Com bubble bursts." He thought of buying a copy but thought the better of it. "Fuck it. This rubbish never ends." The Glenfarclas had gently gone through the gears and had him in cruise mode. "Where are all these people going? Everyone is in such a hurry. Why can't they just slow down to a crawl?"

Thud! Someone had just walked straight into him. He stopped to help Matthew up. "I am sorry, I was not looking. Are you all right?"

A third man suddenly appeared. "Are you all right, Sir?"

"Andrew, are you following me?"

"I have been asked to look after you, Sir. I hope that does not bother you." He helped him up and started walking alongside.

"Not at all, but if you are walking near me, then the best would be to walk with me. Let us go to a quiet bar. Nothing posh; a decrepit dive would do well if no rats are running around."

"Let's turn into the next street and go to Georgie's."

Georgie's was in the basement of an apartment block. It was remarkably quiet compared to the bustle outside. Andrew ordered two beers as he was sure Georgie's whisky stock would be inadequate.

"Sam Adam's? Oh, I like this. Thank you, Andrew. So, are you some sort of ex-marine?"

"Yes, Sir, the hotel employs me to look after special guests. They taught me to butler as well."

"Have you served abroad?"

"Sir, I spent four years in Columbia towards the end of Escobar."

"He was a special kind of businessman but brilliant, daring and ruthless."

"Did you know him, Sir?"

"No, Andrew. I never knew Pablo Escobar. He destroyed far too many lives."

"Are you here for a while, Sir?"

"Yes, I am. You may know that I am here with my daughter. Sally has cancer, and she is going to be treated here. Sally is all I have left. The rest is just a meaningless mirage."

Andrew said nothing and sipped his beer; Matthew looked up at the television hanging from the wall. Dot.com was on a loop. Gold prices were surging. Shipping would not suffer. Some investments would take a major hit, but after the euphoria of the past few months, a correction was needed. Real value creation came from real business, not hot-air concepts. The new economy could not exist by itself. The economy was about real things and merchandise. And the world was still run by humans, not robots.

His thoughts returned to his daughter. "Andrew, I'd like to call the hospital to check on Sally."

Andrew gave him his mobile phone. "Sir, this is a secure phone. All communications are encrypted. I will wait by the bar."

Matthew walked over to Andrew. "Thank you. Sally is sleeping. I also feel the jet lag and should return to my room."

As they stepped out, Andrew hailed a taxi, and they were on their way back to the hotel. "Can I bring you something to eat?"

"Some clam chowder with a roll of bread would be great. Please get some rest yourself. I will see you tomorrow."

The chowder was steaming. Matthew left it on the table while he went to the bathroom to change into the fine pyjamas the hotel had left. He returned to his chowder and relished it with a soft bread roll. Hotels did not get any better, even if the context was bleak. But this was the magic of New York. Everything worked: the hospitals, the doctors, the hotel and the staff. The British had always considered Americans the uncouth new rich. An inferiority complex had manifested itself in tin-pot arrogance. But it would be great if London could be even half as efficient.

He hoped Sally's stay in New York would be curative and palliative. He eased himself into his bed that had already been turned. Jet lag was awful for the body clock, but staying up until local bedtime guaranteed a slumber deeper than any sedative. By the time he woke up, his mind and body felt fresh.

He called for some breakfast and hit the shower. By the time he had dried himself in the bathroom, breakfast and crisp copies of *The New York Times* and *The Wall Street Journal* had been neatly laid on the table. A waiter was standing by and served him a steaming cup of tea. He left when Matthew suggested that he could go. The television was on NBC, and the images and commentary were dominated by trader floors at the stock exchange. Markets were still plummeting.

Since breakfast was now done, Matthew put on some cotton slacks, a pair of moccasins, and a checked cotton twill shirt, combed his thinning hair and made his way down. The chauffeur opened the door and then sped him away to the hospital. The sun was shining on this August morning.

"Good morning Sally, how are you feeling?"

"Morning, Father. I was sedated. That and the jet lag knocked me out. The nurse has just washed me, and I suddenly feel quite fresh, albeit a bit lightheaded. The results of the scans and the biopsy should be in soon. I saw the news on the television while I had some breakfast. Is this going to hurt your business?"

"Not the business, just some private investments. But they were flying unreasonably high. So, it is OK. Do not worry. We still have money for lunch today."

"Maybe you should go to the office."

229

"I have good people working for me. They will monitor things and contact me if something tricky arises." He looked up at the nurse and smiled. "May I please have a cup of tea?"

While Matthew sipped on his tea, Sally looked on quietly. It was an easy, complicit silence, not a hesitant, polite expression of respect. Sally worried about how this was affecting her father's business. Matthew was reflecting on what the doctor would have to say.

Dr Cairns walked in. "Good morning to you both. I have preliminary results from our lab. The cancer has metastasised. We will perform surgery to remove the tumour and the cancer cells around it. We will then attack this with a combination of chemotherapy and radiotherapy. It will be tough, and we will all be in 'war mode.' Sally, you will have to be strong. These treatments are quite aggressive, and you will be in some pain and sometimes feel very ill. We will provide strong anti-nausea medication to keep the discomfort in check."

"Yes, Doctor, thank you for that very frank assessment. I was aware of it being quite advanced for me to be brought here. I owe it to myself, my father and all of you to be brave and fight this head-on." She looked at her father. Matthew could not find words but eventually whispered, "I am here by your side. Doctor? May I please arrange for my affairs to be brought here from the hotel?"

Dr Cairns called Bertram in London. Bertram set everything in motion, and by lunchtime, Matthew was set up in a suite at the hospital. Later that afternoon, father and daughter learnt the schedule.

"The tumours and the breast will be removed as well as the portion of the lung where the cancer has spread. Once removed, the tumour would be tested to determine the drugs for chemotherapy. We will start the chemotherapy when there is some scar tissue on the parts we operate. The radiotherapy sessions will be carried out around the same time. There will be a further assessment to see what is working and what is not. The dosage of the therapy will be adjusted. This will take three to four weeks. If you react unexpectedly, we may have to pause therapy. There will be hair loss and skin depigmentation during the treatment, but this is temporary. Your father can be here with you at any time of the day or night."

Matthew acknowledged the message, asked the nurse to get some tea and biscuits as soon as Dr Cairns left, and wondered if Sally was allowed some. "Yes, Sir, Ms Matthews can have tea and dinner tonight. She will have to skip breakfast tomorrow as we prepare her for surgery. She is booked for 7.30 a.m."

"Are you OK, Father?"

Matthew thought this was typical Sally. "I… of course, I am OK. We are here for you, Sally. Let us just focus entirely on our battle with the cancer. It is going be the biggest fight of our lives."

"Father, I know you are with me, whether you are here or not. I do not want you falling ill with worry and lack of sleep."

"Do not worry about your father. He is old but sturdy. I sleep very well, thanks to my nightcap."

Sally could not help smiling. "So, what are we having for dinner?"

"Now we are talking: a rare Argentinian rib-eye with some chips for me."

"And for me. No idea when I will be able to have another."

"While we are it, a good bottle of Cheval Blanc. If they do not have it, we can ask the chauffeur to pick it up from the hotel."

231

"Now go and get some fresh air, Father."

"Only if you come with me." Of course, she was allowed to go out. They would be back in time for their special dinner.

Father and daughter walked towards the East River from where they could see Roosevelt Island; nothing impressive, but the water was a welcome sight. They sat by a bench and munched on some popcorn. "Not the diet you should be on at all, but we are both alive and, more importantly, together. Do you want to sit a bit longer? A nice breeze is settling in."

"It feels so nice here. I was just thinking I was so anti-wealth, but I now realise how grateful I should be. It is easy to be a hypocrite."

"No, darling, your beliefs are very similar to mine. Wealth is valuable, but it is not the panacea for our pains. You know that better than I."

"Father, with you by my side, I miss Mother. I often think about her. You must really miss her."

"Of course, I do, Sally. One day, we will reunite. She and I were like the two sides of the same coin. I thought that life without her would be unbearable. But the passage of time teaches acceptance. One of us had to go before the other. That is the way life is designed; it is an imperfect phenomenon. We all come, do our bit, and then leave."

"But why do some leave so early?"

"Like I said, life is imperfect. It somehow all balances out at the end. We give and take throughout our existence, but, in the end, there is nothing to give or take. I have amassed so much wealth, but I will leave as a naked soul into the wilderness of eternity while my body will return to the soil. It is a zero-sum game."

"It is a privilege to be receiving such care. It may work, or it may not. What is important is that I would still have lived a full life with moments of sheer joy and deep tragedy.

You have always been by my side. I do not want to cause you pain, but I am ready to leave and join Mother and Catherine."

"Please do not think like that. I want you to hope as much as I do. The treatment will be difficult, and you must keep your spirits up."

Her father would be very alone if Sally did not make it through. He would spend more time on his businesses. That would be his lifeline.

"Father, why don't you write a book about yourself? There is a story to be told. And if you can get a good actor like Anthony Hopkins to play, it would be a compelling film."

"Books are either for self-adulation or for conveying a message. My only message can be that 'life is difficult. Accept it'. That was your message to the people who came to you for counselling in those days at the Town Hall."

They were back at the hospital. "Let us have our special dinner and then get some sleep. Tomorrow, you are in surgery."

The meal was delicious, but there was a heavy silence. Surgery was not something to look forward to. "You know Sally, you qualified as a nurse. Did you ever consider studying to become a doctor?"

"No, taking care of ailing and recovering patients is more interesting. Even here, Dr Cairns is one of the best doctors they have, but I hardly see him. I will get through each day because of the nurses who care for me; we call them sisters for a reason. Doctors have so many tools and equipment at their disposal. Nurses just have their humanity."

"You are so right. When you leave here, we will get them a little something."

"If I get out of here. Yes, that would be nice."

Matthew did not object to Sally's caution. They both knew that things were not in their hands.

Once back in his room, Matthew read a report sent over by his New York office. "Shipping routes remain fluid, and trade flows are up compared to last year. Volume growth of 3% year on year has been matched by corresponding growth in revenues."

Matthew got into bed and was about to switch off the light on the bedside table when he saw an apparition in the armchair. It was Gwendolyn. "Do not worry, Matthew. Sally is a strong girl. I hope she makes it and stays with you for a long time. But if she does not, she will be with your mother, Catherine and myself. She will be at peace here as well."

"You are right, Gwendolyn. But I do not want to live alone."

"You will always have us, Matthew. Now go to sleep. Good night."

Matthew turned to the reading light and switched it off so they could all meet again.

Dr Cairns met Matthew at the elevator, and together they walked to Sally's room. Sally was awake and having a cup of tea. She was looking remarkably fresh.

Dr Cairns allowed father and daughter a hug and waited for Matthew to take a seat. "We removed cancerous cells from the breast and lung. We are now examining the cells to develop a treatment plan. Our senior pathologist will determine the exact type of cancer and its grade to ascertain if any lymph nodes near the tumour have cancer.

"During surgery, I removed some normal tissue around the cancer to ensure that no cancer cells were left behind. I also removed lymph nodes close to the cancer cells. These are being examined to see if they have cancer cells in them. If the lymph nodes had not been removed and they contained cancer cells, these cells could form new tumours and spread to other parts of the body.

"I can confirm that the procedure went without complication, and Sally can rest assured. Once the results from the pathologist are in, we will decide on the course of treatment."

"And what about the breast, Doctor?"

"Ms Stephens, in the case of your cancer, I performed a radical mastectomy. This entails taking out the whole breast along with some surrounding muscles. You are stitched up and bandaged right now, but once the healing progresses, you will feel some soreness. Of course, you can control pain by adjusting the dose of morphine yourself. There is no need to suffer, and there should be no hesitation in managing your discomfort. We will start restructuring your breast almost immediately, as that has no bearing on your treatment. If needed, we can always go back in again."

"What would you start with now?"

"We will start you on chemotherapy as well as radiotherapy. It is called chemo-radiation. The treatment must be quite aggressive. Chemotherapy weakens the cancer cells and allows radiation to work better. But there will be intervals to allow you to recuperate your strength before proceeding with another batch."

"When do I start losing hair?"

"Within days. The nurses can show you some wigs if you wish, or you may wish to make do with a headscarf. But you can decide nearer the time. If you like, you can get some fresh air. You can be taken in a wheelchair until you get some strength. You could start with our own little garden here and see how you feel."

"And what can I eat?"

"You will not feel hungry today because of the anaesthesia and the surgery. But from tomorrow, you can have normal meals. I would recommend that you eat only if you are hungry. If you are religious, we can arrange for a pastor to talk to or read to you. We also have two accomplished musicians, a violinist and a harp player. They can give you recitals individually or jointly for as long or as short as you like."

"Thank you, Dr Cairns, you seem to have thought of everything. I am concerned about the side effects of chemo. Will Sally be vomiting all the time?"

"Yes, Mr Stephens, chemotherapy does cause nausea, but we will be administering a strong anti-nausea medicine. Any vomiting will not damage her health; she will get enough intravenous nutrition to keep her hydrated. Sally, you will start feeling more energetic and like some activity, but we shall take this one step at a time."

"Once Sally is better, can we go for a walk in Central Park?"

"You can, although I would not recommend cotton candy. No ice cream either."

Sally and Matthew both laughed. Dr Cairn asked if he may be excused and left them in the room. Sally pushed back against her bed's inclined back. The nurse eased it to a flatter angle.

Matthew sat on the armchair by Sally's side. There were no words but a shared joy of being in each other's company. Dr Cairn was good. He was neither wishy-washy nor did he offer false hopes. He just laid out the protocols that were in place for treating such a cancer.

"I quite like this chap."

"Yes, Father, he is frank and does not hide the facts. I guess the hospital back in London was also quite good."

"Yes, Sally, but this is the best. Moreover, it was time to get away from suffocating London. There, it is impossible for me to switch off work, although I have a very capable team."

"Do they keep you informed?"

"Only if something is very important. Things are under control. Soon enough, the business will not need me."

"It will always need you, but you must let it go to get some rest. If I survive this cancer, I will be there by your side."

"This is why we have to beat this cancer."

Sally drifted into sleep. Matthew whispered to the nurse that he was stepping out and would have eaten lunch before coming back.

The chauffeur was waiting, but he nodded, signalled that he was walking and set out on foot. It was a warm and humid day. He walked in the direction of Central Park at a brisk pace, his mind full of mixed thoughts. Something told him that Sally was not going to make it. She was a strong girl, but the cancer was grabbing chunks out of her. Losing Catherine had already been a very hard hit for Sally. To be told that she had advanced cancer could have killed off any resilience she had constructed for herself. There had been a very deep and long depression that was still present, but that had somehow been relegated to the subliminal by her inner strength. This was his real Sally, battling against all adversity.

God had given him everything he had coveted but had given her nothing. She had always meant well but had lived a cursed life. Her man had rejected her, she had had to care for her mother at a young age and had lost her mother and her daughter. And there she was, looking into the abyss.

The sight of Central Park brought joy. There was an ice cream vendor. "Sorry, what is frozen yoghurt?"

"It's an ice cream, just healthier."

"In that case, a vanilla please."

If it is healthier, maybe Dr Cairns will allow it. Yum, this tastes just like vanilla ice cream. He walked on until he saw and heard an accordionist. The man nodded, greeting his presence.

"Any request?"

"*La Vie en Rose*?"

"Excellent choice."

Matthew sat down on a bench and heard the skilled musician. An ice cream and delightful music in Central Park! What more could one need? He smiled, left a ten-dollar note and walked on to Central Park's version of the Serpentine, buying some seed to feed the birds. Others were throwing chunks of bread into the water. He scattered his grain for the pigeons on shore. The accordion played on in the background. He needed to make the most of peaceful moments to confront the nastiness. They cancelled each other out even though hurt felt more potent than joy. Pure, unencumbered joy lasted but a fleeting moment; the little boy smiling up at him offering his bread slices was certainly such a moment. Matthew looked up at his mother. She smiled and nodded as he grinned at his little friend. He looked around and saw yet another ice cream man. He excused himself and came back with an ice cone for the boy. They all smiled; Matthew patted him on his shoulder and bid mother and son farewell.

Walking on the concrete path revealed the dulcet tones of a saxophone; the song was Stan Getz's 'A Nightingale Sang in Berkeley Square.' As he got closer, the saxophonist wore dark glasses, a suede jacket and blond plaits—a blond Stevie Wonder without the head movements. The background of grey boulders, some ferns and a little trickle of water streamed down through the creaks put him in a frame worth a great black and white photograph. The next time he would venture there, it would be with a camera.

Gwendolyn should have been there holding him at

the waist with her head leaning on his shoulders. Alas, the bedrock of his existence was no more.

As the musician nodded in acknowledgement of the ten-dollar note dropped into his hat, Matthew turned to walk on the path that skirted the water. Ducks and swans were gliding about, leaving ever-expanding ripples in their wake.

New York, despite its mad hustle and bustle, had preserved its lungs of sanity. However bad it could get in life, this refuge of hope was open to everyone. London had Hyde Park, Green Park and St James's Park, but London was no New York. It needed its own Woody Allen, Ernest Hemingway and F. Scott Fitzgerald. London had a head start, but New York had raced past it. It was rich, it was poor, and it was vibrant. Why did one feel this buzz just being in New York?

'Ooh, what was that?!' Just a pigeon, but its flutter had his heart jumping. Aah no! It had dropped something on his head. Oh no! He took out his silk handkerchief and guided it to where the splash had settled. "Ugh! Naughty bird! Ha! It is supposed to be good luck! My achievement for the day, surely." The hankie was disposed of in the bin as he walked onto Fifth Avenue. The radio at the kiosk was playing 'Baby, I Love You'. They had Aretha Franklin, but Brits thought that there was no culture in America.

Matthew found himself in front of The Pierre. He crossed over and walked in straight to the Gents. His head was clean, but he took a towel, wet it and scrubbed it just to ensure. The attendant looked at him curiously. Matthew smiled and handed him a note on his way out. Matthew then walked to The Perrine. The Maître d' welcomed him as he would. "Mr Stephens, how nice to see you. I was not informed of your visit by guest relations."

"I am not staying here this time, Jacques. Could you find me a table for one?"

"Mais, bien sur, Monsieur. Your table always awaits you."

Once seated at his table, he said, "Lobster with the mousseline sauce? And would you like a glass of Glenfarclas before you start?"

"Oh, thank you for remembering Jacques, but I am just after a good juicy burger with fat chips and extra onions today. I would like a chilled glass of root beer to wash it down. Is that okay for The Perrine?" he laughed.

Jacques smiled his biggest smile. "Well, of course, Sir, an aperitif perhaps?"

"Just some chilled water and lemon."

A man was walking in his direction. It was James Bond. "Mr Stephens, good afternoon. I am an admirer."

"As am I, Mr Moore. Is Her Majesty keeping you busy?"

They both laughed, but Matthew had no intention of asking him to join him. Mr Moore did a polite nod. "*Bon appétit*, Sir. Have a nice visit."

The one weakness New York has is a lack of discretion. He felt eyes preening at him from everywhere. "Fucking Bond! He had to spoil it. Anyway, screw him."

The Chef de Service rolled up his trolley, greeted him, and served him a tall glass of iced root beer. He lifted the cloche with an experienced flourish and placed the plate before Matthew. "Enjoy, Mr Stephens."

There was no need for cutlery here. A burger had to be grabbed by the hand and devoured. 'Mmm, now this was a burger.' The chips were perfect. Not those pommes frites that had become so popular. With the suggestion of light toasting, the brioche bun was a delight. Even the ketchup was great; good, honest indulgence. He should buy the place!

Satiated, he stepped onto Fifth Avenue and returned to the hospital. The pace remained leisurely. The heaviness of the morning had been lifted. It was like floating on the horizon where the sky meets the distant sea. He drifted past a sign with an arrow to the 'MOMA': He needed to go in and check out the Pop Art section before he went back. And then reality hit hard. What if the return home was alone? The tears suddenly surfaced as bitterness knotted within him. The buildings surrounded him from all sides. They were moving in on him. And the ground was sinking. Everything was swirling like a whirlpool; he was being sucked under. Why couldn't he breathe? Ah, a bench. There, he closed his eyes and started deep, deliberate breathing: inhale 1,2,3, exhale, 4,5,6,…1,2,3,…,4,5,6,…1,2,3,…,4,5,6. Mother was smiling, Gwendolyn was smiling, Catherine was smiling.

"You OK, Mister?"

It was the lady from the church. "Ah yes, I don't know what happened there."

It was the lady who had come when Catherine passed away; there was that warmth again. "You are the lady from that church in London?"

She smiled. "You are fine now. Please carry on with your passage." And she walked away. He sighed and closed his eyes, but when he opened them again to look at her leave, she was nowhere to be seen. Was that who he thought it was?

He stood up hesitantly; it felt fine, so he continued towards his destination.

Dr Cairns was with Sally. "She's been sleeping since you left."

"Dr Cairns, may I have a word with you?" he whispered. They left the room towards the seating area next to the elevators and found a convenient space.

"Yes, Mr Stephens?"

"I just had a panic attack on my way here. Can I see someone?"

"Yes, of course. I will check and come back to you straight away. Is there anything else?"

"Apart from the obvious, no thank you."

They both got up to go different ways.

Matthew sat beside Sally's bed and switched on the television, muting its volume. He flicked through the channels till he found NBC. Wall Street was still in the news. 'Did the ordinary man really care? Why was there this assumption that everyone was interested?' The only reason he could think of was the wish amongst ordinary people to see all Wall Street bankers burn.

His eyes spotted a comic digest on the coffee table. 'Archie's Digest.' What a delight. He would look at it later that night. He could also get some of those MAD magazines. These things were rarely seen in England, but it was staple for young and old in America.

"Father!" whispered Sally.

He got up and leaned over. "Sally, welcome back."

"Why? What happened?"

"Oh, nothing. You just fell asleep. I went out, stopped to get a burger and returned after my marathon walk to still find you sleeping. The long sleep must be good for you. Are you feeling OK?"

A nurse came up and stood by, smiling at Sally.

"I feel a bit groggy. Is that normal?"

"Yes, Ms Stephens, it is perfectly normal. Please go back to sleep if you wish."

"Father, are you going to the office to catch up?"

"No, Sally, I prefer to be here with you. However, when you sleep, I wander into a world of anonymity."

She smiled. "That must make a pleasant change for Matthew Stephens."

"For your dad, yes."

"Let us get some tea. I feel like a sandwich, as well. Maybe some cucumber sandwiches."

"Oh, the tea was nice. Was this a hospital or a hotel? Or was it just the privilege of wealth?" Sally had finished the sandwiches and was about to finish her tea when she signalled to the nurse. She heaved. The nurse grabbed a pan and held it in front of her. Sally threw up everything and continued to wretch. Once it stopped, the nurse gave her some water to rinse her mouth and then dabbed her mouth and lips with a wet towel.

Sally looked worried. The nurse ventured some words. "This is very normal. Tea can have this effect. The gastric juices can react quite strongly after anaesthesia and surgery. In an hour, I will give you some anti-nausea medicine and the next time you are hungry, we will try some soup. You are on intravenous nutrition, so there is no harm on that front. It is just unpleasant."

"Sally was a nurse in London. So, she understands."

"Oh, I did not know. Well, then, it makes us both sisters."

Sally smiled. "It does."

Matthew found this ironic: But it must occur all the time. What about an oncologist needing an oncologist? It would be difficult to receive and be comforted by optimism's little white lies. It was easier. Oh, screw it. Why would he even care?

Another nurse walked in. "You have received yet another bouquet, Sally, but this one has very exotic flowers. It looks like it has come from Asia." Sally smiled, took the bouquet and opened the little envelope with it. She read aloud, "Dear Sally, I learnt about your health. Having your father by your side must be quite a tonic. I wish you all the best for a full recovery. Signed: Kung Ling."

"Who is Kung Ling, Father?"

"Aah Ms Ling, yes. She was a competitor from Hong Kong and became a partner. Very impressive lady. We will send her a thank you note."

"But we have not done so for anyone yet."

"Yes, I know."

"You OK, Father?"

"Yes, of course. Why do you ask?"

"Are you thinking of Miss Ling?"

"No, eh… well, yes. But do not worry. I will check it out."

"Father, please feel free to go to the office if you want to. This way, you can have a change from this routine. I will be OK. And you can check with Bertram on how things are at Sanctuary. I will go back to sleep."

"Yes Sally, thank you. I will tomorrow. Now I am just going to pop out and get some air."

He walked towards the waterfront. So, what did Ms Ling have in mind? She was part of the Group. Had there been a change of heart in being taken over? Or was she trying to strike up something beyond the realms of business? He called the free phone number set up for his stay in the US and asked for Bertram.

"I am sorry to bother you. Yes, yes, she is at the hospital, thank you. I am calling about Ms Ling. What? Her office called for a meeting a month ago. So that is how she knows I am here; if she calls again, please tell her she can meet me here. Anything else I should know? Here, the news is rubbish. I will pop into the office. Yes, it would be nice if the chauffeur let himself be known at the hospital's reception. No, I do not need additional security, but you never listen. No, that will be all. Thanks. Good night."

He turned away from the phone booth and walked to the water. The sky was dark, and light smoke billowed from a tourist boat. A tour guide was reciting his routine through a megaphone. A rotating spotlight turned in his direction, and Matthew was caught in it like in a 1950s crime movie. He thought of doing something silly but then just waved at the passengers, who waved back until they were gone. Bloody tourists: they are everywhere. This walk became a bit of a routine in the days that followed.

The hospital routine went on for a few days and Matthew and Sally started talking about other subjects that they did not normally bring up such as the Abode, the Nursing College, the launch of Matthew Stephens and Co, Mr Burroughs and so on. They would only briefly acknowledge the treatment as they both knew that the other was as up to date on developments. Dr Cairn always came along when they were both in the room.

One evening, after a wander along the waterside, he walked back to the hospital. When he entered the reception, a nurse approached him. "Mr Stephens. The doctor has asked to see you."

"That is fine. Please ask him to come to Sally's room."

"Sir, he would rather see you in his office."

"Now?"

"If that's alright with you, Sir."

"Yes, of course."

He was led through the door to Dr Cairn, who got up from behind his desk and walked to him, taking his arm and urging him to take a seat.

"What's wrong, Doctor?"

"There has been a complication, Sir. Sally has developed tumour lysis syndrome. We call it TLS."

"What does it mean?"

"This is a very rare condition that can occur after chemotherapy. It occurs because of the dead cancer cells that flow through the system and find their way to the organs. It is rare for breast cancer. But she had nausea and diarrhoea, which are symptoms. We received her latest lab results, and her readings were off the charts. We have put her on a liquid diet."

"So, what does this mean?"

"Sir, this can be serious if it starts affecting the functioning of her organs."

"Is she going to make it?"

"We are in uncharted territory, Sir. Not much is understood about TLS."

"Can I go and see her?"

"Yes, of course, but she is sedated, and there may be more staff by her side than usual."

Matthew stumbled out of the office and headed to the elevator in the reception. He went straight into Sally's room. The nurses made way for him to get to his unconscious daughter.

He put her hand on her cheek and whispered, "I am sorry, Sally. But please do not leave me."

He left Sally's room and made his way to his own room. He poured himself a large whisky and then lay on his bed. The TV was showing a sitcom. He sipped his drink. What in heaven's name was happening? Why was he suddenly so powerless and hopeless? A good for nothing who could not even take care of his daughter. He had blown it with his mother, wife, his granddaughter and now even his daughter. He was an evil serial killer.

He threw the glass at the TV screen. "Fuck! Damn!! Why am I even here? All I have to show is money, and enough was never enough! And what? A failed son, a failed husband and a failed father; even my granddaughter left me. They all leave. Because I am a murderer, all this is my own doing. The scores are being settled." He took the bottle and swigged straight from it.

The bottle slipped from his hand and rolled on the floor, leaving a trail until it stopped. Some amber liquid was still left along the bottom length, lying prostrate in the face of cruel reality.

He stayed awake through the haziness of alcohol. A knot in his chest seemed to have moved down and settled in his bowels. He changed sides incessantly, grabbing pillows at the end of his tether. He got up, felt his way through his shaving case and found the high dose of Valium while in the bathroom. He let his trousers fall and changed into pyjamas, drank some water and got back to his bed.

The 20mg dose blotted his senses out completely, and within minutes, he was lost to the world's pains. Sleep induced by Valium was not curative, but it provided reliable unconsciousness. The sub-conscience was, however, immune to it.

Sally was six years old in her little Wellingtons, her dishevelled blonde curls prancing rhythmically before her eyes. Armed with her little trowel, she implored her mother to unearth some flowers and replant them elsewhere. Gwendolyn would give in and let her replant from one flowerbed to the next. Gwendolyn had known that most would perish, but occasionally, there would be healthy transmission. When they did survive, Sally would rejoice at the success and forget about the losses.

Matthew woke up, got out of bed, popped into the bathroom to clean his teeth and had a warm shower. He came out in his bathrobe, changed into a simple linen shirt and trousers and slipped on a pair of moccasins. He combed his grey hair back and left the room to take the lift to Sally's room.

"She's sedated Mr Stephens. She has been all night. I will ask the doctor to see you."

It did not sound great, but what else could the nurse say? He sat back in his armchair. "Sister, could you please order me a cup of tea?"

She nodded and dialled the doctor. "Mr Stephens is here, Doctor."

The tea was set on a coffee table. It was steaming. Dr Cairns arrived.

"Good morning, Mr Stephens. Sally's vitals are holding up. May I sit down?"

Matthew leaned over. "What are you going to do?"

"Sir, the dead cancer cells are getting the better of us. With your consent, we have stopped the chemo and want to try a few treatments simultaneously."

"Go on."

"Yes, of course. We suggest a blood transfusion to get clean blood into her and then put her on dialysis to give some relief to her kidneys. If one of her kidneys suffers any damage, then we will propose removal. All this should redress the situation, but we will need to keep tracking her organs; what is good now can change quite quickly. She will be under constant monitoring."

"This is all getting very serious quite rapidly. Please give it your best. She is the only one I have in this world, Dr Cairns."

The doctor nodded respectfully and turned to leave the room. Matthew sat back and poured himself another cup. He sipped and then suddenly broke into a whimper. The nurse came around and held his shoulder from behind. The whimper gave way to weeping. He asked for a napkin and was given one straightaway. He put it to his eyes and then blotted his nose before blowing hard into it. He folded it and put it on his coffee table. Matthew returned to his calm self and got up to drain the tea into the basin before pouring himself another one. He hoped that they knew what they were doing.

The nurse signalled to Matthew. Sally was awake. Matthew got up and walked to her side. Her eyes were open, moved to him and smiled. "Thank you for being here every time I wake up. I hope that you are getting some sleep as well. Please do not worry. If I do not make it, that is OK."

"Why are you saying this, Sally? You are in excellent hands. So please have faith."

"Faith is in short supply at my end. I am ready because I have never spent so much time with you. Thank you, Father. You have always been a caring and attentive father and are here with me until the end."

"Darling. I am not here by duty. I am here out of the respect and love I have for you. You have always made the right decision; you lived your life on your conditions and were never taken in by all the wealth at your command. You took care of your mother, and you took care of me. You set up Horizons and gave purpose to our lives. The moments I was cursed, you made me feel blessed. So, thank you, Sally."

"That is lovely, Father. Thank you. The nurse is waiting, and I need to go for my transfusion."

"I will be here when you are back. God bless you."

Once she was wheeled away, he sat down back on his armchair. He was not moving; he asked for some more tea, buttered toast and *The New York Times*. He needed to switch off a bit. He folded back the newspaper, closed his eyes and pushed himself back in the armchair. Fatigue crept in, an antidote to pain and stress.

There was a nudge at the shoulders. He opened his eyes and looked up at Dr Cairns. "Sorry, I dozed off. What is wrong?"

"Mr Stephens. We had to stop the transfusion as her lungs started to malfunction. The X-rays show that the dead cells have lodged themselves on the membrane of the lung. We must put her on a ventilator to ensure her blood remains oxygenated."

"Ah, OK. Do you need my consent?"

"No, Sir, we can do this as part of her treatment, but we just needed to inform you."

"Please get on with it. And thank you for waking me like you did."

Now she needed a ventilator! This was a sure descent into hell. He would see her as soon as a visit would be allowed. He went back to his room. Sitting down, he saw his mother. "Hello, Matthew. These are difficult times, and health is not something we can control."

"I know, Mother. I failed you, and now I am failing my daughter."

"Rubbish. You took very good care of me, and you are taking equally good care of Sally."

"Will she make it through?"

"That is not for me to say. The doctors are doing their best, so only time will tell. Sally is a brave girl with a pure heart."

"Yes, Mother, but pure hearts are not enough. You left me, then it was my wife and, to top it all, my granddaughter; I cannot lose my daughter."

"This is the equilibrium of life. You have had great success, but you have also learnt its futility. Even the best medical facility in the world can only do so much. No one can alter nature. Illness does not make any distinction."

"Yes, mother. Yes, ill health is universal and democratic, but we seem to have picked the lottery."

"We suffer and discover that life is a two-sided coin."

"So, what should I do now?"

"You must be patient. Let nature take its course, and once this ordeal is over, you should go back and do what you do best. Concentrate your efforts on saving the helpless rather than expanding your business. If Sally survives, she will be by your side. If not, you must do it yourself. I will always be here."

"Yes, Mother, I understand. Thank you." Her apparition had disappeared, but her voice rang true in its message: "Be patient and carry on."

When his eyes opened, the nurse smiled. "Sir, you can visit Ms Stephens. I will walk you there." She explained on their way to the room. "I want to make you aware that it may feel daunting with all the tubes and wires. It is an invasive procedure, but it should raise her oxygen levels."

He stepped into the room. "Hello, Sally. I hope that it is you behind all those gadgets and tubes."

Sally blinked her eyes.

Matthew smiled. "I thought these people would care for you, not put you in a torture chamber. Err… I will just get some air and be back."

Matthew left the room gasping for breath. He sat himself on a sofa; the nurse had followed him out. She looked at him closer and saw no discolouration. She held his shoulder. "Just breathe, and you'll be OK."

He responded with a resigned smile.

"Dr Cairns had briefed me on your panic attacks. It seems that extreme stress triggers this. With your daughter here and all these complications, it is indeed very difficult. I suggest that we give you a sedative and allow you to get some sleep."

"I'd like to see Sally first."

"Of course."

Sally turned her head slightly when she sensed him

come back in, and he spoke as if to respond. "Sorry, Sally, I felt breathless. I should also get myself onto one of your contraptions; the nurse is suggesting a sedative so that I can catch up on sleep. I will just go to my room and join you once I am up. They will let me know if there is anything. I will see you soon."

He took her hand, kissed it, gently laid it back by her side, and then made his way. The nurse walked him to the lift. "Should I order you a light meal? Yes? Ok. I will order some tomato soup with some croutons. Here is the pill you can take either during or after the meal. It is quite strong and should give you some rest." Matthew did not resist and went to his room, got into his pyjamas, ate his soup and then took the pill. Within minutes, he was fast asleep.

Almost three hours later, the pill's effect gave way to awareness. Matthew came back with groggy eyes and mind.

'I am waking up myself, with no nudge from a worried nurse. Sally must be all right. Seeing her with all those tubes and monitors was quite a shock. It was like being part of a movie, a predictable melodrama where the camera pans from sad faces to teary eyes. Well, he was in one of those situations.' This was happening there and then. "Let's go and see how Sally is doing."

"Hello, Mr Stephens. Are you feeling better?"

"Yes, thanks. Is Sally OK?"

"Yes Sir. Ms Stephens is sedated. I will call for a little snack. You can stay here." And suddenly someone shouted: "Code blue!"

And just like that, Dr Cairns rushed in with one assistant doctor and another nurse. They ran towards Sally and started giving her CPR. Matthew stood at a distance without getting in the way. The assistant doctor waited for the battery to charge while the electroshock pads were placed. "Away!"

The chest leapt up only to fall back onto the bed. The ECG line on the monitor had leapt up only to dip down again. An adrenaline shot was administered with a thrusting stab. The next charge was ready. "Away!"

There was little reaction, and the line remained straight until it underwent a prolonged eerie whine.

Everyone stepped away from the bed. Dr Cairns removed his mask and his cap. He placed his hand on Matthew's shoulder. "We have lost her, Mr Stephens. I am very sorry."

Matthew sank back in his armchair, tears and shock blurring everything around him. A nurse stayed with him.

"I do not need to escape this. Just as my wife felt her daughter come into the world, I need to feel her departure; I want to feel this pain." He just stayed there, sunk into his armchair, disappearing into a whirlpool of despair, sucking him in from all sides. There was a silent whine that had settled in his inner ear. It blocked out all awareness that he was alone with Sally.

A nurse came in. "Dr Cairns can see you when you are ready."

"I'd just like to sit here by Sally, if I may."

"Of course, you may, Sir. We have other intensive care rooms, so there is no problem. Sister Grace will stay here with both of you."

Matthew nodded, his eyes still creased and wet with grief.

He walked over to the bed, took Sally's head in his hands and kissed it before weeping like a child. "I am so sorry, Sally. I let you down. I could not protect you. You are gone, my angel." He kissed her head and retreated slowly to sink into the chair, exhausted and resigned.

"It was never easy for you. You suffered all your life but

stood firm. You were our rock of Gibraltar, the unshakeable pillar of our family. Alas, God wanted to put you through the final test. Why, I will never know, but he chose you. He thought you were the only one strong enough to face this ghastly ordeal. I just hope that you did not suffer in the end. I am very proud of you, Sally. You were my daughter, my son, my everything and now you have left. But do not worry about me. Your ideals and strength have inspired me in times of adversity. And I will put your lessons to good use. I hope you meet my mother, Gwendolyn and Catherine soon. I will see you all in due course."

The nurse walked out with him to the lift. Matthew went back to his room. He went onto the balcony and looked up in the sky. He sobbed and wept like a baby, whimpering until most of the poison was out of his body. After blowing his nose loudly, he entered the bathroom and splashed water onto his face. He dabbed his face with a towel and walked out. He asked to be connected to Bertram. "No, Bertram! Sally has left me… Thank you. Could you please arrange for her and me to be flown back home as soon as we are ready and prepared? I would like her to be put to rest next to Gwendolyn and Catherine. No, I do not want a funeral service, just a blessing from the local priest. Yes, I am at the hospital. Thanks. I will come down as soon as I am ready. Thank you."

He next called Dr Cairns. "I will be leaving with Sally to return to London as soon as she is prepared. Yes, it would be helpful if someone could pack up Sally's stuff and get her ready. I will have a shower and then leave. Please arrange for Sally to be transferred to the airport alongside my car. Please call Bertram if you need any help with the authorities. Thank you, Doctor, but I do not have any questions. It is too late, and I understand that we lost our battle. I am sure that you tried your best. Sometimes, the best is not enough."

He put the phone down and started packing his stuff. On this occasion, he diligently folded his clothes and laid them out in his suitcase precisely. He then popped into the shower and scrubbed himself clean of the day's travails. He washed his teeth and rinsed his mouth with the Listerine mouthwash he had been provided. After drying himself, he put on his clothes, packed the rest of his bag and walked down to the reception. A concierge alerted his chauffeur.

The hospital manager came out to bid him farewell. "Sally has been prepared and has been placed in a special ambulance. We have also prepared the paperwork for her body to be flown to England. You can both drive to the airport under police escort. I wish that we had saved Ms Stephens. But this is how it goes. I wish you a lot of courage and heart in the days ahead. Goodbye, Sir."

The ride to the airport was quick. The VIP security entrance was ready to receive them, and the police escort was extended to the foot of the aeroplane. Matthew thanked the police and chauffeur and started climbing the stairs. He then paused to see the coffin loaded onto the plane. He went in, settled in front of a glass of Glenfarclas, and they were given permission to proceed to the runway. Once it reached cruising altitude, a green light came on, and the steward came in with a little sandwich trolley. "We also have some boeuf bourguignon and coq au vin. It has been prepared by your chef at The Pierre."

"For the moment, I will settle for some sandwiches. Some water and another whisky would be great, Alain. Thanks. Do we still have *The Godfather* on video?"

"Yes Sir. We now also have *The Elephant Man,* as you had mentioned."

"No, I do not think I can handle it this time. It will be Brando on this flight."

"Sir, it's not my place, but I am very sorry about Ms Stephens."

"Thank you, Alain. I am sure that she would appreciate your thoughts." He took another sip and then watched familiar images: Sally wanting to go to the Nursing College and lodgings in the Hall of Residence, keeping Catherine, and the passing away of Gwendolyn. And now, there was Marlon Brando. He put on his headset and tried to catch the dialogue, but Marlon's mumble was still hard to catch. Her face looked back at him through a smile of tenderness. "You see, Sally, we are already together. Even Brando could not keep me from joining you in these skies. Let us get some rest, darling." And then he wept again.

'That was the smell of coffee. It was coffee—this button, ah, good.' The seat went back up gently in a mid-upright position. The steward came in with ice towels. Ah, that felt right, and the eau de cologne was invigorating indeed. Even his hands felt like new. He handed the blanket and the pillow to Alain. Why did he never wake up when they reclined his seat and put him to bed?

As Matthew sipped the coffee and took a bit of his warm and flaky croissant, the pilot gently announced they were descending towards London Heathrow and would land in forty minutes.

Back home after so many weeks, to the solitude of an empty house.

Bertram was waiting on the ground. "Oh, Bertram." He hugged Bertram tightly and broke down into sobs on Bertram's shoulders. The latter was taken aback by his boss's hug but supported the grieving father. They waited for the coffin to be loaded into a purpose-built vehicle and then slowly walked to their car.

Sally would be taken to Westminster's Mortuary Services, and the service was arranged for the next day. "The priest will read Romans 6:4, just as he had for Catherine. A violinist and cellist will play 'Albinoni' while we accompany Sally to her final resting place."

"Thank you, Bertram. That sounds perfect. I would like to go home and freshen up, and then I would like to pop into the office."

Home was spotless. There was a pleasant whiff of sweet marjoram hanging in the air. He put Callas' 'Vissi d'arte' on the turntable and turned up the volume while he went to the bathroom, door open. There was no one there. Maria's notes hit highs that pierced the heart. He then stepped into the shower and let the monsoon strength spray cleanse him. The almond milk soap and the coconut milk shampoo were a godsend. The twill shirt, cotton slacks and a light sweater with a pair of brogues may not have been his normal office attire, but this was not the normal Matthew Stephens either. Some sandwiches were on the dining table, alongside a bottle of water. A glass of water was all that was needed before leaving the house. *Tosca* was still playing through the sound system, but he had turned the volume down.

Every member of staff had a sad greeting. "So sorry, Sir." Matthew nodded in acknowledgement.

Single-page summary reports had been placed in a wallet folder on his desk with each pocket tagged:

Finance, Shipping, Freight, Accidents, Human Resources, The Foreign Office, Mr Burroughs, Ling.

The Accident folder explained that the Edward Warehouse had caught fire. There had been no sign of sabotage. The insurer had honoured all the shipping manifests, and all the compensations had been paid with no outstanding customer claims. There had been some injuries but nothing serious. The warehouse had been rebuilt where necessary and had a new fire prevention and handling system. All the other warehouses had also received fire hazard upgrades. The fire at Edward's had been caused by a shipment of tea tree and lavender oil that had reached their flashpoint in the summer heat. The warehouses were not air-conditioned. As part of the upgrade, air-cooling systems were installed in the warehouses. The manager in charge of the whole situation was Richard Marsh, and he was proposed for a promotion to General Manager of Operations to replace the retiring Sean Smith.

"Approved" was written and signed by Matthew at the bottom of the page. He added another line. "Immediate bonus of ten thousand pounds with my thanks, please."

He read a note related to Mr Burroughs and learned that the Indian government had nationalised the tea business in India. They had filed a case against Mr Burroughs' estate for child trafficking dating back a couple of decades. Appeals have been lodged, but the grind of the Indian justice system would presume him guilty until proven innocent. The Marxist government in Bengal was interacting with an organisation of parents and wanted to demonstrate how evil British Capitalism was: *What went unpunished in England would face justice in India.*

The Human Resources folder revealed senior recruitments, promotions and departures. The warehouse hands who had suffered in the fire had been treated and compensated and were back at work. Staff morale was high, although there had been general concern and worry about Ms Stephens. The priest who would be officiating for Sally had already held weekly prayer meetings at the George warehouse.

The financials looked good, as did the shipping business. There was no report on the oil business. "Oh well, I'll look at all this the next time I am in the office." He walked out and said, "Gertrude, I am going home and will not be in tomorrow. Thanks."

The chauffeur drove him back home.

He could see the lights on. Dudley must be in.

"Good evening, Sir. I am sorry about Ms Stephens. I am sorry that I was not here when you arrived."

"That is fine. Could you please get me some tea while I listen to some music? And Dudley, please come to Sally's service tomorrow if you are available. You can drive there with me."

Maria's dulcet tones were the prelude to her piercing notes that would push human possibility towards the divine. If Michelangelo was known as '*il Divino*,' then Maria was rightfully '*la Divina*.'

He had to write his message for Sally. He went to the desk and put pencil to paper. This was not something he had expected to do. No one should have to write a eulogy for one's offspring. It was against the course of nature, against the circle of life. Why would he, at this age, still be around while his beautiful, kind-hearted, oh-so-precious daughter had departed?

The late summer sun shone brightly as the priest read from behind Sally's coffin. He then invited people who would like to say something. Matthew stepped forward.

"Sally, you have been taken away at a time when you were most needed. But then, you were always needed.

You encapsulated the best human traits and showed real character; your conviction in the face of betrayal, pain and adversity makes me proud. You gave us Catherine; you brought her up with kindness and tenderness that only you were capable of.

The souls of my mother, my wife and your beautiful daughter will all be comforted with your presence. I do not know what goes on there, but I hope you all join in celestial communion.

Sally, you taught me that wealth is a futile pursuit. You were right. What really matters is each other; although the circumstances were not ideal, the last months I spent with you were the best in my life. Although I feared losing you, being by your side made me feel whole.

Sally, my baby. I am distraught by your departure but am comforted by the legacy you leave behind; your great work will continue. I promise to look after the helpless for whom we worked together.

If you would please allow me one last indulgence, I would like a small statue installed here, of you as a little girl with your pony. I hope that you will enjoy the memories that we all shared together.

My heart and eyes wept when I saw you on that hospital bed with tubes and wires all around you, but my heart and soul rejoiced at the gentle Sally, smiling through all of the treatment. You were more concerned about me than you were about yourself. Thank you for being my lovely angel."

There was a long pause before the priest asked for them to move to the burial site. The violin and cello strung a sombre melody until they reached the ground. The priest said a gentle prayer, assuring everyone that Sally would always be there. The coffin was lowered into the ground, and Matthew shovelled earth onto it. He started sobbing again, but this time around, there was no shoulder to cry on.

Yet again, he told his chauffeur to drive Dudley back without him. He decided to walk up to Hyde Park Corner and then continue on foot along Park Lane until he could cross over and make his way to his apartment in Grosvenor Square. While on South Audley Street, his eyes were on the pavement, but his mind looked at images of Gail, Gwendolyn,

Catherine and Sally. Are they calling out to me or trying to comfort me in this loneliness and despair?

"Hello, Mr Matthews."

"Oh, hello, David." It was the jovial florist who provided fresh flowers for the flat.

"I am sorry to hear about Ms Sally. My condolences, Sir."

"Thank you, David. How did you know?"

"Everyone here does, Sir. I have had so many calls for flowers to be delivered to you."

"It is best to deliver them to a church, any church. Sally would appreciate that."

"Yes, of course, Sir."

"Flowers are always welcome as long as they come without the well-wishers."

He walked on until he came to the corner café. The coffee came with his favourite amaretti. He thought, 'This is it, Matthew in his corner all by himself while the world goes about its business. Is that Sally walking across? He got up to welcome her, only to see her pass him as she went her way. Why was Catherine waving to him? She looked so beautiful. And just behind her were Gwendolyn and his mother. Why did they all stay on the other side of the road?' He got up and walked across.

The taxi blew its horn as he was in the middle of the room. The girls had vanished, and he sauntered back to his coffee. He had to accept that they had all gone and that he would only see them once he left here. He had to be patient and do what was important before he could walk away from all this.

Sanctuary, Horizon and A House for Oliver needed to be put on a secure path before he could let it all go.

It would not be easy to forsake everything he had created and nurtured. But his dearest had left him, and he would have to leave his interests behind. His misfortunes were for him alone, but he had to share his fortunes with those less fortunate. One had to rise above oneself and embrace a higher cause.

He undid the latch and entered his flat. There was pin-drop silence, and the apartment was immaculate. There were sandwiches under a glass cloche, a bottle of mineral water and a thermos of coffee. He took a plate, put some sandwiches and put them on the coffee table in front of his music system. He poured himself a coffee, brought it back, walked to the turntable, and placed the stylus on the Maria Callas record.

The pathos in her voice resonated with the occasion. Her 'Mamma Morta' was sublime. Just last week, Sally and he hoped they would make it. There he was now, finding himself in the company of his solitude. He got up to pour himself a large whisky and sipped at it. Tears leaked out of moist eyes. He dabbed at them with his handkerchief and then took another sip. What a voice. Had she ever sung for Aristotle? What a couple the golden Greeks had formed. They had been polite acquaintances but had never quite become friends. Matthew had banished himself to a 'glamourless' life, whereas Onassis had chosen a path in the limelight.

Onassis was gone. So would he, but ships would still sail, and singers would still sing. No one was indispensable, apart from Sally. The tears came streaming down again; the whisky had taken the edge off the pain, but the despair had made its way into his guts. The acid that had boiled within made him wretch once, twice and suddenly, his stomach expelled vomit with a force he had never experienced before. And then yet again. He cried, whimpering through leaky eyes and nose. The smell of vomit was potent, but he just took his clothes off, left them on the floor and walked over to his room in his socks and underwear.

A peaceful sub-conscience took over from the bitter void. Catherine was playing with Sally in front of the fireplace. They giggled as the little one tried to caress her mother's hair while Sally tried to avoid her hand. Gail and a heavily pregnant Gwendolyn were having tea at a local teahouse, smiling in complicity.

'What time is it? 2:15! I need some water.' He walked out of his room, switched the light on in the living room, and squeezed his eyes to adjust to the light. The mess from the previous day had been cleaned up. On the table sat a jug of water and two glasses. The room is so clean and so empty. Another pill and I should be ok for the night. Why does everything smell like Sally's hospital room?

Olfactory memory added a fourth dimension to the re-enactment of Sally's last moments. He stood there as the scene played out, a hopeless spectator. But the images were fading away. He was retreating over the edge into the abyss. He kept falling, but he could not see the bottom. How far could he fall? Stan Getz was playing while ducks were swimming in the waters of Central Park. Ms Ling was smiling as she glided through the lobby of the Peninsula; Stephens Vale was gleaming under the sunshine, its citizens walking with big smiles on their faces. Mr Burroughs was writing a note for the Doctor, and he had just passed Mr Striker. His head had a gaping hole, but he was smiling fiendishly; his mother was laying out some meat and a tall glass of ale on the table.

He was sinking into his bed, deeper into nothingness. Where had his will to live gone? He had been a fighter who had confronted so many dear losses. But Sally's departure was the one that hurt the most. He should have spent more time with her. He should have given her advice on her life choices. But he had always taken the path of least resistance, agreeing with everything she uttered. She was his daughter, his child. He should have been forthright. But now it was too late. She was gone.

There was Bertram. He was his employee, but he was the closest Matthew had to a friend. And then she flashed into his mind: Ms Ling. Why had she sent a bouquet to New York? Was it a sign of sympathy? Or was there something else? He picked up the phone and asked to be connected to Ms Ling. She took the phone. "Hello, Matthew? I am so sorry. How are you holding up?"

"It's very difficult, but I have to get through this."

"Yes, I know, but you don't have to go through it alone, Matthew."

"What do you mean?"

"I am in London tomorrow. If you have time, we can have lunch or go for a walk in the park. And Matthew, please call me Bo."

"What, why? Bo, as in Bo Derek?" he giggled.

"No, Matthew, Bo as in 'Kungbo Ling.' Bo is my first name. My first name is not Miss. That is just my status."

"Why is Bo Ling a Miss? Never mind, Bo, call me when you get in. Have a good flight over."

What was he doing? He should be grieving, not flirting with one of his senior executives. Was his grief pushing him into something that had remained subliminal?

Bertram did not go to the airport to receive Miss Ling on this occasion, although he was aware of her visit. The offices had been in touch. Bertram did not see anything untoward in Ms Ling coming to London so soon after the funeral. In any case, Matthew may be grieving, but he would not let anything blunt his business sensibilities.

Ms Ling called Matthew when she got to her hotel, and they arranged to meet in the hotel's courtyard. They crossed over to Hyde Park.

"Thank you for coming, Bo; I must confess that this time around, I am feeling particularly bruised."

"You have had quite a lot of tragedy to deal with, Matthew. I am not a parent myself, so it is impossible for me to imagine the pain you are feeling now. I never met Sally, but I understand she cared for your wife when she was ailing. And then she had to suffer the loss of her daughter."

"Well, Bo, you seem to have kept tabs on my family. Should I be reading something into this?"

"You have always been a mentor, Matthew. After meeting you for the first time in your office, I tried to learn as much as I could about the people in your life. I am sorry if it seems like an intrusion to you. I do not mean to offend you."

"No, not at all. My family was my most precious achievement, and Sally was the jewel in the crown. She had a pure heart. She wanted to be loved for just being Sally rather than a wealthy heiress. The only time glimpses of her leaked into the world was when she was trying to solve the problems of normal people through her project. Her whole life was about serving others. As a child, she cared for Gwendolyn, became a nurse, and brought up her daughter all by herself. Her counselling was about empowering people to sort a way out of their misfortunes. She also helped put Sanctuary on a firm footing. It would be nowhere had she not been there."

"She was a saint, Matthew, and she will always be by your side."

"She certainly was, oh Sally!" Tears streamed back into his eyes. Ms Ling took hold of his arm but did not say anything. They walked a few more steps and then settled down on a bench. Matthew was weeping. Ms Ling sat by his side and let go of his arm. She sat there quietly, choosing absolute silence and immobility over anything else. Whether he said something or not, Bo wanted to be by his side on that bench.

She believed that he should be allowed to weep, without any disturbance. Matthew Stephens had lost the most precious person in his life. Succumbing to his daughter's advanced cancer had destroyed him.

Matthew took out a handkerchief from the breast pocket of his jacket and dabbed at his eyes, and then uncaringly, he blew his nose hard into it before getting up and walking to the nearest bin to dispose of it. He stood there next to it, looking at Bo. She got up and walked towards him. They then walked along the path that kept them parallel to Park Lane before veering right at Hyde Park Corner. The bustle of the traffic was kept at bay as the walkways allowed for a respectable distance from the road. Bo Ling took in the crisp autumn air and fought off the spasms of jet lag, slowly seeking to seep their way into her.

As if on cue, Matthew remarked, "You must be on Hong Kong time. It is time to walk back to the hotel instead of prolonging your agony in the presence of an inconsolable father."

"Not at all, Matthew. I am here if you can bear my presence."

"Thanks, Bo, I appreciate this. We do not know each other well, but it is very gracious of you to be here at this moment. Thank you."

"Matthew, this is the only reason I am here. I had thought of seeing you in New York but then thought the better of it."

"Oh, you should have. You would have met Sally."

"I would have loved to, but it would have been awkward."

"Maybe, but she would have approved." That came out a bit unexpectedly. Approved of what?

"Well, I am your employee, like so many others. So, she would not understand."

"What is there to understand? You are a genuine well-wisher. And no, you are not an employee. You are an associate, a partner."

"It doesn't matter, Matthew; it doesn't matter now."

"It does, Bo. For some reason, you understand me. I am older than you, but we connect."

"Yes Matthew, we do. And you were right about the jet lag. It is hitting me quite hard now."

"Let's walk back."

Matthew Stephens and Bo Ling traced their steps back up the track they had trodden. It was quiet all the way. They arranged to meet for lunch in South Audley Street the following day.

"Try to get some sleep, Bo. I am going to take a pill and switch off for the night."

They looked at each other and then turned away in opposite directions on the hotel's porch.

There would be no meeting at the office as this was not a business visit. It was more, friendly support; a companionship visit when someone seeks to comfort another. Matthew was seething with emotions related to his immense loss, and she was the right antidote. He returned to his Grosvenor Square flat and found Dudley in the kitchen. "Oh, hello! Thank you for being here. It will be great if you could warm up some of that asparagus soup for me with a couple of breadsticks, please."

"Of course, Sir. I will stay here for a few days while things settle down."

"Sally's loss will not settle down, Dudley, but it is very kind of you to offer. I must admit that it is nice to have someone around. After supper, why don't we both have a drink? There is no obligation, of course, if you have plans."

"Not at all, Sir. I will certainly have that drink with you. As I said, I will be here over the next few days."

"Oh, OK. That would be nice. In fact, a friend of mine, Ms Ling, is over from Hong Kong for a few days. I can call her over for dinner. I hope that it will not be too much trouble."

"Not at all, Sir."

The walk through the park in the company of Ms Ling had alleviated the angst he had felt since New York, and he recovered some of his appetite. This was the first bit of food he had been able to ingest since the flight over. This was followed by a drink when neither spoke much. The only matter that came up was the disposal of Sally's house and the need to go and look to see if any work needed doing. Dudley would take care of it. It was gratifying to have competent staff reacting to the slightest suggestion. They had a job to do and performed it to the best of their ability. It was all very professional and reliable. Wealth had not prevented pain, but it had delivered worldly comfort.

After washing his teeth, Matthew retired for the night and stepped into his bedroom. It was empty. He walked out to the living area; it was beautiful and clean but also empty. Even Dudley had retreated to his service quarter.

He walked over to the record player and checked if the Callas album was still on the turntable. He looked for 'Mamma Morta' on the album sleeve and then guided the arm and its stylus onto the appropriate groove. He walked back to the sofa and listened to the cello accompanying the pathos of Callas. His heart felt heavy as he closed his eyes. Sally's face filled his vision. She was smiling, but the pain only deepened. He opened his eyes and saw a wavy blur all around. The waves were moving around him, towards him. They were closing in from all sides. The song was at a crescendo as if goading on the waves towards their onslaught.

Matthew realised that this was another panic attack. He forced himself to lie down on the sofa but, in doing so, tripped the table lamp on the side table. The table lamp fell on the marble floor, just missing the carpet. The light exploded in a loud bang. Matthew stretched out and started breathing heavily: inhale, exhale, inhale, exhale, inhale, exhale.

"Sir, are you alright?" Dudley had heard the table lamp. He called the doctor. He turned off the music and slipped a pillow under Matthew's head, covering him with a blanket.

"It is nothing Dudley. I have these panic attacks. It started in New York. I just have to breathe myself out of it. I am okay now. Thank you for coming to my aid."

The doctor confirmed Matthew's own diagnosis and gave him a tranquilizer. He asked Dudley to be within earshot, just in case of another episode, but assured both men that nothing was serious. "Please come to the clinic tomorrow. We can run some precautionary checks."

Dudley sat in the armchair next to the sofa and settled in for the rest of the night while the tranquilizer put Matthew to sleep.

The doctor put Matthew through some tests and concluded that nothing was wrong physiologically. He suggested a referral to a psychiatrist. "Mr Stephens, the last few months have been extremely stressful for you. Parental stress is very different to business stress. Even you are human, Sir. I suggest you talk to a counsellor and start thinking about yourself. It is important to think about your own well-being. I would not suggest reducing your work commitments as they provide your raison d'être, but perhaps some meditation and spirituality could provide some relief. The counsellor will be able to point you in the right direction. Otherwise, please carry on with your day-to-day life."

So, it was back to the shrink. And yes, Matthew Stephens was human. He was alone.

Bertram came by the flat to ask after Matthew. He was aware of the panic attacks. "Matthew, you really need to take things easier. Dealing with Sally's passing away is going to remain difficult. But the business is running well. You have put in a great team; they are all there for you. We all want you to be well. So please want the same for yourself."

"Thank you, Bertram. I will stick around here until I get bored to death. And then I will come to harass you at the office. I am not worried about the business at all. That is the one thing that I feel fine about. My problem is that I am lonely. Sally was a companion and a confidante, the only one."

"Yes, Matthew. You do know that you have many well-wishers."

"Oh yes. Oh, Bertram, before I forget, did you know that Bo Ling is here? I met her yesterday, and we went for a walk in the park."

"Excellent. You see, you have well-wishers everywhere."

"I was hoping to have her over for dinner. Why don't you join us?"

"Thank you, Matthew, but that would not resemble a walk in the park. It would be more like boredom in a boardroom. Plus, you have always been fond of Ms Ling all along. So, it is best to have some time with her yourself." Matthew realised that Bertram had defined the sentiment so precisely. And it would indeed be a wearisome crowd if he joined them for dinner.

Bertram finished his tea and left Matthew in Dudley's company. Matthew requested to watch *Godfather Two*. Dudley set it up and placed a hot cup of camomile tea and some shortbread within Matthew's reach.

"Thank you, Dudley. It is great. I have you here and Bertram at the office. What do I have to worry about?"

"Sir, you mentioned dinner with Ms Ling. Would you like me to set it up for tomorrow evening? That is if you feel up to it."

"Yes, yes, excellent idea. I hope she likes your cooking. Can you cook Chinese? No, no, better to stick to British food. You are fantastic with that Dover sole and that rack of lamb. Please make both so she has a choice."

"Yes, Sir." Dudley was bemused by the enthusiasm of his employer. It was refreshing to witness him emerge from the sadness he had sunk into since the passing away of Ms Sally. It did not matter what their friendship was about, but the fact that it provided welcome relief to his master was remarkable. He would summon his best butler and chef skills to ensure that the food and drink matched the occasion.

"Sir, it's Ms Ling on the phone."

"Matthew, hello, how are you?"

"I am fine, Bo. How are you? Are we still on for tomorrow?"

"That is what I am calling about Matthew. In fact, I am flying back to Hong Kong today. My uncle has suffered a heart attack."

"Oh dear, is this Hua Ling, our chairman?"

"Yes, Matthew. It is Hua Ling. It is a family as well as a business issue. The Board has called an extraordinary meeting to appoint a new chair. It seems that some directors have proposed my cousin, Hua Ling's son."

"Oh dear. What a time for boardroom theatrics. Do not worry about our dinner. You need to go back. But on the matter of the chair, do you want to be chairperson? If so, you have my backing."

"Thank you, Matthew, but as this is also a family matter, I will support the path of least resistance. If there is broad support for my cousin, I will request you to please acquiesce."

"Of course, Bo. I have never had to deal with family

issues in my business, but I understand this could be quite sensitive. In any case, it will be good for your uncle to have you by his side, even if he may not be fully aware of what is happening. We will catch up the next time you are here. Also, please feel free to call Bertram or me if you need anything. Have a restful flight over."

He knew Dudley was around, although he had made himself scarce after passing on the call.

"Dinner with Ms Ling is off, Dudley. She must fly back today to be by her uncle's side, who has suffered a heart attack."

"I am sorry, Sir. I hope things work out."

"I will pop into the office. Please let Bertram know."

Sanctuary and Horizons were rechristened *A Home for Oliver*. The charities had a senior executive, but they reported to the Managing Director for A Home for Oliver, Bertram Powell.

Bertram would manage with a team that he would handpick. The ownership of A Home for Oliver would remain under a trust tasked with the mission of perpetuating its work. The institution would stay in private ownership of the Trust and never be listed on any stock exchange. Matthew Stephens' dividends and his Company's profits would finance the charity's running expenses and, at the same time, provide the investment for expansion. The Queen would remain the Patron unless she relinquished her sponsorship to Prince Charles.

Bertram Powell would be the man in charge, and, to the extent possible, senior managers would be recruited from the business itself. The financial press reported the "change of order" and the rest of the media followed shortly. The tabloid predictably led with: "Heirless tycoon starts settling his interests."

The public had no real interest as they were wrestling with the realities of the here and now. But they did wonder why the disaster of the dot com bust that had reduced many a billionaire had left this man untouched. This man was richer than the Royal Family's combined wealth and was quite literally on another planet. But life had levelled him.

Matthew reflected that he had started with nothing but had had a strong and loving mother. He had had an exemplary wife, his life partner. Hard work and a few fortunate moments had catapulted him to the pinnacle of the business world. He had been given the gift of making the right move at the right time and had been lucky with his ventures. Winning had come so naturally that it had not even seemed like victory.

And Mr Strike? He had tried to justify it, but the fact remained that he had taken his life. His mother should have found a way to kill him instead. But that is not the way it worked. His whole life had gone by with its many ups and downs, but the one constant had been the malignant lump in his belly. It had refused to budge, "We have no right to kill. Or else we spend our existence in retribution. Losing every family member is a cruel price to pay. Yet, they have all gone. It has been a lifetime of penance. Acts of ignominy must be repented. The riches need to be sacrificed, and I need to seek oblivion. Only then will my sins be absolved. Ashes to ashes, oblivion to oblivion."

The decision was taken in a rare moment of lucidity. Everything had suddenly fallen into place. The act of the biggest personal dispossession in history had been decided within less than an hour. His people would take it up from there.

"I want Emily Westbridge to do this, Bertram. She is a chat show host on one of the minor cable channels."

"Yes, Matthew. The press is going to have quite a day."

"Oh well, if it means going out with a bang, so be it."

"I do not want to interfere with your thinking, Matthew, but you have thought this through? I cannot imagine you retiring in this fashion."

"Yes, Bertram. I have thought this through. We need to relinquish everything before we die. You know that I am not attached to all this business and wealth stuff. I was attached to my family. And they have all left."

"But this is all your creation. Plus, you have got used to a certain way of living. There is no need to embrace poverty at this juncture of your life. Even if you retire, you should do so in comfort."

"Bertram, I have not found comfort here. I am restless. I sleep badly, and I worry all the time. I need to escape into simplicity with a very basic life. It does not matter to me if I no longer have these worldly comforts. You know that my mother was poor, and we lived a very bare existence. So, it would be like going back to where I come from. That is the only reality, Bertram. All the rest is an illusion."

"Yes, Matthew, but your achievements and success are real. They are no illusion. Plus, your trust in me goes way beyond the reasonable. I am just an employee who has tried to serve you, as have many others. You could have chosen someone more deserving, someone of stature, like Ms Ling, for example."

"Bertram, I am very fond of Ms Ling, but she has her life in Hong Kong. I am not even sure she aspires to step up to take over the whole business. Even if she did, it would be wrong for me to place her in a position that she would earn out of favouritism on my part. I trust you, Bertram. You are the only one I know who can run the business and look after A Home for Oliver. And I know that you will carry my mission out with utmost devotion. Trust is the main currency in any relationship, business or personal. So please do not question my choices. I know that you have my interest at heart. But I have certainly thought all this through."

The Renunciation

Emily Westbridge was waiting for her elusive exclusive; the richest man in Great Britain had avoided the media like the plague. And then suddenly, his office had called to grant her a forty-five-minute face-to-face. There would be no script, and the programme would go out live.

The door opened, and an elegant Matthew Stephens stepped in, looking many years younger than his seventy-seven. He still had a full head of grey hair. Unlike the few pictures in the media, he did not look serious; he looked pleasant and relaxed. He wore an open-collared white shirt, a khaki linen jacket and a pair of blue trousers. Neatly laced dark brown suede shoes completed his attire. Matthew Stephens wore no glasses and looked straight at Emily through his deep-set turquoise eyes.

"Please sit down, Sir. Could I offer you something to drink?"

"A scotch would do nicely, thanks."

It was three in the afternoon, but who was she to argue with Matthew Stephens? This was an exclusive that would have been an unprecedented scoop for any major channel. Yet here they were on a marginal satellite channel. Emily was only thirty-four, and the biggest guest she had ever had before this day was an Olympian who had won silver at the 1992 Olympics.

Once the scotch was placed on the coffee table, Matthew Stephens bent across to take the glass in his hand, sniffed the contents and then let the glass rest in his hand without a sip.

"We can start, Ms Westbridge."

The countdown to airtime started, and Emily Westbridge looked into the camera.

"Today, we have the honour and the privilege of talking to one of the most enigmatic personalities in Great Britain. His achievements have straddled the worlds of big business and philanthropy. Here is a man who started with nothing in an England run by aristocrats. Here is a man who beat all odds to become the wealthiest person in the British Isles, a man who, as a teenager, lost his mother to deprivation and illness, who lost his beloved wife and business partner to muscular dystrophy, who lost his only child and daughter to cancer and who also lost his only grandchild."

The camera panned away from her and zoomed in on the subject.

"Mr Stephens, welcome!"

"Please call me Matthew."

"Yes, Sir."

"Just Matthew, please."

"Matthew, Sir.. sorry… Matthew, it is difficult to introduce a guest such as yourself. Although you have remained out of the media, your life has always generated immense interest. Of course, your eponymous business is written about everywhere."

"The business is part of the economic landscape, so it gets attention. But my personal life is different. It is private. The media vultures do not understand this because they look for scandal and gossip. Their perennial excuse for public interest is the biggest lie of our times. How can it be in the public interest to invade an individual's privacy?

"Here is a fact that I learnt last night; I was informed that I am not only the richest man in the UK but also the third richest in the world. These chaps have estimated my fortune at almost forty-five billion pounds. Astonishing, isn't it?"

"How do you feel about all this, Matthew?"

"Ah! This is exactly why I am here. I need to clarify something important; if we were to take the figure of last night, then I can confirm that at this very moment, I am forty-five billion pounds poorer than I was last night."

"What? How is that possible?"

Matthew paused for a moment, a long moment.

"The reason I had insisted on a 3pm show was that I had arranged for two meetings this morning. The first was with my Board, where I resigned as Chairman, and the second was with my solicitor and Trustees. Everything I owned was given away from 3pm this afternoon, apart from a small cottage in the West Country purchased this morning from my chauffeur. And I will receive an allowance of two thousand pounds a month. The Trust will pay my removal expenses, as well as the cost of purchasing a sturdy bicycle."

"Matthew, wow! This is shocking news indeed. There are lots of questions I would like to ask; the most obvious one is why?"

"Emily, before I answer that, let me explain why I chose your show when I could have gone to any of those arrogant wankers who believe they are doing you a favour by talking to you, who believe they are bigger than the subjects they tackle. I loathe them all equally." He winked at Emily. "I will also be covered for any legal costs and libel damages that come out of this show. But you, Emily, are the outsider: no private school, no Oxbridge for a black girl from Brixton. The only interesting person you ever had was your distant relative who had won a medal at the Barcelona Olympics. I have seen one other show of yours: the first one was when you had on some inner-city kids who carried knives. You tried to find out why they were doing this. You came to the sober conclusion that this is a world where such kids have little choice. Strangely, I related to them because I could well have turned out like them. But they need a chance. We all do. I also wanted to do this on my terms, and what easier way than to bully a minor channel? How many people are watching? Three hundred, tops?"

"Maybe more since you announced your newfound poverty. I have just been told that our ratings are going through the roof as we speak."

"That is why I am here. In the next twenty-four hours, there will be many who will have heard and read every little word we utter during this chat of ours."

"Matthew. But why the decision to give it all away?"

"Oh, that! The answer is quite simple. Why not?"

"Well, it is yours to give away, but a small house, a bicycle? You look remarkable for your age, but most people…"

"Emily, you and I are not most people. You and I have both come up the hard way. In a way, the two of us are very similar. After this show, you will reach the status you have always desired. To answer your question, I would like to ride a bicycle for as long as possible. But for now, I wish to just talk, a sincere chat with someone who is neither my mother, wife, nor my daughter and, for that matter, not even my granddaughter, who meant the world to me, each of whom I lost.

"You know, when my mother was alive, I had promised myself that I would never be poor and that no one I would know would die in those circumstances. Granted, I am not poor and granted that those circumstances were erased from my life forever. But my money saved neither my wife nor my daughter. It did not even help my granddaughter. And here I am, approaching my eighties, alone in the final stretch."

"It's sad; not just sad, it's tragic."

"Sad, happy, no Emily, it is none of that. It is just life. We do what we must and then we succumb to the inevitable."

"That sounds defeatist for a man who overcame all odds."

"At my age, there is neither victory nor defeat. There is just acceptance."

"How did it all begin, Matthew?"

"A benefactor helped me when I was desperate to save a very sick mother. There is a lot of evil in this world, but there is also some real good. And this good has been the source of my motivation. Each time I was struck down by tragedy, I knew that something would happen that would pick me up. As someone considered as a very successful businessman, I have suffered quite a bit. I never set out to change the world. And quite frankly, all the wealth I amassed did little good for the public. If I had not shipped all that stuff, someone else would have. The competition was always cut-throat. My employees flourished, but some also died at work. And my wealth did nothing for those knife-carrying youths you had on the show."

"But Sanctuary and A House for Oliver now operate in twenty-seven countries worldwide."

"Yes, Emily, they do, but our business operates in over a hundred countries. There are many more countries in the world. A House for Oliver spends an average of two thousand pounds per child per annum. With the money I have planned to provide, we should be able to help over twenty million children during their formative years. And if the money is disbursed and invested wisely, the benefits could roll on for decades. But even all this is just a drop in the ocean."

"Is there any reason to focus only on abused children and not on simple orphans?"

"I do not believe we have any rigid line distinguishing between the two; orphans can often be abused. The abuse angle is more important to me because I could have been abused myself had I not encountered a benefactor. I was not an orphan; my mother was ill but alive. But I was poor and desperate: ideal bait for someone without scruples. Although I got lucky, most do not. Many lose their innocence within a few ruthless moments of callousness. The real world is a lot uglier than books and movies make it out to be.

"Without naming names, more to protect the victim in question, there was this boy around the same age as I was when I had to ask a favour of someone to keep my mother alive. When I found him, he was scared, bereft of all dignity, and ashamed of himself. He had run away from his master's house because his master had invited some close friends, each of whom had had a go at him, sodomising him repeatedly, while others were stubbing out their cigarettes on the spot of their choosing on his body. We have rights for animals, and we have rights for humans, yet we have humans who are not even accorded animal rights."

"And how did you deal with this boy?"

"Our team of doctors, nurses and psychologists looked after him, and I engaged with the perpetrator to ensure this did not happen again. He no longer lives in the country."

"Yes, Matthew, there are rumours that you blackmail the wealthy for financial gain."

"Blackmail is illegal, and I would never break the law. I deal with people the way I deem fit. As far as wealth is concerned, I have been successful due to acumen and luck, not extortion. But I have an acute sense of right and wrong and believe wrong should be avenged; redemption should have a price. For predators of innocence and helplessness, money should not play a role in avoiding disgrace.

"You know something, Emily? Social standing is a very potent motivation. People go to great lengths, especially in Mayfair and Belgravia, to preserve their social circles and maintain their access to private clubs. A façade of camaraderie remains even if someone sleeps with another's wife. It is a twisted societal norm, one that I have close knowledge of. Although strangely enough, I was never really accepted as landed gentry. Well, it is not that strange. I have origins in destitute East London, son of a single mother and no noble name to claim aristocratic links.

"Notwithstanding, those who aspire to remain an integral part of high society would go a long way in preserving their status and would rather leave London or even England if they risked a smudge on their worldly reputation. I will let you know that some have sought redemption by supporting A Home for Oliver. The wisdom is that this would temper the ravages of Mathew Stephens' fangs. It is true, sometimes it does."

"Well, if they have done serious damage, they should be punished. But there is the law. Does it not work?"

"Emily, the law is great but based on evidence, procedures, and long-winded processes."

"But you got Samuel Burroughs off the hook."

This was a bit unexpected, but he had to reply. "Samuel Burroughs was accused of doing wrong, but the justice system did not uphold the case against him. What was omitted in the media was that Mr Burroughs did a lot of good and served humanity better than most. Had it not been for him, I would not be here today. I did not get him off the hook. Our legal system acquitted him."

"Yes, Matthew, but is the police not doing its job in protecting the vulnerable?"

"Emily, youngsters fear the police and do not report violations. What is even worse is that these kids think that they have done something terribly wrong themselves. On the other hand, the assailants are highly respected members of society whose sense of hubris is impenetrable. This is where I come in."

"Like some sort of superhero, high society vigilante?"

"I would not go that far. Let us say I would come in as the man with the mission and the means. These villains fear me because I bring their victims quick justice, extricate them from their presumed disgrace and rehabilitate them away from this evil. A Home for Oliver aims to make these youngsters realise that it is not their fault and that they can still make a comeback, that one day they will be able to trust others again and aspire to a normal life.

"You may have heard of the recent case where the single mother of a five-year-old girl helped her boyfriend rape her daughter by holding the little girl's hands while the man had intercourse with her. Can you imagine a greater evil? Here, the police did indeed intervene very quickly and quite conclusively.

"You know, Emily, I have seen quite a lot of life, and from where I am sitting, abuse is the biggest misfortune. It is a phenomenon that scars and smoulders for life. It kills trust, confidence and self-respect."

"Matthew, you have made your strong feelings very clear. We hope that your efforts eradicate the scourge of youth abuse. But tragedy has played an important role in your own life. You have had more than your share of personal calamities. Does wealth have a role to play in coping with tragedies?"

Matthew smiled, closed his eyes and bent over to sip the whisky.

He did not say anything for what seemed like an eternity. The world knew this man had lost all that was dear to him. He put his glass back on the table, looked at Emily, and squeezed his eyes shut. Another thirty seconds passed. Emily started getting a sign from next to the cameraman, a board held up with a rushed scribble, "Say something, we are on live." Emily did not.

Matthew opened his eyes and smiled. "No, Emily. One cannot hop onto a private jet and escape misery and grief. Wealth plays no role whatsoever in coping with tragedy. It is obvious. With all the money in the world, I was helpless. I lost them all one by one: mother, wife, daughter, and granddaughter. What did the Matthew Stephens' billions do? Nothing!"

He continued, "Human beings need health and companionship. Add a roof over your head, a bed to sleep and two square meals daily. One does not need to be super rich to survive. I was extremely fortunate in business, but everyone I loved remained untouched by my wealth. My wife lived a simple life and then she lived a very ill existence. She and my girls derived very little, if any, benefit from my wealth. My mother passed before I became wealthy, my wife became terminally ill when I became wealthy, and when I had been wealthy for some time, my daughter and granddaughter feared being identified with my wealth.

"They were devoted to me, of course, just as I was to them, but my daughter hid the fact that she was my daughter for a long time. She was worried about not having genuine relationships. She shunned her social peers to find a life amongst what she called 'real' people. My granddaughter never knew her father and her own husband did not know which family she came from until the day of their engagement. So, in a strange way, the wealth I had accumulated never really brought any of my family either pride or joy. Rather than bringing them comfort, it brought them discomfort. In a way, I can understand the insecurity that goes with wealth. Wealthy people are always fearful of being dispossessed. We all know that we will leave all this behind, but we still attach so much value to the ephemeral status of possession." He paused.

Emily decided to wait it out again.

This time, Matthew took less time. "You know, the happiest moment in my life was when I was with my wife at a hospital in London. We were both in the room where my daughter had just delivered Catherine. That was the defining moment for me. My world was complete. Then I really had it all. The rest just did not matter.

"But then, I kept accumulating the billions; the spread of my business was like a cancer, not dissimilar to my daughter's tumour. My business was invincible, just as cancer is. But nature mocked me; my daughter's cancer spread as quickly as my business grew."

"Are you saying that your success was a cancer?"

"In my case, it probably was."

"Matthew, do you believe this was somehow related to offsetting your success?"

"Emily, I will never know if I was being punished for my rewards or if I was being compensated for my misfortune. All I know now is that it is time to move on."

"And where do you go from here, Matthew?"

"Away from everyone and everything; I could have moved abroad to France or Italy, but I realised I love this land too much. Moreover, my French and Italian are unremarkable, and I did not want to end my life as a foreigner. There are things I need to do before I leave this place for good, things I have never had a chance to do. I have always wanted to do some gardening, ride a bike and read. I will try all three. If my body does not cope for some reason, then reading is what I will latch on to. And cooking. And most of all, try not to think about business. I would like to die alone, at peace with myself. I want to disappear into oblivion. And this, your show, is the prelude to that final curtain call."

"How fascinating! And thank you for choosing this show to announce the next chapter in your life. I do not believe you will ever disappear into oblivion, but we wish you well, Matthew. On behalf of the millions you are helping, I would like to express a deep sense of gratitude. Ladies and gentlemen, Matthew Stephens!"

Emily Westbridge's show with Matthew Stephens was distributed to 893 channels, voiced over in seventy-three languages and was estimated to eventually have a viewership of over a quarter of the planet's population. Emily became the hottest ticket in town. Calls from rich and famous publicity agents flooded in for interview requests.

The message that money does not equal happiness had universal appeal.

Emily would always remember how it had all started. Each interview would contain a respectful reference to the break Matthew Stephens had given her. She would always say, "Did you ever experience a defining moment in your life? Did someone suddenly knock at your door to bless your life?" She always ended the show with a thank you to the guest and signed off, looking squarely at the live camera, "Thank you, Matthew."

The world had found a new messiah: the 'ex' richest man appealed to everyone. What was there not to like? Many had envied him, but everyone now felt sympathy.

Priests and religious leaders used Matthew Stephens as an illustration of metaphysical equilibrium. Never had a man who possessed so much been dispossessed of even more. Never had so much power been impotent in the face of personal tragedy. Never had so much grief accompanied such riches.

The *Financial Times* ran a special Sunday supplement on Matthew Stephens, analysing what his departure from day-to-day business would mean for the business world. They also ran an editorial on philanthropy amongst the super-rich. What set Matthew apart was that his was neither a project for health nor a scholarship initiative. His was a project for the dignity of youth.

Time magazine named him Man of the Era.

While all this was happening, Matthew had quietly moved to his cottage, his whereabouts known only by Bertram. He was not contactable by phone. He had a mobile phone that he could use to make outgoing calls, but the number was not revealed to anyone, nor was it traceable. Any communication with him had to go through Bertram. He would determine the urgency of the matter and send a letter to him. The postal address was in the house's name and had no mention of the name of the Occupant. The incoming mail was always in an unmarked, plain brown envelope.

He received a weekly report on A Home for Oliver every Monday morning. The information had a summary table on the first page laying out a breakdown by how many additional Olivers had been received. He would also get monthly reports. Bertram was making sure that the organisation grew while keeping the focus on each victim's well-being.

There were figures by country. The concept had caught on in other countries. Governments provided premises, and local business people readily contributed to the financing of the noble cause, some out of philanthropic motivations, others out of guilt, or both. The United Nations gave it the seal of a humanitarian project. There were rumours that the Nobel Foundation was in the process of short-listing Matthew for the ultimate recognition.

Matthew was not aware of the media rumours. All that interested him were the performance reports. He was not interested in overall numbers. He was only interested in additional numbers. For him, this was one of the main indicators of the effectiveness of his Foundation. The other detail that he examined with obsessive interest was the conversion rate of Olivers identified to Olivers enlisted and the average conversion period. His guidance to the operatives at the Foundation was that the conversion period should not exceed four days and that the percentage of 'enlisted Olivers' to 'identified Olivers' should not fall below eighty per cent. This way, he could ensure that the criteria he had laid out were respected right from the outset while at the same time ensuring that there was no bureaucratic hurdle in the conversion process. Conversion entailed the immediate deployment of legal and social workers to establish the child's predicament and direct access to counselling, boarding, lodging, medical examination and spiritual teaching. The idea was to restore an identity and, in doing so, re-establish the victim's dignity.

He was particularly pleased with one Monday morning report. There were two new countries, Haiti and Afghanistan.

Everyone had a right to dignity.

He cycled to the morning market in the village square on Monday. He bought the usual vegetables, fruit, cheese and treated himself to a bottle of local cider. His regular groceries would be ordered at the 'Father and Son' grocery store next to the bicycle stand. He would leave the foodstuff he had purchased earlier at the village market at the store, and they would arrange for it all to be driven over to his house later in the day.

He would then walk over to the local newsagent, buy himself a copy of *The Times,* and settle down at the teashop with a pot of freshly made tea and a big slice of carrot cake. He rarely spoke to anyone; the occasional exchange would remain within the confines of a remark on the weather or a discussion about the next event at the church. Sometimes, he looked around and smiled at this place's serenity and simplicity. Occasionally, that smile would turn into a mischievous grin. 'This place needs drugs, sex and rock and roll. Maybe I should ask the chaps in London to send some lap dancers and male strippers to shake things up a bit.' He would laugh out aloud, to the bemusement of others, and then walk over to the bicycle stand to retrieve his black pushbike.

And so it went on for months.

Until one Monday morning, the sky was an exceptional blue, a morning when the village grocer did not see the old man swing through the entrance doors with his brown paper bags from the market. When, until late afternoon, the owner of 'Father and Son' grocers had still not seen him, the son walked over to the teashop and asked after their client. They said that they had not seen him either. The father asked his son to stay at the shop while he took his delivery van and drove off to Matthew's house. His bicycle was leaning against the fence. He knocked. "Mr Stephens, are you there?"

There was no reply. He lifted the latch as he always did. There was no lock. "Mr Stephens, are you there?"

There was a ray of light coming through the bedroom door. The man walked over, into the room. Matthew Stephens was lying on his back, his eyes shut, in his pyjamas under a quilt. There was serenity on his face, his lips smiling under a stagnant nose.

The grocer looked up at the wall and saw a small, embroidered message hung up in a modest wooden frame.

The obituary column in the local newspaper had a small entry:

"We do what we can, but it's never enough."
Matthew Stephens
1930–2010

Epilogue

Emma was having a cup of tea, mildly aware of the television. She tuned it into one of the Flemish Channels; each weekday morning, they would transmit an English programme on buying houses with Dutch subtitles. She was fascinated that house buying had become a national obsession. She thought this was the more posh, more socially acceptable version of the much-derided phenomenon of reality television. It seemed palatable that people expressed their likes and dislikes openly to the public. Not only that, but they were also actually taking the whole nation with them on a house hunt And the viewers enjoyed it: some were envious, others were amused, and others plain nosy. Voyeurism had become a legitimate pursuit.

That show ended inconclusively; the prospecting owners did not settle for any of the four houses they had seen. Emma made another cup of tea while the commercials came on. When she settled near the TV again, the screen had blue and pink titles running diagonally across the screen: *The Emily Westbridge Show*. It was a rerun of one of her older shows.

There was a very pleasant-looking black lady smiling into the camera. "Today, we have the honour and the privilege of hearing from one of the most enigmatic personalities in Great Britain."

Later that evening, she asked Chris, "Do you know anything about this chap Matthew Stephens?"

"Of course, he's Ian's father-in-law."

"The Ian I met at that drink."

"Yes, the Ian you knew."

"Ohh, I get it. Ian's wife?"

"Spot on; Ian accidentally strangled Matthew Stephens' only granddaughter to death."

"And this man, he is still around? I saw him on television."

"*The Emily Westbridge Show*?"

"Well, yes, how do you know all this?"

"Emma, *The Emily Westbridge Show* is on a par with Oprah in the ratings. She has now moved to the US as part of a deal with NBC. In fact, the firm Ian works at advised Ms Westbridge on her contract. I even know the London partner who led the negotiations with NBC.

"The show created history. Media polls estimate that more people have seen that interview than the Martin Bashir interview of Princess Di on the BBC."

"Have you seen it, Chris?"

"No, I have not, but I am sure it will pop up on some channel one of these days. So, what did you think?"

"Before I found out about the link to Ian?"

"Before and after."

"He is fabulous. He exuded power and vulnerability at the same time. I felt sad for him. All that wealth and no one to continue the legacy."

"Well, I would not say that. A Home for Oliver is the fastest-growing charity on the planet. What is more, with the means and the quality of the management he has put into place, the Foundation will see many generations of Olivers, far beyond our own lifetime."

"You seem to know a lot about him."

"Well, he is one of the richest men in the world, or rather he was. His television appearance was a strategic masterstroke; he used the personal tragedies he had suffered to gather support for his Foundation. And he provided a live illustration of what he meant by deserving a chance; going with the giants of prime-time interviewers would have deprived Emily Westbridge of the rarest of interviews."

"But she is brilliant."

"Yes, of course, but Emma, many deserving people just do not get a break. This was exactly the point the old man was trying to make."

"Well, that and he avoided going into too many details about his personal tragedies; He skilfully avoided getting into the details of each loss. Losing his daughter and granddaughter after all that could not have been easy. The granddaughter was our age."

"Not only that, but she also apparently had a strange upbringing. Her mother had fallen in love with a doctor while she was a nurse. When the doctor found out that she was pregnant with Catherine, Matthew Stephens' granddaughter, he just dumped her; from what I understand, they did not have the social standing, which was important for this doctor."

"But she was Matthew Stephens' daughter."

"Yes, but he did not know that."

"What? How is that possible?"

"Sally Stephens, the daughter, left home to become a nurse. But to do this, she wanted to live like any other nursing student in London. Her surname was not a giveaway, so it was easy. In any case, in London, anonymity is not a difficult thing. Also, I guess people with immense wealth sometimes feel unable to develop genuine relationships because of the wealth obstacle."

"The doctor would have found out at some stage and claimed his daughter."

"Now this is where wealth comes in handy; Matthew Stephens made sure the doctor would never come near them, and he would leave the UK to go and work in a hospital in Melbourne."

"So, he may be around."

"Yes, but with enough shackles to ensure he does not return to the UK."

"Chris, how do you know so much about Matthew Stephens? Through Ian?"

"Only partly from Ian. Mainly from our own business. For as long as I can remember, Matthew Stephens has owned every oil tanker that carries our oil. And as if that were not enough, he became our company's second-largest shareholder after the Canadian government."

"But you said that Ian was your adviser; you work for Matthew Stephens. How does all that work?"

"Matthew Stephens has always believed that Ian was not guilty. So, although he was extremely angry, he never wanted to persecute the man. In fact, he just did not want the perpetrator of the accident anywhere near him; the firm understood this. Moreover, they wanted to avoid controversy and moved him from London. If Matthew Stephens had felt otherwise, he would have ensured that Melbourne would play host to yet another exiled professional."

"So, there's a moral in all this?"

"I don't know; there must be."

"Chris, it just shows that no one has everything. We complain. I know I have about our misfortunes, but then you realise every happy story has another side."

"I guess. Just staying with the story, apparently, Ian was also never aware of the family he was going to marry into. He had always thought that Catherine Stephens was a book editor. The reality of wealth was only revealed when Ian proposed to her; she accepted on the condition that she would first reveal certain secrets."

"Quite an unexpected secret that. He was expecting some sordid detail from the past, and there he was suddenly marrying the richest granddaughter in the world."

"Matthew appreciated that Ian insisted that he and his wife live within their means. He was a successful young lawyer, and his wife had a job in publishing. Their marriage had been a small affair with just immediate family."

"How do you know all these details?"

"Well, Ian and I have had quite a few lunches together. We have always got on well. And when you hear from him, you realise what extraordinary circumstances people can find themselves in. And now it turns out that you knew him as well."

"I would not say I knew him, but it is a small world. I remember his father. He ran the stables. He was the archetypal country gentleman. Did you ever tell him about us?"

"Well, he knew that I had an English wife. But no, I never reciprocated with our life story. That is for us and us alone. And quite frankly, he needed to relate his story. He has no children and no partner that he has mentioned. He lives a very different life to mine."

"You have a wife."

"Yes, a stunning one at that."

"So, you are a lucky man, aren't you?"

"Am I?" he whispered.

"Please check on the boys, and we'll see."

Chris tiptoed to the rooms, checked that they were fast asleep, closed their door and found his way back to their room; Emma had switched the lights off. He slipped under the quilt and went over to Emma's side. She was naked. Her soft, smooth skin was lightly perfumed. He moved her hair and kissed her neck while she turned to face him. Her leg and arm moved to pull him closer. In an instant, she moved on top of her husband. Chris put his hands behind her, holding her firmly and pulling her towards himself. Emma did not resist and put her hands on the headrest as her thighs rested on either side of his chest. And then she moved herself higher.